# Sins of the Forefathers

## Volume 1: A Chained Awakening

# Sins of the Forefathers

## Volume 1: A Chained Awakening

J.D. Campbell

Published by Level Up in the United Kingdom in 2024

Cover illustration by Sippakorn Upama

ISBN: 978-1-83919-685-0

www.levelup.pub

J.D. Campbell writes Fantasy fiction. Based out of Texas, he grew up wishing the dragons in his childhood books were real. After graduating from Texas A&M University with a degree in Environmental Geoscience, he promptly stumbled into writing about dwarves and magical robots. He is the author of the *Sins of the Forefathers* series on Royal Road, Scribble Hub, and Patreon under the name PreCursive.

# Chapter 1
# Arrival in Green

From one moment to the next, I was somewhere else. There was no in-between frame, no flash of light, or expository dialogue to explain my change in circumstance. I didn't get a reason for the complete ruination of my life.

No, I got to fall on my ass in the middle of a forest clearing in-between eye blinks.

At the very least, I wasn't naked at the time, being out and about and wearing regular worn clothes and worn shoes. I couldn't even imagine how much more confused I would have been if I had been transported in the middle of the night or in the dead of sleep, instead.

I like to consider myself a fairly level-headed person most of the time, but this went beyond the norm. Bearing my new, extraordinary circumstances in mind, however, I'm willing to forgive myself for being stunned enough to not realize I wasn't alone. To be fair, I don't think they had noticed me yet either.

Maybe fifteen feet away from where I was sitting, there was a scene out of a historical period piece happening. What appeared to be a train of perhaps thirty wagons with covered roofs had created a circle around a bonfire. Inside that circle, I could see a mass of people in rough-spun clothing going about their day, setting up a camp, and doing chores. On the outskirts of the camp, however, the most visible people, to judge by their appearance, had to be guards. They didn't look to be very attentive, as it appeared that the guards of this camp were the restless teenagers given a spear and busy work.

At the same time that I noticed the nearest 'guard', he noticed me. With a shout, the nearest one attracted the attention of the others and started towards me. Scrambling to my feet, I tried to make myself look non-threatening to the pissed-off-looking teen by raising my hands and speaking calmly.

"Hey, uh, I don't really know what's going on, but I'm not looking for any troub—" I started. Before I could finish my sentence, the teenager had gotten close enough to me that he could ready his spear, point it at me, and start shouting.

The problem was, I didn't understand a word of what he was saying. Frankly, I couldn't even identify the language that he was speaking.

That did not have great implications.

The shouting of the guard had not only drawn the attention of the other guards, which were starting to stream over to me, but it appeared to have drawn attention from the camp itself. Appearing at the edge of the camp was an older man in more functional-looking armor than the leather gambesons over simple woolen clothing that the teenagers had. This guy was wearing actual chainmail, a steel helmet, leather vambraces, and carrying a sheathed sword at his waist and a shield over his back.

Making his way over to us, the older man barked a command at the other guards and made a dismissive motion at them. As they started to return to their posts, what I could only conclude was their overseer had reached the guard still pointing a spear at me.

Taking his eyes off me to speak to the older man, the teenager started jabbering away at the older man excitedly. As he started to speak, the overseer turned a suspicious glance my way based on

2

whatever the guard was telling him. However, whatever he was being told was clearly not making him very happy. Before the teenager was finished speaking, the older man snapped something at him that made him fall quiet.

Taking a closer look at me, the older man suddenly began to frown harder than he had been. For some reason, he just kept awkwardly looking at me, as if something would change if he stared long enough. Several minutes passed in this way before the man turned and spoke to the teenager again, suspiciously keeping one eye on me. Suddenly, the teenager was staring intently at me as well, but whatever they were trying to do was clearly not working. The teenager squinted suspiciously before he turned to the older man and said something to him.

The older man was quiet for a few seconds before glancing at me again. Suddenly, in a startlingly fast movement, the overseer grabbed a wooden truncheon he'd hidden in his belt behind his sword and swung at my head with blinding speed.

I was only able to recognize what was happening as the club neared my temple. Before I could react, from one moment to the next, I was unconscious.

***

I couldn't tell how long I'd been out of it. For all I knew, I had been out for days.

As I slowly started to come to, I was barely cognizant of my surroundings. Frankly, I felt like total shit. I had a massive, pounding headache and a ringing in my ears like I had never experienced in my life. I hadn't even opened my eyes yet and wasn't even sure I was able to considering how groggy I was feeling. I barely retained enough presence of mind to wonder if this was what a concussion felt like.

What had actually awoken me, however, was the feeling of a wet rag being gently dabbed on my face.

Slowly cracking one eye open, I tried to look at whoever was touching me. I couldn't manage it, as my eyes weren't able to focus properly. All I was able to see was a vague human shape gently wiping my face with a rag.

And then I passed out again.

\*\*\*

When I woke up for a second time, I felt fine. Which, frankly, startled me awake very easily once I realized that fact.

Jerking my head up from where it had been resting on my chest and opening my eyes, I was actually able to take in my surroundings this time.

It was nighttime when I woke up and I must have been in the back of one of those wagons I had noticed earlier. I was sitting in the back of one of them with my arms tied behind my back to a post built into the wall of the wagon. Furthermore, I had a rag tied around my mouth in order to prevent me from speaking. Glancing around, I guessed this must have been one of the supply wagons considering the number of food products I could see sitting in crates around me.

At the back of the wagon, the opening had been left uncovered to a view of the outside. This didn't help me very much however, the way the wagon was situated meant that all I had was a view of the forest not very far away. Looking at the forest, I could guess that this caravan had moved from the place I had arrived in, however. From what little I could see; it looked like a much smaller clearing.

It must have been very late when I woke up because I didn't hear any activity from the camp where I was. I could see a faint amount of firelight from what remained of the bonfire, but other than the fara-way crackling of logs and the call of faraway insects, that was all I could hear.

Taking stock of myself, I felt surprisingly fine. Despite being hit in the head extremely hard, by my standards at least, I don't think I even had a scratch to show for it. The only aches I could complain about were the ache in my arms from being tied, and the ache in my ass from sitting on wood in one place for who knows how long.

Relaxing now that I didn't seem to be in immediate danger, I let my head fall back against the wagon wall with a thunk.

What the fuck was happening to me, I thought to myself. I had to wonder if anything that was happening to me was even real. Was this all a dream? Did I get hit by a car, and this was a coma? Recollecting the series of events that had brought me to this point, I stifled a hys-terical laugh from exploding out of me. First, I get teleported some-where else completely out of the blue instantaneously. Second, I get threatened with a spear by a skinny teenager. Third, I get knocked the hell out by some medieval LARPer and then tied up in the back of an honest-to-God wagon.

I couldn't comprehend how this was happening, and I didn't want to.

I must have spent the next hour staring blankly at the other side of the wagon before something knocked me out of it. Raising my head, I was able to put my finger on what had unsettled me. The insects had stopped, and the forest had gone silent.

Something must have caught my eye in my peripheral vision be-cause I looked out to my right at the forest through the wagon's back.

There was movement in the trees.

Freezing up in immediate terror like a mouse before a cat, I tried to look more closely at what was happening at the tree line. As I watched, several indistinct man-like forms started to slink out of the darkness and into the clearing. It was hard to focus on them, however, as the forms of these creatures were blurred somehow. It reminded me deeply of a movie I had seen as a child about an alien stalking an army platoon.

Whoever or whatever was getting closer to the caravan was extremely cautious, even with their ability to become semi-translucent. Squinting, I was able to make out over a dozen forms slowly crawling along the ground, making their way towards the caravan.

For a moment I considered trying to call out to try and wake the caravan or even alert any potential guards that had missed the coming danger. But, for whatever reason these paranoid idiots had put a gag on me. Beyond that, I didn't even have much room to thrash about to try and make some noise, being bound to the wall the way I was.

That decision seemed like it would come back to bite them in the ass shortly.

Before long, the forms that were creeping across the clearing had passed beyond the limited sight allowed by the portal of the wagon. I tensed up, dreading what was surely going to happen soon. These people, this caravan was undoubtedly in real danger right now. Nobody that had any kind of pure intentions would be trying to approach a camp so stealthily. I made the decision to try and hunker down closer to the wagon floor and behind the crate of vegetables I had been looking over the top of.

For long minutes, I didn't hear anything but the suppressed sound of my own breathing. Then, a stifled scream, as if it had been cut short somehow.

After that, the camp erupted in a riot of noise, too difficult to parse all at once.

The sound of banging and shouting, as if someone was pounding on a metal object.

The high-pitched scream of a woman, stifled.

The cry of the horses, frightened by the noise.

The cacophony of steel upon steel.

Considering everything that was no doubt happening in the camp, the attack didn't take overly long. Ten, perhaps fifteen minutes after the ambush had occurred, the furor died down. Outside the wagon, I could hear a harsh, guttural voice in that same language I didn't understand earlier. There was an intonation to one of these voices, louder than the others that I couldn't place, as if every word they spoke had an undertone.

It didn't in any way sound human.

They were yelling and screaming at other people, hitting them as well from the fleshy noises I could hear. I couldn't really tell what they were doing, but most of the voices seemed to be congregating near the bonfire.

After a few moments, one of the harsh voices yelled loudly, causing most of the moans and crying to quiet down. Then, what seemed to be a long explanation from the same voice that had yelled.

This seemed to spark something in the humans, as one masculine voice spoke up, angry and frightened. This caused the harsher voices to erupt in even harsher laughter.

Then, a slicing noise. And two separate thuds.

More screams and cries from the gathered humans, before harsh yelling and screaming caused them to cease.

After that, things moved quickly. I heard struggling as the surviving humans were separated out and moved around the camp. I heard people rummaging through the items left around the camp. I heard the wagons and horses being readied to move out.

I heard the heavy sound of boots moving to the back of the wagon I was trapped in.

With a growling laugh, the figure at the wagon opening tossed something into the wagon that landed in front of me.

It was a woman. Hogtied.

Our eyes met.

She was younger than me perhaps, but only by a few years. Brown hair, brown eyes, tanned skin, and the build of a woman that worked for a living. She could have been anyone back home, the veritable Jane Everywoman.

Right now, she was covered in mud, blood, and tears.

After a moment, the woman seemed to dismiss me. Turning on her side away from me as best as she could, I heard her start to sob silently into the gag that they had fitted her with. Much like my own.

As the wagon started to move out, no doubt being directed by one of the raiders, the end oriented itself towards the bonfire I had seen and heard. I risked a quick peek over the top of the crate I was cowering behind.

Fading in the distance, I could see a vision of horror. The raiders had callously tossed over a dozen human bodies on top of the bonfire. Men, women, those teenage guards, and even a few children were visible.

Burning.

Crackling.

An indescribable smell of burning human meat reached me, even at this distance.

Slumping back down to hide behind the crate once more, I helplessly stared at the wall over top of the still sobbing woman.

Captured twice since I'd gotten here, wherever here was.

What the hell was going to happen to me now?

# Chapter 2
# Sadism Trek

I was jolted awake by a boot to the ribs.

Somehow, I managed to get some fitful sleep in the aftermath of the caravan ambush. It didn't feel like more than a handful of hours. I was still exhausted.

Looking up from where I had been slumped over, I finally managed to get a good look at the people that had attacked the caravan last night.

Tall, was my first impression. I wasn't a short man by any measure, but this man towered over me by at least a foot. He was visibly stooping over in the cramped confines of the wagon. Lithely muscled, pale-skinned and completely bald, they were wearing a combination of rough leather armor and simple leather clothing, all a uniform brown. One of the most striking things about them had to be the mask. They had a finely detailed wooden mask covering their face, carved into the shape of a wolf's head. I could still see his eyes though, an intimidating amber, through the appropriately placed holes. However, what caught my attention the most were the ears.

They were long, extending perhaps six inches from their head and pointed, in an upwards manner.

Catching sight of them, I wasn't as surprised as I perhaps should have been. Obviously, of course, the murderous raiders that killed over a dozen people were some kind of fantasy elf.

Booting me in the ribs again, the elf shocked me out of the stupor I had fallen into staring at him. This time he also barked something at me, obviously a command of some kind. Realizing that the elf had untied and ungagged me at some point, most likely before he woke me up, I raised my hands in a plaintive manner and tried to talk to him.

"Look man, I don't understand what you're trying to say to me," I said slowly, even though I realized he most likely didn't understand me any more than I did him. Hopefully, the tone at least would tell him I didn't intend to try and fight him. Right now, at least.

Even though I couldn't see his face under his mask, I could still tell that the elf was surprised by what he had heard. He stared at me blankly for a few seconds before a small laugh escaped him. That small laugh quickly escalated though, as before long the elf was veritably howling in laughter, even slapping his right thigh for good measure.

I didn't understand what was so funny, and I didn't get a chance to. Darting a hand my way, the elf grabbed my right forearm in an iron grip and yanked me to my feet roughly. Putting me before him, he jerked the arm he was holding behind me and started to march me forward toward the exit of the wagon.

I yelped like a struck dog from this sudden movement. Before I could even try and say something to the elf, we had reached the exit. Suddenly, a boot struck me in my back with force, launching me out of the wagon.

I landed painfully on my front from the sudden booting I had experienced. Laying there dazed, it felt as if the world had gone white for a moment, preventing me from seeing or hearing anything going on around me.

Out of nowhere, a hand grabbed me by the hair and yanked me to my knees. I grunted from the pain, unable to see from the dust that had gotten into my face from the throw. I could hear an excited chattering coming from what must be the elf that had manhandled me, though. He called out, and I could hear some answers from what must be the other raiders.

Rubbing the dust from my eyes, I could finally see what had been going on outside the wagons. Once again, the wagons had created a circle once the raiders had stopped for the night. However, what was happening inside that circle was far different from the near idyllic period piece scene from yesterday.

The elven raiders had brought out all their captives from yesterday and forced them to their knees to sit in a group. For some reason, just like me, everyone had been unbound and ungagged. I could see the woman from last night in that group. Guarding them were four other raiders, nearly identical to the elf that had roughed me up. All of them were bald, all of them had wolf masks on, all of them had amber-colored eyes, and all of them were male. The only difference that could be distinguished between them were the types of leather armor and clothing they wore or didn't wear, and the different weapons they were holding.

With the limited amount of vision that I had from the elf holding my head tight by my hair, I could see other elves ransacking the other wagons. They were tossing things out of the wagon that they didn't want or need or could sell I suppose, and keeping what they wanted.

At the words of the elf holding me, I could see some of the elves going through the wagons look our way. Stopping what they were doing, three of them wandered over in our direction, curious about whatever my captor was saying to them.

When they had reached us, the elf holding me seemed to start explaining something to the others, ending in another laugh. Whatever he was saying to them must have made them as shocked as he had been earlier, because the elven raiders looked at each other in a dumbfounded manner before erupting into laughter. The elf holding me by my hair shook me like a dog, as if to punctuate the joke.

Wrenching me back to my feet by my hair, I was shoved into the group of other survivors and down to my knees. Looking around at the others, I could see that they were mostly women, with only a few other men. I suppose that most of the men had been killed in the fighting.

A shout directed my attention to the front of the group. Another elf, different from the others was standing in front of our group, holding a spear planted firmly in the dirt. Looking closely, I could see that this elf had slightly higher quality gear than the others, with a distinct red marking on his mask's left cheek. A single claw mark.

Now that he had the group's attention, the presumed leader began speaking to the group in the disturbing voice that I had noticed last night. He explained something to them in a matter-of-fact manner in short sentences. He clearly didn't care what the group thought of what he was saying, because whatever he was saying caused some of the women to start crying. He just talked over them until he was finished.

Something he had said must have frightened one of the surviving men past the point of reason, as with a shout he surged up and ran out of the circle of survivors. Not looking back once, he made a break for it towards one of the gaps between wagons. Surprisingly, the guards were fairly nonchalant about this and didn't make any effort to chase him.

The elven leader laughed and took a stance. Hauling the massive spear he had been holding above his shoulder, the elf looked more like an Olympic javelin thrower than a bandit. The spear took on a slight red glow somehow, and with a shout the leader threw the spear with a crack of air, faster than I could see.

Straight through the fleeing man.

With the momentum of both the spear and the man running, the spear ended up pinning the man through the chest to the ground. The man gave a short, weak scream before trying to scrabble at the instrument of his death lodged in him.

Then he stopped.

This caused more than a little bit of crying and wailing from the group of survivors, particularly from one older woman that bore a resemblance to the now-dead man.

I understood now why the group had been untied. It was so that he could frighten us so badly that he could make an example out of someone for the cost of disobedience. And looking at the cruel delight I could see in his amber eyes, I could take a guess as to why he had ungagged everyone.

He liked the screams.

The leader stood by patiently as the sobs of the group began to quiet down, and then motioned to a group of elves that had been standing off to the side. As one, they began to move in towards the group while at the same time the guards pressed in tighter, as if to remind everyone of the consequences of disobedience.

The extra elves and the guards began to separate out the group and rebind and gag the group of survivors. I was singled out by who I could tell was the same elf that had laughed at me earlier. He bound and gagged me before mockingly patting me on the cheek and laughing once more.

After that, all of the survivors including myself were hauled up over the shoulders of individual elves, one on each shoulder as if we weighed no more than a five-pound sack of potatoes. Instead of taking us back to individual wagons like we had been in, the elves took us to one of the wagons that they had cleaned out. Tossing us in, they didn't even tie us to posts on the walls like I had been earlier.

Nobody really struggled, we had all been disabused of the notion of resistance.

I struggled my way into sitting up against the wall of the wagon before trying to take a better look around the wagon at the survivors. Now that I could concentrate on it, I could tell that there were ten women and four men, not including me. Fifteen people, cramped together like rats in one small wagon.

The others were able to really take note of my presence now as well, and they clearly didn't care that much for me. They congregated into groups away from me as best they could, eyeing me suspiciously. I was an outsider after all. Not too long ago I had been a prisoner of their own, some stranger one of their guards had pulled in from nowhere. The only person that didn't seem to care all that much about my presence was the woman that had shared a wagon with me last night. Instead, she just stared off into space mindlessly, unable to care for the world around her and out of tears.

The elven raiders snapped the small wooden gate at the back of the wagon closed, leaving us to an uncertain fate.

***

After a while, the caravan started moving again. I could hear the raiders out there, directing the horses.

As the caravan got underway, I started to wonder what these murderous assholes wanted with us. Objectively, I could understand why someone would raid a caravan, even if I found it reprehensible. Some people didn't care about what happened to others, they just wanted their stuff. But why had they taken prisoners? Were they intending to ransom us off to some presumed human authority? Eyeing the number of female captives with me, I tried not to think of why the raiders could want them.

I supposed eventually I would find out why they'd taken us.

The day passed slowly for us survivors. The only thing of note was that one of the men was unable to help himself anymore and shit his pants. I tried not to hold it against him, even if it caused the wagon to stink.

There was nothing for us to do, no conversation to be had with these gags in. All they could do was huddle together in search of a minuscule amount of comfort. All I could do was stare off into space and think about what was going to happen to me next.

Eventually, night came, and the caravan didn't stop this time. The raiders drove through the night.

***

The next morning, I woke to shouting.

One of the surviving men was being dragged out of the wagon by one of the raiders by his still-bound feet. The man was trying to struggle away from the elf, but he was clearly no match for the strength of the elf. As he passed me, I could see that it was the man that had soiled himself.

There was another elf at the entrance of the wagon that was doing the shouting. As the elf and the struggling human got closer to him, both elves grabbed the human man and bodily tossed him outside the wagon.

The elves followed him and from outside came the sound of what was unmistakably a beating. I could hear the sound of fists on flesh, a mix of shouting and laughter from the raiders, and the muffled screams and cries of the man.

Nobody inside the wagon made a sound.

Once the beating was over, the elf that had been shouting earlier appeared at the entrance once more. This time he was clearly address-ing the whole group when he began to shout again. I suppose he was telling us to hold it or pay the price.

After that, we were picked up and taken outside once more. This time, the caravan had stopped next to a stream. I suppose this was why they hadn't stopped last night, they wanted to reach a source of water. One by one we were carried out of the wagon and down to the stream. Once there, they unbound and ungagged us again.

One of the captors barked a command at the group before gestur-ing to the stream. First, the survivors took great gulps of water, and then they began to do their business.

I followed their lead, making sure I was upstream of everyone else.

When we were done, each of the survivors was given a small loaf of bread and given instructions once more. We ate as quickly as we could, so as not to annoy our captors.

After that, we were bound and gagged once more and tossed back in the wagon. Once there, we were finally able to lay eyes on the man from earlier. He'd been stripped naked and then beaten black, blue, and bloody before being tied up again. Frankly, he'd been beaten so bad I wasn't sure he was going to survive. They must have broken some ribs, because it was obvious he was having difficulty breathing.

There was nothing any of us could do for him.

The caravan started moving again.

***

The man didn't survive the night.

***

This pattern would repeat itself for the next week or so. Honestly, it was hard to keep track of time with the inconsistent way that the raiders drove the caravan.

It was also hard to keep track of time because of how weak everyone was getting. We were being given so little food and water that it was difficult to keep our strength up. Increasingly, I found myself spending more time asleep than I was awake.

But no matter how weak we got, none of us forgot the lesson learned from the dead man.

***

Eventually, the raiders must have reached where they were intending to go. I was too out of it from weakness to notice initially, but the caravan had been stopped for much longer than usual.

But I noticed when the raiders appeared at the back of the wagon for the final time.

They marched into the wagon and started to grab us one by one before taking us out of the wagon. Even if we had the inclination to struggle against them, we were too weak to do so at this point.

They took us outside before unceremoniously tossing us to the ground in what seemed to be a prepared spot.

Struggling to my knees, I finally got a look at the destination that the raiders had been driving us towards.

It was a farm.

# Chapter 3
# Haggling Before the Gates

Actually, farm didn't do it justice. It was more of a plantation.

Stretching out in vast fields in front of me were crops, as far as my eye could see. From a cursory look, it didn't appear to be a mono-crop being grown. Ordered in neat plots, I couldn't quite tell what was being grown from my position. From a distance, I could see a great many different people working in those fields. However, those same people gave me a sinking feeling in my chest, even exhausted as I was.

They were obviously slaves.

All of them were wearing threadbare clothing, with what appeared to be dull black metal collars clamped around their neck. None of them appeared to be in amazing shape, with sunken cheeks and emaciated forms. Toiling away in the fields before me, they were to a fault, as silent as could be.

Each plot had what could only be an overseer or perhaps a guard, to keep an eye on the 'property'. These were slaves as well if not slaves in better shape. The overseers were dressed in slightly better clothing and were obviously better fed. These guards also carried a truncheon at their belt, while trotting around upon the back of a horse in order to keep a better eye out. They still had the collars on, though.

They were, all of them, human. Even the overseers.

Several of those overseers were sitting on horseback in a group not too far away from us, eyeing the raiders uneasily. They didn't seem to care overmuch for those of us that had been dumped in the dirt.

Tearing my eyes away from the overseers before me, I noticed the dirt road snaking its way in between two different types of crop fields. In the distance, I could see a cloud of dirt making its way in our direction rapidly. As the cloud got closer to us, I was able to make out the vague shape of what was coming our way. It looked to be a horse-drawn carriage.

After perhaps five minutes of waiting, I was finally able to get a better look at the carriage as it stopped not far from us. It was, in a word, gaudy. Painted a dark green color, it was covered in gold ornamentation. Even the horses seemed more expensive than the simple workhorses that the caravan and the guards were using. No, these were pure white despite all the dust they had kicked up, with an almost disdainful bearing to them. What caught my attention the most, however, were the two people sitting on the carriage's driver's bench.

I think they were dwarves.

One was obviously a servant of some kind, based upon his almost comically stereotypical butler uniform. With short-cropped brown hair and clean-shaven cheeks, he didn't at all match my mental image of a fantasy dwarf. The second one must have been a guard of some kind, based on his gear. He was wearing, of all things, a full suit of shining silver and gold ornamented plate armor. His breastplate was covered by a green and gold cloth tabard cinched at his waist, with an image of a bull mid-rear painted across it. He had a gaudy-looking longsword belted at his hip, with golden bull horns functioning as a cross guard, and a kite shield slung across his back. I couldn't make out any features under his helm.

Both dwarves hopped down from the seat of the carriage. The servant hurried to the door of the carriage, while the presumed guard leisurely hopped down and ambled over to stand next to it. The armored dwarf stood to the side of the door, with a visibly bored posture, while the servant went to open the door. With a bang, the door opened before he could, sending the servant dwarf flinching back.

Striding down the steps of the carriage was a dwarf that was equally as gaudy as the carriage he had rode in on. Pale-skinned, he wore rich forest green silk robes with a shining golden cape secured to his shoulders with a golden chain. He had much longer hair than the servant dwarf, pitch black in color falling well below his shoulders. He also had a voluminous beard, reaching mid-chest length that had several braids in it, capped with golden rings. In fact, gold seemed to be a theme with him. He had golden rings on each of his fingers, several golden chains around his neck, multiple golden earrings, and he even had golden ornamentation on his belt. Even his shiny black leather boots had golden clasps on them.

Catching a glimpse of his eyes, I could see that they were a bright gold as well, with a slight glow to them. Striding in our direction, he had a walking stick painted as green as the carriage, equally as decorated.

Stopping perhaps twenty feet away from us, the lead dwarf made a show of looking at the lineup of caravan survivors arrayed in the dirt. As he looked over us, I caught his eye briefly. Despite their warm color, they were anything but friendly. He looked at me like I was a bug he had crushed underfoot, with a slight curl of disgust to his lip.

Finished with his inspection, the leader of the dwarves spoke into the crowd of raiders that had arrayed themselves behind us. Hearing boot steps behind me, I saw the leader of the raiders that I hadn't seen in days step out.

He said something back to the dwarven leader before they seemed to enter into some kind of back-and-forth exchange. Whatever it was that the elven leader was saying didn't seem to make the dwarven leader very happy, as he raised his voice briefly, making the armored dwarf lay a hand on his sword. This didn't seem to sit well with the raiders, as I heard some shuffling and mumbling behind me, which only stopped when the leader raised his hand without looking backward.

He said something again to the dwarven leader, which seemed to calm him down. Not taking his narrowed eyes off the leader of the raiders, the richly dressed dwarf held a hand out to the servant dwarf to his right behind him. The servant stepped up briefly, took a small bag off his belt before handing it to his master, and stepped backward with a bow. Looking down finally, the dwarven leader opened the bag and spilled its contents in his hand revealing a pile of gold coins. Taking some away, he deposited exactly fourteen gold coins back into the bag.

Exactly the number of survivors arrayed before him.

As the lead dwarf tossed the bag of coins to the elven raid leader, I closed my eyes briefly in despair. I suppose I knew now why we had been spared in the ambush upon the caravan.

We were meant to be sold as slaves.

Opening my eyes again, I risked a quick glance at the other survivors to my left. The numb look on their faces told me that they already knew that this had been the fate that awaited them.

\*\*\*

After that, the elven raiders left, taking the caravans that they had stolen along with them without a backward glance at the people they had sold into slavery.

As they left, the servant dwarf hurried around to the back of the carriage before unlocking something. From behind it, I heard the servant bark a command at the slave overseers that had been standing off to the side during the entire exchange. They hurried to obey, moving over to where he was. I could hear the clank of chains as something was unloaded.

From behind the carriage, the overseers carried out lengths of chains with manacles and collars attached to them. As they got closer to us, a few of the other overseers unsheathed their truncheons before moving in to hover over us with fearsome scowls on their faces as if to intimidate us. They needn't have bothered, as we were all too weak from hunger and dehydration to even consider resisting them.

One by one, the overseers began to truss us up in shackles and chains. When it came to be my turn, all I could do was limply let them do what they wanted. Even if I hadn't been weak from neglect, I had never been very physically inclined in my life, before I'd been dropped in this hellhole. I was placed at the very back of the line.

Yanking us to our feet, we were just in time to see the richly dressed dwarf from earlier climbing back into the wagon and slam the door behind him. Hurrying back to the carriage from where he had been directing the overseers, the servant dwarf climbed into the driver's seat, while the armored one sat next to him. Shouting a command back down to the overseers, the servant dwarf gestured back down the dirt road in the direction that he had come from. The overseers bowed to him before performing some kind of salute, thumping their right closed fist over their hearts.

The servant dwarf reared the horses and the carriage around, before setting off at a breakneck speed down the dirt road back the way they had arrived. Watching them fade into the distance with unfocused eyes, I was nonetheless startled when the chain attached to my neck was yanked on. Jerking my head to my right, I saw the dirty face of one of the overseers shouting at me. He pushed me forward with the truncheon as the procession of chained slaves started to move.

The overseers marched us for miles in the heat, weighed down with chains, collars, and manacles. No matter how much they shouted, they seemed to catch on that we were too weak to move any faster.

As we proceeded down the dirt road, I could see that we were surrounded by crops. I didn't personally know much about farming, but there seemed to be a larger variety of goods being grown here than I would expect. I only recognized some of them, but wheat, corn, and cotton were among the crops I was able to discern. Something about the huge variety of crops that I could see didn't seem right to me, but I was too exhausted to think about it.

After perhaps an hour of continuous shuffling at our slow pace, buildings began to come into sight in the distance. These were ramshackle things, that looked like they were made from driftwood than any kind of sound material. From those ramshackle buildings, I could see dirty faces peering out at us. Primarily women both young and the elderly, I could see some elderly men as well. All of them wore threadbare rags. All of them also wore those same black collars the overseers were wearing. The overseers yelled something at them, and the other slaves disappeared.

I suppose these were the slave bunks.

As we moved further up the road, I began to see what appeared to be a wall in the distance. Made of carved wooden logs with points at the top, the wall had a gate in front of us that had two guards manning either side of it. These guards were also in full plate with the same tabard as the armored dwarf from earlier, but far less decorated and without a helmet. These dwarves were also carrying spears instead of a sword and shield. Strangely, they were clean-shaven to a fault as well.

When our procession reached the gate, one of the overseers stepped up. With lowered eyes and a deferential bearing, they tried to speak to the guard. The guard cut him off with a wave of his hand before moving off to the side and opening a smaller door rather than opening the gates. Gesturing at us in an impatient manner, the dwarf began to wave us in.

I couldn't muster up the energy to be surprised when the other side of the wall contained a full-blown dwarven settlement.

# Chapter 4
# A Panicked Squint

As we were marched in, I took in my surroundings as best as I was able.

Honestly, the way the small town was set up reminded me of an old west reenactment. Off to the side, I could see that the main road extended away from the closed main gate we were denied entry. In the distance, I could see that the main road extended to what appeared to be a palatial estate that was barely visible from where we were. Wooden buildings that were either single or two-story with signs spelling out unintelligible words lined either side of the main road. I suppose they were stores of some kind.

Going about their day in the midst of all of this were more dwarves than I had seen before this point. Mostly male, I could see a few females bustling about. None of these dwarves were filthy rich looking like the dwarf that had bought us earlier, to my eye. These looked like tradesmen or crafters based on their simpler clothing. None of them gave our procession of manacled slaves more than a disinterested side glance.

I noticed once again that none of them had beards like the rich dwarf from earlier.

As we moved through the town, I was able to get glimpses of what lay beyond the main thoroughfare in the gaps between buildings. Residential buildings, it looked like. Beyond the bustle of the main road, I could see houses laid out between green fields of grass. I could even see an extension of the wall in the distance. It looked like this entire settlement including the residential district was encircled by the wall I had seen earlier.

The overseers moved us farther into the town, towards the end of the row. There, they directed us to the back of a large building that had a line of dwarves leading out of the doors. I guess this was some kind of administration building.

Around the back, one of the overseers knocked on a door set into the building. A few moments later, a harried-looking dwarf in some kind of uniform opened it. Before the overseer could even say a word to him, the clean-shaven dwarf audibly groaned. Ducking his head back in, the dwarf shouted something inside the building. Emerging again, the dwarven clerk waved us in impatiently.

We were brought to a back room where two other dwarves in uniform were preparing. The first dwarf was sitting behind a small desk, going over a large ledger book.

The second dwarf was warming up a branding iron in a cast iron oven.

We were directed to stand against the far wall from the dwarf at the desk, where we were unchained from each other and chained to the wall instead. After perhaps five minutes of tense waiting on behalf of us survivors, the dwarf at the oven said something to the dwarf at the desk. Looking up, the desk dwarf pointed to the first person in line and waved them closer to him. It was the woman who had been thrown into the wagon with me that first night after the attack. Unchaining her from the wall, one of the overseer's force-marched her to stand in front of the desk. The woman was trembling in fear.

The dwarf at the desk didn't say a word to her, he just looked at her strangely for a few moments. After that, he looked down back at his ledger and wrote some things down. When he was done, he waved her away to his left. Where the dwarf with the branding iron waited.

With a stifling hand on her shoulder, the overseer marched her over to the dwarf that was stirring the iron around in the red-hot coals. The overseer shoved her to the ground, before turning her on her face. The woman was audibly sobbing.

The overseer grabbed her arms, while the dwarf grabbed her legs. The oven dwarf took the iron out of the fire. Walking over to the terrified woman disinterestedly. He sat on the small of her back. Yanking down her dress to expose her left shoulder. The man brought down the branding iron.

I looked away, but I couldn't block out the sound of her piercing scream or the sizzle of her flesh as she was branded.

I looked back up just in time to see the branding dwarf stand up from where he had been sitting on the poor woman's back. The overseer and door dwarf let go of her arms and legs as well. Setting the iron back in the oven to warm up again, the branding dwarf grabbed a small piece of cloth out of a metal bin that I hadn't noticed earlier. Striding back over to the woman he had just branded, he slapped the apparent bandage on her blackened branding mark callously, drawing a fresh wail of pain from her. Yanking her back to her feet, one of the overseers took her back outside for some reason.

I looked back up at the dwarf at the desk and felt dread begin to pool in my stomach. I was barely able to stop myself from shaking at the realization the same thing was going to happen to me.

Over the next hour, the pattern would repeat itself for the other twelve remaining survivors. First, they would be brought to the desk dwarf to get eyeballed, and then they would be branded. The first male survivor they brought to be branded somehow found the strength to struggle, but a swift punch to the back of his head stopped that. He, like everyone else, was branded anyway.

Finally, I was the last one left. Everyone else had been branded and marched out of the building by an overseer. Looking up at me from his ledger, the desk dwarf motioned in my direction. Grabbing my chain, an overseer shoved me forward till I stood in front of the desk, shaking in fear.

The dwarf gave me the same strange, appraising look as he had everyone else.

And then something happened that hadn't every other time someone had stood before his desk.

He frowned.

He sat back in his chair for a second, before leaning forwards and looking at me strangely again. By this time, the other dwarves in the room had noticed his pause and were looking at the desk dwarf in confusion. Abruptly, the desk dwarf stood up from his desk before hurrying over to stand in front of me. Reaching up, he grabbed the length of chain that was attached to my collar before yanking me down to his eye level. This time, he looked straight into my eyes with an intense look.

Whatever he was looking for he didn't find because he stepped back before turning around, shouted a single word, and kicked his desk. The other dwarves hurried over in his direction before the desk dwarf pulled them into a huddle and they started whispering to each other. Whatever they were saying to each other caused one of them to pop his head out of the huddle and shoot me an astonished look before he was pulled back down.

Chancing a look up at the overseer holding my shoulder, we exchanged confused looks.

I guess this fucker didn't understand what was going on either.

After a few minutes of frantic whispering, the dwarves exited their huddle looking anxious. The desk dwarf rushed over to me before leading me back to the wall. There, he fumblingly reattached my collar chain. Turning around, he started saying something menacingly to the single overseer left in the room. Whatever he said to him caused the overseer to bow frantically and start babbling. Raising his voice, the desk dwarf cut him off and pointed to the door. The overseer hurried out of the building without a backward glance.

The desk dwarf turned back to me with a frustrated look and stabbed a finger downwards to the ground. I just stared at him un-comprehendingly. With a growl, the dwarf grabbed a handful of my shirt before yanking me to the ground and pointing downwards again. He wanted me to sit.

Looking up, I was able to see the dwarves moving quickly out of the room through a door that led further inwards. I guess they didn't give a shit that the iron was still in the oven. Gazing around the room confusedly, I tried to get my bearings.

What the fuck had just happened?

*\*\**

I waited in that back room for hours, surrounded by the fading smell of charred meat. The only way I had to keep track of time in that room was from a small slit window situated near the top of the outside wall. From what I could tell, it was twilight.

Despite how exhausted I was from hunger and dehydration; I wasn't able to take a nap during the wait like I wanted. I had a feeling that the dwarven clerks from earlier weren't done with me.

I was proven right; the door they had left through earlier creaked open slowly as if nobody wanted it to make any noise. Two of the dwarves from earlier slunk into the room surreptitiously and closed the door behind them gently. With no source of light in the room, I couldn't tell who they were from this far away.

As they got closer, I could make out that it was the desk dwarf and the door dwarf from earlier, with the door dwarf carrying a bag over his shoulder. The desk dwarf came closer to me, while the door dwarf walked over to the outside door to gently unlock it. When the desk dwarf reached me, he looked down at me, scowled, and made two extremely understandable gestures.

He put a finger to his lips in a shushing motion and then slashed that same finger across his throat.

Alright then, message received.

I nodded and kept my mouth shut.

Slowly, in order not to make too much noise, the desk dwarf unfastened my collar chain from the wall. Once done, he tugged me to my feet and led me to the back door. The two dwarves conversed briefly in whispers before leading me out the back.

As we left the building, I was surprised that they seemed to abandon all attempts at stealth they had been exhibiting earlier. They made no attempt to conceal what they were doing as we started to move up the road. If I remembered the orientation of the town from earlier, it seemed as if we were heading in the direction of the estate near the end of the road. Despite not attempting any kind of stealth, I could tell that the two dwarves were still somewhat tense. They only got tenser as when we neared the end of the back road, a dwarf in plate mail came around the corner carrying a torch.

The guard-dwarf called out a friendly-sounding greeting to the two dwarves before saying something in a questioning manner. When our group reached him, the desk dwarf started speaking to the guard in a friendly manner. As they conversed, I saw the desk dwarf gesture to me. With a glance, the guard made a sound of understanding before looking away from me. When we were about to leave, the desk dwarf smiled and held out a hand for the guard to shake. From the angle that I was at, I could see the glint of a gold coin in his palm. The guard smiled as well and shook the desk dwarf's hand.

As we got underway and the guard went down the way we came from, the door dwarf let out a sigh of relief and slumped over slightly. The desk dwarf snarled something at the door dwarf under his breath, causing him to stand back up straight.

The two dwarves lead us around to the left side of the wrought iron fence that surrounded the palatial estate at the end of town. There, I saw that there was a smaller path that led up and along the fence with dense tree cover along the other side. Our group traveled up and along that small path for perhaps fifteen minutes in tense silence before the dwarves stopped again. Looking around to see why we had stopped, I was jolted out of my inspection by the desk dwarf jerking my chain again. Glaring at me, the desk dwarf led me towards the tree cover and a small foot path in the trees I had missed in the dark. We proceeded down it.

After another five minutes of walking down the path, surrounded by forest on both sides, we emerged into a clearing.

There was a house in the clearing.

It wasn't enormous like the estate that we had passed, but it wasn't tiny either. Two stories and made out of what seemed to be red brick, it was almost quaint in comparison. Off to the side, there was a smaller structure that nonetheless had a chimney on it. There was smoke coming from that chimney and hammering noises coming from the building.

The two dwarves started to make their way over to the smaller building, tugging me along with them.

For some reason, the dwarves stopped some twenty feet away from the open entrance to the building. It was too dark out for me to see far into the building. I couldn't make out what was making the hammering noise. For the first time, I heard the desk dwarf sound nervous as he called out a greeting into the structure.

The hammering stopped.

I heard the clomp of boots as someone started to make their way out of the building, making the two dwarves tense up.

Emerging from the building was perhaps the biggest dwarf I had seen so far. While most dwarves only came up to about stomach high on my five-foot-eleven inches frame, this one came up to shoulder height for me. He was bare-chested except for a heavy brown leather apron pockmarked with burns, and a pair of leather pants, boots, and gloves. Heavily muscled, broad-shouldered, and soot-stained, he had long, bright red hair and a long, bushy beard. I noticed that he was the only dwarf other than the one that had 'bought' me that had a beard.

He was also scowling.

When he came out, the two dwarves that had led me here bowed to him at the waist and started to speak to him once they had risen again. Even though they were speaking in a deferential manner to him, whatever it was they were saying clearly didn't make him any happier. Noticing me for the first time, he scowled harder.

Glancing back to the two dwarves, he finally spoke to the two dwarves in a rough, deep voice. Whatever he said to them caused the door dwarf to panic, as he literally fell to his knees and started to beg the large dwarf. The desk dwarf didn't stop him and started to speak to the large dwarf again in a pleading manner. Whatever it was that the desk dwarf said to him caused the large dwarf to visibly recoil in surprise. This time when the large dwarf looked at me, it was with clear pity.

Sighing, the large dwarf covered his eyes with one large hand. Dragging his hand down his face and smearing more soot on it, he said something to the two dwarves in an acquiescing manner. Visibly brightening, the two dwarves bowed to him again and began to babble. Cutting them off with a gesture of his hand and a gruff word, the large dwarf waved at us to follow him.

The large dwarf led us to the door of what must be his house before stopping. Turning around, he said something to the two dwarves. They clearly didn't care much for whatever he said, as they began to protest. Raising his voice, the large dwarf said something to make them go quiet. The large dwarf opened the door before glancing at me and gesturing me closer. Hesitantly stepping forward, I was surprised when the desk dwarf defeatedly let go of the chain attached to my collar. For a wild, stupid moment I considered trying to make a break for it before the reality of my condition reminded me of what a shit idea that was.

Slumping forward, I stepped through the door that the large dwarf had opened.

# Chapter 5
# Awakening

I emerged into the entryway of the house, too tired to even be apprehensive. The march from earlier combined with my generally poor state had led to a case of complete exhaustion that I had never experienced in my life.

From where I was standing, I could only make out a few things in the entryway. There was a staircase leading up to the second floor on the right side of a hallway that led to the back end of the house. On either side of the entryway, I could make out two closed doors that led to other rooms. It was too dark in the house right now to make out anything else.

The large dwarf shut the door behind us and locked the door, barring the two dwarves that had taken me here from coming in. I didn't turn my head, but I could feel his intimidating presence behind me. I was barely aware of my surroundings enough to put one foot in front of the other at this point, and I think the large dwarf realized this. Coming up to stand at my side, the large dwarf said something to me in a much kinder tone before putting his hand on my shoulder and led me into the house.

We didn't go very far, as he only led me to a door situated underneath the staircase. Looking back at me with a small frown, the large dwarf opened the door.

I shaded my eyes with my chained hands as well as I could from the light that spilled out.

Despite being in an awkwardly situated location, the room inside was fairly large. It looked lived in, with big bookcases and dressers along the wall. I could also see a large workbench situated along the far wall covered in papers, materials I couldn't place, and tools I didn't understand the purpose of.

There was also a human man inside. Wheelchair-bound.

If I had the energy, I would have been more shocked at the incongruity of seeing what appeared to be a high-backed wicker wheelchair in a fantasy setting. As it is, I was just numb.

As he turned his wheelchair to face the door, I could make out the man inside. He was elderly, looking to be at least in his seventies with a completely bald head. From the collar around his neck, I could guess that this man might be a slave as well. But there were two things about this man that stood out. The first thing was the reason that he was in a wheelchair.

He had no legs. I had some experience with amputees, and with a glance, I could tell that both of his were above the knee. He had tied off his loose pants high up enough to tell.

The other peculiar feature was his eyes. While his irises were pure black, he nonetheless had a distinctly colored pupil. A pure, shining silver. The oddly reversed combination seemed almost inhuman.

As I took him in, he did the same to me. Unlike the large dwarf that had strode into the room before me, he didn't look at me with pity. It was sympathy, instead.

Looking away from me, the man in the wheelchair addressed the dwarf in an inquisitive tone. The large dwarf looked awkward for the first time I had seen, rubbing a hand behind his head as he began to explain something to the man in the wheelchair. As he spoke, the large bushy eyebrows of the elderly man shot up in surprise.

Taking a quick glance at me again, the elderly man asked a question of the large dwarf. Nodding his head, the dwarf spoke to the man again.

Turning back to face me properly, the elderly man smiled at me before gesturing to come inside. As he did this, I realized that I had just been standing just outside of the doorway, staring exhaustedly at their conversation. Too tired to even consider doing otherwise, I stepped into the room.

As I did, the dwarf dragged a chair from the corner of the room and placed it directly in front of the wheelchair-bound man. Guessing what they wanted, I sat down in the chair. Slumping into it, I closed my eyes for a second. I was surprised when I felt large, rough hands grab my own.

Jerking my eyes back open, I could see that the large dwarf had laid a hand on one of my manacles. With an intense look on his face, the dwarf spoke a single word. Both the manacles on my wrists and the ones on my ankles fell off onto the floor with a thunk.

My collar didn't though.

Stepping back, the large dwarf moved behind the wheelchair-bound man and leaned against the workbench on the far wall. I was frozen in surprise for a moment before the voice of the elderly man ripped me out of it. He must have understood that I didn't understand him, so he was speaking to me in a calm soothing manner. Reaching for me, the man took my hands into his own, longer-fingered ones. Even if they weren't as rough as the dwarf's, I was surprised by the strength I felt in them.

Finished with whatever he had been saying, the elderly man closed his eyes and began to visibly concentrate. As he did so, I could feel a small wind start to kick up in the room. Taking my eyes off the man for a second, I tried to find the source of it and couldn't. The window in the room was closed.

Looking back at the man, I was astonished that he had started to glow in the brief second I had glanced away. A growing aura of shining silver energy had started to radiate out of the man, growing larger every moment. As the glow around the man grew larger, the wind inside the room began to pick up as well, until there was a vortex of loose papers from the workbench flying all around us.

Starting to panic, I tried to yank my hands away from the elderly man, but to no avail. No matter how hard I tried, it was like he had the strength of a steel vice grip. In my panic I stood up. I knocked the chair I had been sitting in backward. I prayed the increased force from standing could help.

Throughout all of this, the dwarf just leaned against the workbench and observed calmly.

Furrowing his brow, the elderly man concentrated harder, making the silver glow surrounding him intensify until it was painful to stare at him. After a few more seconds, he must have been satisfied because he smiled slightly before opening his eyes.

As the man looked directly at me and caught my eyes, I screamed in pain. It was incredibly painful to meet his eyes, as they were shining even brighter than his aura. All I could think was that this had to be why they tell people not to look directly at an eclipse. My eyes felt like they were on fire, but I couldn't look away.

Staring into my eyes, the man sat up as much as he was able to and adopted a stern look on his face. Slowly, the man began to recite something that I couldn't understand in a solemn manner. As he did so, the silver glow began to move from the man to me. Creeping along his hands, it slid up my own.

With a surge of energy that I didn't know I was capable of in my exhausted state, I began to yank on our conjoined hands even harder, screaming incoherently all the while. But no matter what I did, I didn't even budge him.

As the silver energy began to completely cover me, the man began to speak louder. By the time that the energy had completely covered my body, he was practically shouting.

With a single shouted word, the man finished whatever he was doing, and when he did, I could feel the energy surrounding me surge inwards, penetrating my skin.

It felt like a bomb had gone off inside my head.

Stumbling back, I didn't even realize that the older man had let go of my hands. I was too busy screaming in pain. Clutching my head. I fell to my knees.

Something was happening to me, but I couldn't tell what. It felt like something was reaching down into the very depths of me, somewhere I couldn't explain, and electrifying it. At a point, it became too much for me to withstand.

I passed out.

*\*\**

Sometime later, I jolted awake upright with a coarse scream.

Despite just waking up, my blood was pounding in my ears like a drum. I couldn't even see properly for a few minutes. Slowly, my blood stopped rushing through my ears and I started to calm down. As it did, I hunched over and put my head into my hands.

"Good afternoon, young man."

Jerking my head back up, I turned in the direction of the voice.

Sitting off to the right of the bed I had been laying in, was the old man in a wheelchair from last night. From the look of it, he had been there for some time. He had a blanket over his lap that he had laid a book on.

At the sight of the man, memories of last night rushed through my head. I remembered the silver light burning my retinas and inflicting an ache that I could still feel even now.

I stiffened, eyeing him warily, saying nothing.

The man must have noticed my reaction to him because he softened his expression before raising a hand.

"I assure you; I mean no harm," The man softly began. "I regret the intensity of your Awakening, but such a reaction is common in cases of your age."

"W-what?" I stuttered, speaking for the first time in days. "What are you talking about? What the hell are you talking about?"

Wait.

I could understand him? He could understand me?

What the fuck did this guy do to me?

So, I asked him.

"Who the hell are you, and what did you do to me?!" I shouted at him, trying to climb out of the bed. I tried to at least, but when I tried to move to any degree, I nearly passed out.

Despite getting some rest, I still hadn't eaten or drank anything in days.

I began to topple forward, face forward off from the bed. Before I could, I felt the man catch me.

"Calm, young man." The man said soothingly as he began to help me sit up. "I will be glad to explain your situation, but I do not believe you have the strength to stand just yet."

After he helped me to the edge of the bed, the elderly man gestured to his left. Looking over, I could see that there was a bedside table to my right. On it was a plate with a glass cover over the top of it, with a glass of water accompanying.

"Firstly though, I believe that you need to regain some strength after your ordeal," he said with a smile. "Please, help yourself."

Still wary of the man, I nonetheless scooted up the bed to hunch over the plate of food. Taking off the opaque glass cover, I beheld a plate of eggs and toast, still steaming hot.

Suddenly aware of how ravenously hungry I was, I started to shovel the food into my mouth with my bare hands, uncaring of the days of collected filth on them. Only pausing to guzzle the water in between handfuls, I finished the food in record time. Frankly, I was past the point of caring if the food had been tampered with in any way.

When I finished the food, I flopped back onto the surprisingly comfortable bed with a sigh. I luxuriated in the feeling of a full stomach for the first time in days before sitting back up with a groan.

Directing my gaze to the old man, I opened my mouth before closing it when he raised a hand to stop me.

"Perhaps, before we begin, we should introduce ourselves." The old man said.

I looked at him for a second before shrugging.

"Alright," I started. "I guess I'll go first."

"My name is Nathan Hart."

# Chapter 6
# A Grey Introduction

"A pleasure to meet you, Mr. Hart." The old man began, placing a hand over his heart and bowing at the waist as best as he was able. "You may call me Grey."

I raised an eyebrow at him. "Just Grey, huh," I said skeptically.

"For now, Grey will suffice," he replied unblinkingly. "Anything more than that is merely window dressing."

That's not suspicious at all, I thought

"Okay, I guess," I said to him, clasping my hands together in front of me and leaning forward. "Now what?"

The older man smiled at me again and mirrored my position.

"Mr. Hart, I understand that you might have undergone somewhat of an ordeal since your capture. So, I can appreciate it if you are wary of extending even the slightest amount of trust. To that end, you are welcome to the use of my washroom in order to cleanse yourself of the road dust and collect your thoughts." He gestured off to the side of me as he was speaking. "Inside, you'll find a clean pair of clothes that you are welcome to as well."

Looking in the direction that he had motioned towards, I noticed a door that I had missed when I had first entered the room. Turning back to the older man, I opened my mouth for a second before closing it. Scooting forward to the edge of the bed, I gave Grey a nod.

"Thanks, that, uh, that sounds pretty nice actually."

"Indeed," he said, returning my nod. "Feel free to avail yourself of the facilities, meager as they may be. Take your time, and consider what questions you may want to ask me. I'm sure you have many, and I'm perfectly happy to answer what I'm able to."

Walking around the bed, I made my way to the door Grey had pointed out. Once I did so, I looked back over my shoulder at him somewhat uncertainly. Once he saw that I was looking at him, he gave me an encouraging nod.

Turning back around, I opened the door and went through, closing it behind me.

***

Grey had called his 'washroom' meager, but it didn't seem so bad to me.

It wasn't very large, and it didn't resemble a modern bathroom very much, but it seemed usable. Inside, I could see that it had what appeared to be a bronze washtub, a small dresser with a large bronze bowl sitting on top of it. Above that was a surprisingly clear mirror attached to the wall above the bowl, a rack that had a few rough spun woolen towels on it. The far wall was what I could only assume to be some kind of toilet.

The problem was, the tub didn't have any water in it, and I couldn't see any way to fill it if I wanted to take a bath. It didn't have a spigot of any kind, and there didn't appear to be water pipes in the room. Looking down at myself, and more importantly, giving myself a sniff test, I could tell I needed a bath badly, however.

Standing around aimlessly for a few moments, I decided that I would need to ask Grey. Somewhat embarrassed, I turned back to the door and opened it.

Poking my head out the door, I glanced in the direction of Grey. I found him staring right back at me, as if he had been waiting for me to come out.

"Hey, uh, Grey right? I don't, uh. I don't see how to, um," I said sheepishly, starting and stopping. "Where's the water for the tub?"

"I see," he said calmly. "Am I to understand that you do not know how to operate the facilities, Mr. Hart? Do you require assistance?"

Feeling my face grow red in embarrassment, I nodded.

"Certainly, Mr. Hart. I would be happy to assist." Grey said, wheeling over to the door.

As I stepped out of the way to let him through, Grey entered the washroom. It may have been small, but there was still room enough inside for the two of us.

"Firstly, I believe you wish to take a bath, Mr. Hart?" he questioned.

"Yeah, but you don't have to keep calling me Mr. Hart, you know?" I said to him. "Feels weird. You can just call me Nathan, or even Nate if you want."

"I see," he said thoughtfully. "Well Nathan, let's begin with the washbasin."

Wheeling over to the washbasin, Grey pointed to three separate bronze disks about the size of my fist that were physically attached to the side of the tub somehow. Leaning closer to get a better look, I was able to see that each of the disks had a symbol scratched onto them in a language that I didn't understand. Each of the disks had a different symbol on them.

Looking back at Grey, I gave him a curious look. "What? What's up with those?"

Nodding thoughtfully to himself, Grey answered me. "These disks are how you operate nearly any form of washbasin, no matter the size. Look here," he said, pointing to the leftmost disk. "This disk will control the amount of water that is added to the basin."

Having said that, Grey pressed his thumb down onto the disk. Hearing a bubbling noise, I looked over the rim of the tub and looked down. When I did so, I was able to see that there was water coming from seemingly nowhere filling the basin from the bottom up. Within seconds the tub was filled nearly to the top.

Taking his thumb away from the disc, Grey gestured to the water. "As you can see, the basin is now filled with water. However, you'll find it to be quite cold. Not at all suitable for a refreshing bath, now is it?"

Pointing to the second disc from the left, Grey continued. "This disc is the one that controls the temperature of the water. Now I say temperature, but what I really mean is heat. This basin does not possess a Plate of Cold, and thus cannot lower the temperature of the water. It merely possesses a Plate of Heat to raise the temperature of the water inside. Like so."

He pressed his thumb to the middle disc like he did the first one. Within a similarly short amount of time, the water had gotten so hot that steam was visibly rising off of it.

"Be cautious, however," Grey said to me, taking his thumb away from the middle disc. "Plates of Heat determine the temperature it exerts based upon how long you lay your finger upon it. If I had left my thumb upon it much longer, the water would have begun to boil. I do not believe that would have been conducive to a comfortable bath, no?"

Glancing at me, Grey smiled slightly.

"Lastly, we have a Plate of Dispersion. Slightly more esoteric in function than the Plates of Water and Heat, this simplified rune will empty the basin when you are finished." Finishing, Grey pressed the third button in the row. When he did, all of the water in the tub simply vanished, instantly.

Jumping slightly, I couldn't help to gape stupidly at everything I had witnessed. I had seen some pretty wild stuff since I had gotten here, but this had to have been the most overt display of magic I had seen. I thought I had internalized the fact that magic had to have been real, otherwise how could I have ended up here? But everything else up to this point had been more subtle than the magically appearing and disappearing water. I suddenly felt dizzy.

Leaning up against the tub away from the magical discs, I crossed my arms, closed my eyes, lowered my head, and murmured to myself. "Magic is real, huh."

I felt stupid immediately for saying it. Obviously magic had to be real, you dense moron. Feeling overdramatic and silly, I opened my eyes and looked over at Grey.

He was staring back at me with a raised eyebrow. "Indeed. Magic is quite real, young man," he said dryly.

Coughing into my fist, I desperately searched for something to say. "So, uh, how safe are those things? If I had been sitting inside the tub when I pressed the Plate of, um, Dispersion right? Would I have been vanished or destroyed or something?"

"They're quite safe Nathan, no need to worry," Grey reassured me. "Every commercially available Enchantment Plate has inbuilt safety mechanisms that detect the presence of a soul, and will not trigger if one is detected in its bounds. Besides, it would take something far more powerful than a simple washbasin Plate to disperse a living being."

"Additionally," Grey continued. "The water was neither vanished nor destroyed, as you put it. It was merely dispersed, as the name suggests, back into free-floating Aether. Indeed, nothing can ever be truly destroyed, as you so put it. Not even Aether."

Nodding thoughtfully to try and show that I understood what he was talking about, even though I didn't, I nonetheless did catch what he said at the end. Nothing can ever be truly destroyed, huh. That sounded an awful lot like a very important law of physics.

Maybe magic didn't completely spit in the face of the universe after all.

Wheeling away from the basin, Grey continued his explanation. "Moving on, if you inspect the washbowl," he said, gesturing over to the bowl on the dresser. "You'll notice that it possesses the same trio of Plates."

Walking over and looking at the bowl, I was able to see that he was right. The bowl did have those same three discs attached to it, even if they were smaller than the ones attached to the tub.

"Additionally," I heard Grey say from behind me. "If you feel the need to ah, relieve yourself. You'll find that the privy also possesses a Dispersion Plate. I implore you to use it."

Turning around and fixing Grey with a weirded-out look I said, "So these plates can even disperse, um, 'waste'? You don't…breathe it in or something afterward, right?"

Bringing his hand up to pinch the bridge of his nose, Grey sighed wearily. "No Nathan, you are not breathing in any waste after using a Plate of Dispersion. You are not the first to ask that question, and I somehow doubt you will be the last. Any material dispersed in this manner is neutrally aligned and carries no hint of its previous state."

Okay, but I still didn't like the fact I could potentially be surrounded by poo magic being in this room.

Straightening back up in his chair, Grey fixed a smile back on his face. "Well! I hope this was helpful to you, Nathan. If there's nothing else, I'll leave you to your bath."

With that, Grey began to wheel out of the room. Stepping aside to let him out of the room, I told him, "Thanks man, I appreciate it."

"No problem at all, Mr. Hart," Grey said, staring at me thoughtfully once he had exited the room and turned about. "No problem at all."

\*\*\*

I must have been in the bath for nearly an hour after Grey had left, but it was impossible for me to tell the time. Relaxing in the steaming hot bath after the crazy week I'd had and just letting my mind drift felt amazing. Even though I realized this wasn't the end of my troubles, I badly needed to decompress in some manner where I wasn't in mortal danger.

Getting out of the bath and toweling off, I went rummaging through the drawers of the small dresser the bowl was sitting on. Eventually, I found the change of clothes that Grey had mentioned. There were a pair of brown linen ankle-length pants and a matching white linen short-sleeved shirt with a lace-up neck. I was surprised to find Grey had set aside some linen socks and a type of underwear I wasn't familiar with. They resembled boxers, to a degree, but with a drawstring built into them. Everything fit surprisingly well.

After getting dressed I moved over to the mirror to get a good look at myself for the first time in a while.

In my professional opinion, I looked like shit. Even after the bath.

I looked haggard, honestly. I still had the same brown hair as always, which I had brushed backward like I usually did with a bristle brush I had found in the dresser. Still the same dull green eyes, even if I had massive bags under them. Still the same pale skin, even if it looked paler than usual considering everything I had been through. I was surprised I hadn't sunburned, considering how easily I usually burned.

However, peering into the mirror I eventually noticed something strange. In the upper right-hand corner of the mirror, I could see a small blue box moving around. Trying to get a better look at it, the box seemed to be moving around in the mirror in relation to the movement of my eyes.

"The hell…" I murmured to myself, reaching out with a finger to try and touch the blue box.

When I finally managed to touch the glass right over the blue box, I heard a short chime inside the washroom. Jerking in surprise, I glanced around wildly to try and find the source of the noise. It was as if the noise had come from nowhere.

When I looked back at the mirror, I jumped in surprise again. In front of me on the mirror was a large blue box with words on it in a language that I couldn't understand, similar to the runes on the Enchantment Plates that Grey had taught me about earlier. The blue box was so large that it was preventing me from even seeing my upper body in the mirror, even if I could still see the background around the edges of it.

As I watched, astonished, the symbols in the blue box began to rearrange themselves into words that I could read.

**Your Soul has Awoken to Mysticality
Welcome to the System
Would you like to review your Status?
Yes/No**

"What the fuck…" I breathed.

# Chapter 7
# Welcome to Vereden

Alright, okay.

I didn't know what this was, but I had a theory. I'm guessing that whatever this is, it was a result of whatever Grey had done to me last night. Beyond that, I was going to have to figure it out for myself.

I mean, I suppose I could go back out and ask Grey again what this was, but I was still feeling embarrassed from earlier. There's nothing like having an old man explain to you how to work a toilet, as if you were a particularly dim toddler, to make you feel emasculated.

Was it a smart decision to mess around with this myself? No, not really.

Was I going to do it anyway? Yes, yes, I was.

Let's start from the top. 'Your Soul has Awoken to Mysticality'. Was that what Grey had done to me last night? Did he somehow inject magic into my soul? Why the word 'Mysticality'? Was that something distinct from magic? Was I going to be able to do magic now?

I'll admit, I was a little excited at the thought. Since I was a child, I had always been drawn to the typical swords and sorcery style fantasy. I'd always dreamed about the possibility of magic. I had grown up on stories of wizards, elves, and dwarves. Although, my experiences with the latter two had been less than stellar.

The second line was less clear to me, though. 'Welcome to the System'. What System was this blue box trying to tell me about? Some kind of computer system? Wherever I had ended up, it seemed like one of the sword and sorcery settings I had read about in books. But I suppose that it was possible that they had computers as well, even if I hadn't seen one yet. I tried to inspect the mirror, moving my hands around the edges of it. I couldn't find anything to suggest this was some kind of magical smart screen. It seemed like a fairly clear mirror to me.

Finally, the last line was directly asking me a question. 'Would you like to review your Status', with two smaller blue boxes underneath it with the words Yes and No in them. I had little idea what it meant by Status, but I was getting tired of fruitlessly contemplating the mirror without doing anything about it.

Well, whatever.

I pressed my index finger to the blue box with the word Yes on it.

As I watched, the three lines from earlier disappeared, and more text appeared in the blue box.

| | |
|---|---|
| **Name** | **Nathaniel Eugene Hart** |
| **Titles** | **N/A** |
| **Level** | **1** |
| **Age** | **24 Sol** |
| **Race** | **Human (Precursor)** |
| **Affinity** | **Terrestrial** |
| **Class** | **N/A** |
| **Professions** | **N/A** |
| **Health** | **100/100** |
| **Stamina** | **100/100** |
| **Vitality** | **10** |
| **Strength** | **10** |
| **Spirit** | **10** |
| **Dexterity** | **10** |
| **Perception** | **10** |
| **Intelligence** | **10** |
| **Wisdom** | **10** |
| **Free Points** | **0** |
| **Options** | **[Talent Page], [Skill Page], [Profession Page]** |

Okay.

First of all, nobody has called me Nathaniel since I was ten years old. Second, how dare you remind me I have a middle name.

Thirdly, I did not expect Status to essentially mean RPG status. Jesus, it was like I was looking at a tabletop RPG class sheet. I had never been into tabletop RPGs, but I was familiar with the concept. I had always been more of a video game guy, honestly.

Looking over my "Status", there wasn't much in the way of an explanation. Maybe there was some way to get one. If this was a Status page straight from an RPG or an MMO, perhaps there was a help function? There wasn't a button or anything I could press for that, so maybe it was verbal? I gave it a shot.

"Help!"

"Contact an admin!"

"Uh, open a ticket!"

"Customer support!"

I tried not to speak too loudly, conscious of Grey, likely still in the other room. But nothing happened. The blue screen was still the same with no changes. Looking over the screen again, I came back to the last line. 'Options'. I guess these were the only way for me to interact with my Status right now. Talents, Skills, and Professions. Of the three options available to me, only one of them was accessible to me. The Skill and Profession page options were greyed out. That left the Talent Page if I wanted to inspect this any further.

I gave it a shot.

The Status screen changed again, wiping out everything that had already been on it. Instead, this time it rearranged itself into three distinct columns that were divided. The left column had a header titled "Racial Talents", while the middle and right columns were titled "General Talents" and "Class Talents". I noticed the Class column was greyed out as well, while the General column appeared blank. However, there were four entries under the Racial Talents column.

**Racial Talents        General Talents        Class Talents**
**Hidden Amidst the Spheres: Veil your Status**
**The Scintillant Blade: Strike the root**
**Dream of the Infinite:    Allows unshackled Aetherial growth**
**Language Adaptation: Allows understanding and communication with all discovered sapient species**

I totally understood all of this, one hundred percent.

Of the four "Racial" talents that I had, two were completely vague, one was opaque, and the last was obvious. I guess that Language

Adaptation was why I could suddenly understand Grey after he had apparently 'awoke my soul to mysticality'.

I had questions about this, and I'm guessing that Grey knew the answers. The way he had spoken to me earlier most likely meant that I was supposed to discover all of this while in the washroom. Especially considering I could only see this stuff in the mirror.

I guess it was time to go and ask him.

Giving one last glance at the mirror before I left, I tried one last command. "Close Status?"

Surprisingly, that one worked. The blue box vanished from the mirror. It didn't leave the smaller version I had noticed in the corner of my eye from earlier.

Shaking my head, I opened the washroom door and stepped out.

\*\*\*

Entering back into what I had guessed was Grey's bed/workroom, I saw that he hadn't left while I was in the washroom. He was reading the book I had noticed from earlier; I suppose to pass the time. When I exited the washroom, he looked up at me and gave me a slight nod.

Closing his book and folding his hands back over it, Grey motioned to the bed and spoke. "Done with your bath, then? I believe that now is as good a time as any to continue our conversation. I'm quite sure you have questions."

Nodding back at him, I said. "Yeah, you could say that. I have a lot of questions."

When I walked back over and sat back on the bed, I resumed my posture from earlier, clasping my hands together and leaning forward. Looking at Grey, I opened my mouth for a second and then closed it.

"So." I started and then stopped.

"So?" Grey repeated, arching an eyebrow at me.

"So…Where am I, exactly?"

"Ah, I see." Grey nodded. "You are presently within the house of my, shall we say, chaperon and friend, Azarus of House Savoy. This house resides in a small town that exists solely as a hub for the plantation and to support the master of the manse, Magnus of House Savoy."

"Okay", I began. "That's…nice, and opens up for some other questions, but I was thinking more broadly than that."

Grey raised an eyebrow at me again. "Very well," He began. "This plantation is, I believe, located somewhere in the general vicinity of the southwestern portion of the Dwarven Principality of Velancia, which is located to the northwest of the Human Kingdom of Herztal. I believe that we're not far from the Barren Forrest, which, if you're unaware, exists as a general buffer between the two states."

I lowered my head and clasped my hands tighter. "Broader than that."

Grey nodded and sighed as if a suspicion of his had finally crystallized. "These two kingdoms, the largest remaining extant powers, exist on the mainland continent of this planet. That planet is named Vereden."

I nodded, still staring at the floor, not trusting myself to speak.

It's one thing to be surrounded by things and people you don't understand, with the suspicion that you're very, very far from home. It's another thing to be told by another person you're on another planet.

We sat in silence for a moment.

I appreciated it.

After a few minutes, Grey sighed again and put his own hand on my tightly clenched ones.

"I believe, Nathan," Grey started compassionately. "That you are a Precursor."

I finally raised my head to look at him. "I'm guessing you know I don't know what that is."

"In truth," Grey said, leaning back into his chair. "Not many would know what a Precursor is. They're a rare phenomenon, only seen once every few centuries. Even then, there have been long gaps in the appearance of one."

"Alright, then what do you know about what a Precursor is?" I said to him.

"A Precursor, to the best of academic knowledge, is someone from outside the known realms. You are likely unaware of this, but the people of Vereden know of six other planets that are known to harbor life. For many, many reasons, we no longer have contact with five of them, but the point is that we know there exists life outside of our own."

"A Precursor," Grey continued. "Is not from any of these known planets. They are always human, even if described as a variant. They always appear randomly, somewhere upon the mainland continent of Vereden. They have no knowledge of us, nor us of them. They are always Unawoken. And they possess strange powers, even by the standards of the System, once they are Awoken."

"Awoken, huh," I said softly.

"Indeed, Nathan," Grey answered me compassionately. "By your reactions earlier, I am gathering that you have no knowledge of the System. Or even, perhaps, Mysticality in general."

There's that word again.

"No, I don't," I said, straightening back up. "Mysticality. What is that?"

"Ah," Grey finally smiled again. "By your reaction, I can assume that you noticed the System prompts in the mirror. I did hope that you would."

"Yeah, yeah I did," I replied, eager for at least one thing. Even if I was on another planet, getting magical powers had to at least be a consolation prize.

"Mysticality," Grey said, adopting a lecturing tone. "Is the general term that encompasses the tripartite supernatural structure that the sapient races can draw upon. These three parts can be defined as, roughly, Mind, Body, and Soul. The method of drawing upon the powers of the Mind and the Body can be termed as the Art of Magic, and the Art of Cultivation respectively. As Arts, these two disciplines exist as refinement tools. By practicing either Magic or Cultivation, you are essentially refining either your mind or your body into a more perfect state of existence. These two Arts can draw upon two differing energies, that are nonetheless equal in potential. These energies are Mana, for Magic, and Ki, for Cultivation."

"Wait, you mentioned that Mysticality had three parts," I interrupted. "You only mentioned two. What about the soul?"

"Be patient, young man," Grey scolded me lightly. "I was getting to that. Now, as a member of the sapient races you and I have the capability to draw upon either Mana or Ki to practice Magic or Cultivation, past a certain threshold. However, these two are mutually distinct. You cannot draw upon both of them, to the best of modern understanding. The process of unlocking either Mana or Ki excludes the other. However, that does leave the Soul, does it not? What then, if Magic is the Art of the Mind, and Cultivation is the Art of the Body, is the Art of the Soul? That leads to the System."

"The System," Grey continued his lecture. "Is opaque to us. It is imperfect. It has flaws and inefficiencies. We have no knowledge of precisely how it came into existence, even if the precise moment of its initialization is a matter of historical record. There exist only theories about how it came to be, despite knowing that its origins must lie in a certain conflict. What is known is this. The System is a method of

Soul refinement, open to all members of the sapient races. As Magic refines Mana, and the Body refines Ki, the Soul refines Aether. At the moment of its initialization, all members of the sapient races were Awoken and given the knowledge of how to Awaken the System in others, but that gift was never repeated. The System cannot be Awoken naturally, and can only be Awoken by another person. The minimum age to do so is ten years old, or the rough equivalent of that age. However, it is highly, highly recommended that you do so at that age. After age ten, it becomes progressively more difficult to Awake the System in another. The power required in order to Awaken another grows greater every year that they are Unawoken."

Grey paused for a second to take a drink of water from a glass on the nightstand. I jerked out of the trance I had been in listening to his explanation and took the chance to ask a question of my own.

"So, that's what you did to me last night? You Awoke the System for me? Is that why there was a huge light show? Why did it hurt so much?"

Grey set his drink back down and answered me. "Indeed. Your Awakening was perhaps the most violent I have ever personally witnessed, much less done. I do apologize about the discomfort involved, but in Awakenings as late as your own, there does tend to be an element of pain as your Soul shakes off its shackles. Normally, a child only experiences a slight pinching sensation during an Awakening. However, I have to ask. Did you perchance   examine your Racial Talents while in the washroom? Was there perhaps...anything amiss with them? Out of place characters, or missing explanations?"

I looked at him strangely and replied. "I mean, they seem fine from what I could tell. No strange characters, and they all had explanations. Though, the explanations didn't help all that much. I can't tell what most of them do."

Grey sighed in apparent relief before speaking. "Thank goodness. I was worried because of how late of an Awakening yours was."

"Uh, could something have gone wrong?"

"Yes, something could have gone wrong, very much so. Another hazard of late Awakenings is the potential for corrupted Racial Talents. I mentioned before that the System is imperfect. Well, this is one of those imperfections. In cases such as those, the talent in question could end up either simply not working in the best case, or actively hindering the owner in the worst. When that happens, the only hope for that person is to visit a specialist and pay to have the talent removed. There has never been a recorded case of a Precursor with a corrupted talent, but I didn't wish to assume."

I stared at Grey wide-eyed for a moment. "Well, thank fu—"

Suddenly, I could hear the front door open before I heard someone start stomping through the house. Whoever had come in sounded like they were heading in our direction.

"Ah," Grey smiled again. "That must be Azarus. Come, I'll introduce you to him. I don't believe you had the best introduction, but I assure you he's quite kind in his own way."

"Alright..." I said, skeptically. My experience with dwarves haven't been great so far.

After a few moments, I saw the door handle turn and the door swing open. As it was opening, I heard that same voice from last night speaking, this time in a language I could understand.

"Grey," what could only be Azarus said gruffly. "I finished what you asked, but are you sure this—"

When the dwarf entered the room and I saw what he had in his hand, I shot to my feet.

Noticing me, the expression on the dwarf's face fell. "Ah," he said. "Bugger."

Clasped in his hand was a branding iron.

# Chapter 8
# Misdirection

Grey sighed and pinched the bridge of his nose. "Azarus, I asked you to leave it in your workshop to prevent this exact situation."

"Aye, well," Azarus said, not taking his eyes away from me. "I forgot."

Shaking his head, Grey turned back to me. "Nathan. Nathan! Please, look at me."

Dragging my eyes away from the branding iron in the huge dwarf's fist, I looked back down to Grey.

Grey met my gaze.

"Nathan, I promise you," Grey said pleadingly. "I *promise* you that you are not in danger right now. Nobody is going to harm you. Please, sit back down so that I can explain our situation."

My blood was still pounding in my ears from the adrenaline rush of seeing a branding iron again. I don't think I'll ever forget seeing all those people from earlier getting branded by those dwarves, and I had no desire to go through that same experience. Still, something in me, maybe my gut, was telling me that at least Grey was trustworthy.

To a degree. Even though I was one hundred percent sure he gave me a false name.

Maybe my gut was just telling me I was hungry again.

Whatever.

I sat back down on the bed and clasped my hands after one last look at the branding iron before focusing back on Grey.

"Okay," I said, controlling my breathing to tamp down my anxiety. "What's up?"

Grey looked confused for a second before disregarding it. "So far, Nathan, I've explained to you broad topics. Where we are, very basic information on the System and Mysticality. You absolutely need to know these things as a Precursor—"

"You were right!? He's actually a Precursor!?" Azarus interjected excitedly, staring at me with wide eyes. I noticed he had set the branding iron down against the wall. Uh. That's not really something I'd expect from such an intimidating-looking guy.

Grey closed his eyes. "Azarus, please," he said frustratedly.

"Right, right. I'll be quiet." Azarus said, wincing.

Taking a deep breath, Grey continued. "And although those things are terribly important, what matters most right now is the situation that we are all in. You," Grey gestured to me. "Have been captured and sold as a slave to the lord of this estate. Magnus, Heir of House Savoy."

Out of the corner of my eye, I could see Azarus fold his huge arms at the mention of that name.

"I, however," Grey continued, placing a hand over his heart. "Am a political prisoner that has nonetheless been collared and branded like any other slave. This was done in order to hobble me and prevent me from being able to interfere in…a variety of things."

Grey scowled slightly.

For a moment, I could swear that the room darkened as much as his expression.

"At this point, I have no doubt that my imprisonment was something that was orchestrated by certain high-ranking individuals in both the Kingdom and the Principality. As such, once I was captured, I was handed off to the Prince of House Savoy, Magnus's father, in order to hide me away. From what I understand, the decision was then made to ship me off to a remote location. Enter, then, both Magnus and Azarus." Grey said, finally turning to look at Azarus.

"Right," Azarus said, nodding. "I'll take over from there."

Azarus shoved off the wall he had been leaning on during Grey's speech and walked over to the far wall. Picking up a chair, he carried it over and set it down on the right of Grey before sitting down. Leaning forward, Azarus stuck his hand out for me to shake.

Startled to see such a familiar gesture from someone that wasn't even human, I automatically put my hand in his. When his hand closed around mine, I could feel the power in it. It not only felt like he could crush my bones to powder, but that he could do the same to stone as well.

"Nice to meet ya," Azarus started. "Azarus, House Savoy."

"Uh, nice to meet you too? Nathan Hart." I said, somewhat confusedly.

Nodding, Azarus dropped my hand. "Right, okay. So, my situation is a bit complicated," he said uncomfortably. "Magnus, the shite, is my first cousin. When my uncle was thinking about who to hand Grey off to that he could trust, he thought of his own son. Who's just as much of a dumb bastard sadist as he is. Well, the problem is that Grey might not stay a prisoner forever. He's too powerful, too experienced. The Prince figured that if anyone could figure out a way to escape, he could."

At that, I turned to look at Grey with a raised eyebrow. "Just Grey, huh."

Grey looked back at me with an innocent smile on his face, as if butter wouldn't melt in his mouth.

Shaking my head, I turned back to Azarus.

Looking nonplussed at the exchange, Azarus nonetheless continued his explanation. "Well, he figured that if Grey escaped that he would naturally go home and tell everyone that the Savoy had been holding him captive and had even enslaved him. Hell, I'm not convinced that the people that set this whole thing up didn't intend for Grey to get out sooner or later. So, the problem that the Prince had is that he still wanted to hold onto Grey, but didn't want to catch the blame for it if and when he got loose. Enter ol' Azarus, the designated scapegoat." Azarus finished, pointing his right thumb to his chest.

"The plan," Grey picked up. "As we have deduced, is to claim that I was captured by Azarus single-handedly, without the knowledge of House Savoy, in order to ransom me back later. Which is, frankly, ridiculous. Azarus does not possess either the ability nor inclination to do such a thing."

"That ain't gonna matter to either the Council or the Human High King though," Azarus said with a frown. "Both sides would know that it's horseshit. Both sides would know that it was just backroom dealing to get Grey out of the way. Publicly though, it would be a way to avoid war over House Savoy kidnapping the Hea—"

Grey coughed into his fist.

Azarus paused to look at Grey before realization stole over his face. "Right," He nodded. "So, House Savoy would offer my head up on a platter to Herztal in order save face over holding Grey captive. All the while enjoying the benefits holding him captive could bring. And I gotta tell ya, I ain't too pleased to be anyone's scapegoat, especially not that fucker Magnus."

"Benefits?" I said, glancing at Grey. "What kind of benefits? Or can you not tell me that either?"

Grey winced slightly before answering. "I possess some small ability in both Enchantment and Alchemy. As you can see," Grey said, turning his chair around and gesturing at the workbench against the wall. "I am given weekly quotas of artifacts and potions that I must accomplish by my 'owners'."

"Small ability, huh," Azarus muttered under his breath disbelievingly.

Pretending that everyone in the room hadn't heard him, Grey continued. "If I do not finish what I have been assigned, my handler, in this case, Azarus, is meant to punish me in whatever way he sees fit."

"Oh aye," Azarus said sarcastically. "I'll whip ya good if you don't make enough tat for the Prince to hawk and line his pockets with."

"And I am lucky indeed for your forbearance," Grey replied with a nod.

"Okay," I said. "I get some of that. I have some questions though, 'cause that sounds like a lot of assumptions."

"Feel free to ask," Grey said.

"First, if everyone is so certain Grey is going to escape sometime, why haven't you yet? If he's so badass, why doesn't he just blast his way out? Second, if this Prince is so certain that Grey is going to escape, why would he put him in easy reach of his son? I mean, I don't know about you Grey," I fixed my gaze at Grey. "But I don't know how happy I'd feel with my slave 'master'."

Azarus and Grey exchanged a glance at that.

Grey coughed and then answered. "To begin with, we don't know **why** Magnus was given my metaphorical leash. As you say, it's unusual for the Prince to risk his Heir in this manner. It's far more in his character that he would hand me over to one of his underlings and let them catch the blame for his misdeeds."

"As for why I haven't escaped, is because I can neither physically nor magically do so in my state," Grey said with visibly buried tension. "As you can see, I no longer possess legs. I assure you; this is a recent development that was deliberately inflicted upon me. Presumably to make it more difficult for me to escape this trap."

"Oh, Jesus…" I muttered, horrified.

"As it is, I'll have to wait until I can escape to have them regrown. Truly, I never—"

"Wait, what?" I interrupted Grey. "Magic can do that? Just regrow limbs?"

Grey smiled kindly at me. "Indeed. It is an expensive and laborious process, but it is perfectly doable. I possess neither the ability nor knowledge of healing magic to do so myself, even considering this collar I have been forced to bear."

"As for why I cannot simply 'blast my way out', as you so put it Nathan," Grey smiled wryly. "That is due to the nature of how a slave bond works. They suppress both your Virtues and your Class, in a manner so that you are unable to utilize any skills or abilities you may possess, including Magecraft. However, they do not suppress one's Professions, as a slave without access to their Profession might as well be useless. As I am right now, I'm of little use. Luckily for you, the Awakening process is so fundamental to the System that it can temporarily bypass these restrictions. I'm likely the only person in a thousand miles that would have been able to Awaken you."

"Furthermore," Grey continued. "The collars that you and I currently wear are only one part of a functional slave bonding. The branding is the second part, using a specifically enchanted iron. They are useless alone, as neither function fully without the other."

I nodded before pausing and considering. "Wait," I said haltingly. "Wait a second. If they're useless alone, and I'm only wearing a collar, then I don't have this slave bond?"

Grey smiled predatorily. "Oh yes," He practically purred. "In their haste to bring you to Azarus so that I could Awaken you, it seems Messrs Finly and Luca neglected to either brand you appropriately or supply us with the necessary iron. Truly, how sad. As it is, you are only a slave in a legal sense, Mr. Hart."

I couldn't help but feel relieved.

But…

"Okay then," I started hesitantly, glancing at what was still leaning next to the door. "Why did you apparently have Azarus make a branding iron then?"

Grey's smile vanished and I could see Azarus shift uncomfortably.

"Ah…" Azarus rubbed the back of his head before looking away.

"Nathan, you must understand." Grey began. "You may not be under a slave bond currently, but all that is required for you to be forcibly placed under one is to be discovered. It is not uncommon for slaves to be checked by the slave drivers or watchmen in order to root out potential infiltrators. They wish to prevent any of my allies from potentially rescuing me. After all, my presence in this settlement is an open secret among the dwarven populace. That's why Messrs Finly and Luca knew to come to Azarus in the first place."

"So, the plan Grey and I thought of," Azarus picked up, speaking for the first time in a while. "Is that you need a dummy brand."

Azarus gestured over in the direction of the brand he had brought in.

"That garbage is just a piece of shaped pig iron. It doesn't have the slave enchantment on it, and we ain't gonna put it on. Your average flatfoot can't tell the difference between an actual enchanted brand and a fancy-looking scar."

"But what you're saying is that you still want to brand me," I said, tensing up.

"Nathan, please, calm yourself," Grey said soothingly. "I will not lie to you. Yes, we believe that placing a dummy brand on you is the best way to protect you from a full slave bond. However, we aren't monsters. We do not intend to brand you as if you were a common unfortunate slave. Azarus, if you would?"

"Alright." Azarus nodded before getting up out of his chair. He walked over to Grey's workbench before opening a drawer and taking out three bottles and carrying them back over to Grey. When he did so, I could tell that each of the bottles were filled with differently colored liquids. One liquid was midnight blue in color, one was yellow, and one was red.

"This," Grey said, holding up the bottle with a blue liquid in it. "Is a potion of sleep. We intend for you to be asleep during the process, in order to make the ordeal easier for you. The other two potions are meant to numb the area that the brand will be applied to, and to heal the brand afterward."

Grey showed me the yellow potion and the red potion respectively.

"These two will need to be applied to the area that is to be branded, in order to be most effective."

"So, if I agree to this, I won't feel it at all?" I said, relaxing somewhat.

"Indeed, Nathan. We truly believe that this is the best way in order to protect you from being constrained by a slave bond." Grey said compassionately.

"And hell," Azarus interjected. "It'll just be a scar when we're done. Nothing stopping you from getting it healed if we ever get out of here."

I leaned back on my hands. "Escape, huh. You've mentioned that before. You think we could pull it off?"

Grey and Azarus exchanged a glance.

Grey cleared his throat. "Well," He started awkwardly. "Right now, any plans for escape are a tad unclear. So far, we have several irons in the fire, so to speak, but nothing firm. It is actually *your* presence that has given us some small amount of hope, young man."

"He's right," Azarus nodded. "Precursors are supposed to be able to do some unusual shite once they're trained up. So, general idea is to get you leveled up a bit, teach you a thing or two, and hope you help grease the wheels."

I stared off into space for a few moments.

They were depending on me to pull some kind of deus ex machina out of my ass, huh. Let's pin all of our hopes on the mysterious 'Precursor' that we just met. Not exactly prime plan material, right there.

We were so fucked.

"Okay." I sighed eventually, leaning back forward. "Fuck it. Let's do it. I'll let you brand me. How do we do this, and where do you need to put it?"

Azarus untensed his shoulders while Grey let out a slight sigh of relief.

I raised an eyebrow. "You two look pretty relieved for something that was mainly to benefit me."

Azarus rubbed the back of his head again. "Ah well," he said. "What we didn't tell you, 'cause we didn't want to put too much pressure on ya, is that I could have gotten into some major shit with Magnus if it was discovered that I was harboring an unbound slave."

"Yeah?" I said curiously.

"Yeah," Azarus replied seriously, dragging his index finger across his throat.

Ah.

"If I may," Grey interrupted. "We'll need to place the brand on the back of your left shoulder, Nathan. If you would, I would appreciate you taking off your shirt and then drinking the potion. After that, Azarus and I will begin the procedure."

"What, here? In this room?" I said surprised, looking around. "Don't you need something to heat it up first?"

There wasn't an oven of any kind or even a fireplace in Grey's room.

Azarus smirked. "Don't ya worry about that. I've got it covered."

Right, right, magic.

"Okay," I said, standing up. I then took off my shirt and hung it over the foot of the bed frame. Sitting down, I found that Grey was holding the sleep potion out to me. I took it from him before taking a sniff of it experimentally. I don't know what I was expecting, but I didn't expect a magic sleep potion to smell like a pleasing mix of lavender and blueberries.

"The potion will take effect nearly immediately," Grey said reassuringly. "Make sure to lay down directly after drinking it."

I nodded before holding it up. "Well, bottoms up I guess."

I knocked the potion back, trying to drink it in one go. Trying to at least, as it sure as *hell* didn't taste like blueberries at all. In fact, it was pretty goddamn vile. I managed to drink it all without gagging, but it was a struggle.

As soon as I had drunk all of it, I was already starting to feel woozy. Somewhat drunkenly, I managed to lay back down without falling off the bed.

After that, there was only darkness.

# Chapter 9
# Breakfast and a Choice

I woke up feeling completely fine.

Groggy, I didn't open my eyes at first. For a moment, I didn't remember anything of what had happened to me over the last week. I just luxuriated in the surprisingly comfortable bed that I found myself in. I couldn't tell how long I laid in bed, but after a while, I gradually opened my eyes. I was greeted by a room adorned with plain wooden paneled walls and a similarly wood floor illuminated by an open window.

I didn't recognize the room that I was in.

Turning my head in confusion for a second, still half asleep, I jolted when I suddenly remembered everything. I sat bolt upright with a rush of adrenaline, making my head swim.

That's right. Grey and Azarus said they were going to put me under and brand me.

They said they were going to put it on the back of my left shoulder, so I tried to feel around back there with my right hand. Someone must have put my shirt back on me after they'd finished, I noticed. I thought I might be able to feel something under my fingers, but it was slight. Whatever they had done afterward must have healed it enough to not feel like a raised scar.

Looking around, I guessed they, or rather Azarus, moved me to a different room after they'd finished. It was a much smaller room than the one that Grey had, I could tell. Maybe about half of the size, it only had a bed, a small dresser, and a desk and chair in it. Glancing out the window that I could see from my bed, I could tell that this room must be on the second floor of the house.

Swinging my legs off the side of the bed, I decided to go looking for either of them to ask how the procedure had gone. As I stood up, I grimaced. Either the adrenaline from earlier or the amount I'd slept in the last twenty-four hours had given me a slight headache.

Opening the door to the room, I stepped out. Glancing around, I could see that there was another door across from me that presumably led to another bedroom, and a door to the right. Maybe it was another washroom. On my left was the staircase down to the bottom floor.

As I moved down the stairs, I thought that I could hear something coming from the back of the house. Once I got to the bottom I headed in that direction. As I got closer, I could tell that what I had been hearing was the sound of someone eating. I stepped through the open doorway at the back of the house into what could only be the kitchen.

The kitchen was a bit sparse, honestly. It didn't seem like it had been built with being a kitchen in mind. There were a few tables, presumably for food preparation, a large cupboard, and a small table. There was also a wood-burning cast iron stove with a small chimney that led through the roof. The kitchen also had a few windows along the far wall and a door that led to the outside.

Grey was sitting at the table eating a bowl of something.

As I stepped through, Grey looked up at me and gave me a slight smile and a nod.

"Ah," he said to me. "I thought that I heard you shuffling about. How are you feeling?"

"Fine, I suppose. So, the whole branding thing went well, I guess?"

"Well enough, well enough. Once we had finished and healed the mark, Azarus moved you to his guest room. He wished for me to tell you that the room is yours, for the foreseeable future."

I walked over to the table and sat down on one of the chairs.

I looked around the somewhat sparse kitchen. "So, where is he anyway?"

"Hmm?" Grey made an inquisitive noise, a spoon of what looked like oatmeal halfway to his mouth.

"Azarus," I said. "Is he out back or something?"

"Ah," Grey said with a grimace, setting down his spoon to answer me. "He's stepped out. He had some unpleasant business he had to attend to."

I raised an eyebrow at him. "Anything relevant to the whole, I dunno, situation?"

"Yes, very relevant. You see, when one considers dwarven society," Grey said, adopting a lecturing tone. "Messrs Finly and Luca overstepped their authority, bringing you to Azarus first. What they should have done is take you to Magnus instead. It's understandable why they did so, as they wished to avoid his potential wrath at his inadvertent purchasing of an older Unawoken slave."

"And that's bad? Being Unawoken, I mean? Why would he be pissed at them, anyway? He was the one that did it."

"Bad, in the sense that an Unawoken slave would not be as productive as one with a full Status. In a sense, through their wish to avoid angering him, they may well have saved your life. Magnus may well have simply ordered you…disposed of, shall we say." Grey said with a distasteful look on his face. "As for why he would be wroth with them, well. Let us just say that Magnus is not well known for logical thought."

We sat in silence for a few moments before Grey continued.

"Since Messrs Finly and Luca essentially went over Magnus's head taking you to Azarus, Azarus needs to register you into his legal, ah, ownership shall we say. As a noble, Azarus is the only other dwarf in this settlement legally allowed to own a slave. He needs to settle with his cousin for having finagled a slave out from under him, and so he went to visit Magnus. He's settled on a somewhat believable fiction to explain how you came to 'belong' to him."

"Which is?"

"Simply that he needs a house slave to assist him in his work. Well," Grey said, forcing a smile onto his face. "Enough of that for now! Are you by chance hungry? There's still some porridge left in the pan if you'd like some."

"Yeah," I said, nodding. "I think I'd like that."

***

Grey and I were still eating when we heard the front door open and someone wearing large boots stomped in.

Looking up, Grey said. "That must be Azarus. Azarus! We're in the kitchen!"

We heard the stomping stop for a moment before reorienting in our direction after shutting the door. In moments, Azarus appeared in the kitchen doorway with a huge scowl on his face.

"And how did it go?" Grey said, unfazed.

Taking a moment to take a huge breath, hold it, and then let it out, Azarus seemed to calm down.

"All gods piss on that shite," Azarus replied, still frowning. "But it went fine. He didn't give a rat's arse about one lowly human slave, but it's better than him making trouble later. I stopped by the admin building too on the way home to have a little conversation with the bean counters from last night."

Azarus smirked a little. "Long story short, they understand how things are." He nodded in my direction. "Even got you registered proper. Don't need to worry about some uppity stickman coming by to pound on the door about an unregistered slave."

Azarus walked over to the table and slumped into the last chair available with a sigh.

Grey cleared his throat. "Well," He started. "Since we're all here, it's a perfect time to consider our next moves."

I looked between the two of them for a moment. "And that is?"

Azarus straightened up in his chair. "Gettin' you some levels, I reckon. Which will be a mite difficult if we try and go about it the usual way, so we'll have to be careful."

"What's the usual way?" I asked. "No, wait, let me guess. Killing monsters or something?"

Grey quirked an eyebrow my way. "Indeed. I'm surprised to hear you say that, Nathan. Does your world perchance have some knowledge of the System after all?"

"Ah, no actually," I said, somewhat awkwardly.

How the hell are you supposed to explain the concept of video games to a fantasy wizard and a dwarf?

"It just fits in with similar, ah, stories from back home."

"Very well," Grey said confusedly. "But you are essentially correct. The primary method that the system grants to advance in level is by killing monsters."

"Okay," I said, leaning forwards. "But how does that work? I mean, why does killing something give you XP?"

"XP?" Grey muttered to himself. "No, never mind. To answer your question, let us return to the topic of souls. Through the experience of life, a soul accumulates Aether, the energy of the soul. At the moment of death, as that soul begins to transition into whatever comes afterward, the Aether that the soul has accumulated is dispersed. As a refinement tool, the System collects the Aether that the soul disperses, refines it, and adds it to your own."

Grey paused for a moment.

"However," he continued slowly. "Because I know that you will ask. This does mean that the act of killing another sapient being, such as a human or a dwarf, will disperse the Aether that they have accumulated over their life. However, thankfully, this Aether is largely inaccessible. The refinement that the System introduces is extremely personalized, and thus means that the Aether that another user of the System disperses is incompatible with someone else's."

"Can't imagine the fuckin' mess there would be if people could just go around killing each other and get a bunch of levels," Azarus grumbled.

"Oh indeed," Grey agreed, nodding. "As it is, you can only absorb a fraction of the amount of Aether dispersed by another sapient. As such, the primary way to level is to go out and cull the monster population, which are themselves large amounts of unrefined Aether solidified around a physical proto-soul. Monsters cannot possess a Status or be Awoken after all, even if they can be assessed in a manner as if they did."

I tilted my head a bit in thought. "Okay," I said consideringly. "What about animals then? Do they have souls that accumulate Aether as well? Can killing them give you levels?"

Grey nodded. "They do, yes. However, not as much as a monster. Consider a simple sliding scale if you would," he said, holding up his hands parallel to each other with a large space between them.

"On the far end," he said, wiggling his right hand. "You have the sapient races, such as humans or dwarves, which do not release much refinable Aether upon death. In the middle," He continued, moving his right hand closer to his left. "You have wildlife, which only releases a small amount of refinable Aether. It's not considered an efficient method of advancement, however, nor is it an environmentally sustainable one."

Grey paused to reach for a glass of water next to his bowl of porridge and take a sip.

Setting it down and putting his hands back up, Grey continued his explanation. "Finally, we have monsters," he said, wiggling his left hand. "They release a large amount of unrefined Aether upon death, depending upon the Aether density of the environment they form in. As monsters are largely composed of Aether, their physical form disperses as well. They leave only one thing behind, which is the physical proto-soul composed of solidified Aether they're formed around. These are colloquially referred to as monster Cores."

"For you though," Azarus picked up. "Getting you out to kill monsters is going to be a bit of a problem. Legally, you're a slave. You can't be going off on your own or the flatfoots will catch you, beat you black and blue, and carry you back here. Now, I can take you with me into the forest, but I can't go out often. I haven't been going out much meself, to be honest. Magnus doesn't want me to, so he's instructed his guards to only let me leave town twice a month. The fucker."

"Presumably, this is to make sure he can keep a better eye on me." Grey piped in. "But in reality…"

"It's because the little shite is jealous I'm higher level than he is," Azarus told me. "So, he's trying to get ahead with an excuse like that. He can't bar me from going out at all, or he'd get in legal trouble. What with me bein' another noble and all. He doesn't have the authority of his father to do that. As it is, I can only go out to the forest about twice a month. It's not much, and even then, this area isn't much use to me. The Aether density around here doesn't produce beasties strong enough to help. But it would work for you, so I'll try to take you with me when I can."

"In the meanwhile," Grey picked up. "We'll introduce you to the second method of advancement. Professions."

"It's safer to get started with," Azarus said. "But it's much slower—"

"In fact, you only refine as much as one-seventh of the amount of Aether from crafting a similarly leveled item as you would from slaying a monster. That amount grows to two-sevenths of the Aether you would gain with a second profession." Grey cut in enthusiastically.

"Aye," Azarus said exasperatedly. "Two sevenths then, 'cause you should always take two professions. Between me and Grey, we've got four of the seven professions, so you have some good choices. We'd be able to teach you decently in them. I'm a Smith and an Engineer, myself."

"I am an Enchanter and an Alchemist, as well," Grey said cheerfully. "All that's left is for you to choose what you wish to learn."

# Chapter 10
# Unexpected Circles

I looked between both Grey and Azarus, somewhat bewildered. "Alright, that doesn't help me much, you know. Can't just tell me to choose a couple of Professions when I don't know anything about them. I'm not from around here, remember?"

Azarus glanced away, rubbing the back of his head and mumbling something vaguely apologetic.

Grey coughed into his fist, embarrassed. "Apologies. I let my enthusiasm for the subject get away from me." Shaking off his embarrassment, Grey straightened in his chair. "Let us begin with an explanation of what Professions are and their importance then, shall we?"

Looking back over to Grey, Azarus grunted. "Do ya want me to go get the book, then?"

"Yes, thank you. That would be helpful." Grey smiled at Azarus. "However, I'll start with a cursory explanation."

Azarus nodded before getting up from the table and exiting the room.

"Professions," Grey started, drawing my attention back to him. "Are the unexpected cornerstone of the System. They are the myriad of different pseudo-classes that allow the user to meticulously create whatever their soul desires if they have the creativity for it. In this world and beyond, there are seven categories of Professions. Ah, thank you." Grey said to Azarus, who was coming back into the kitchen.

He was carrying a leather-bound book under his right arm. Nodding at Grey, he put the book down on the table in between Grey and me and then sat back down at the table. I also noticed that he was carrying a small handheld mirror. He set that down next to him.

Looking down at the book that Azarus had brought in, I saw that it was embossed with a stylized rendition of a heptagram. The book was titled rather simply *Professions of the World*, with the initials *S.V.G.* engraved underneath it.

Grey smiled fondly down at the book. "Ah, Silvain von Gradon's magnum opus. A wonderfully intelligent man, but he was sadly lacking with his naming sense." Looking back up at me and tapping the cover of the book, Grey smiled mysteriously. "Care to take a guess on the meaning of this marking, Nathan?"

Leaning over and taking a closer look, I frowned in thought. "Hmm," I muttered. A heptagram, with seven points...

I looked up at Grey. "I'm guessing this symbol has something to do with Professions?"

"Indeed," Grey nodded. "The heptagram represents the Profession system. At each point along the symbol lies one of the seven Professions. Those Professions are Smithing, Wildshaping, Enchanting, Alchemy, Artistry, Fleshcraft, and Engineering," he said, tapping each point on the symbol in a clockwise motion with each name he said.

"They're just categories though." Azarus piped in. "You don't end up with one of those on your Status. When you're taught the base Profession by someone that knows it, one of two things happens," he said, holding up one finger. "One, you can influence what Profession you end up with. Say your pa' was a Carpenter and you want to learn how to be a Carpenter from him. First, he would teach you the base Profession of Engineering, and then you would concentrate on becoming a Carpenter. System is a'ok with you choosing your own Professions like that. Two," he said, folding down one of his fingers. "You let the System choose the Profession you end up with. The System is burrowed deep into your soul, right? Supposedly, it knows you best and can choose what would suit you most."

"It's considered the more romantic option," Grey said thoughtfully. "But I recommend it. Generally, those who let the System choose for them are more likely to express satisfaction and joy in their work."

"Hey now, I chose me own Professions and I enjoy them just fine," Azarus said to Grey.

"Of course," Grey said, conceding. "However, this belabors the point of why everyone, even serious Classers focus intently on their Professions. It isn't because they have a deep devotion to the art of creation, after all. It's because the more you create, the more complex and powerful your creations, the more Impact you create for yourself."

"Impact?" I asked.

"Understand, Nathan, that Impact is merely what the academic community calls it. We cannot measure it in any true way, as the System will not communicate the weight of your Impact. The Impact theory is merely the generally understood mechanism that determines your Class choices at the selection break points. Impact shapes the choices and rarity of the Classes that will be available to you at selection. What you create through your Professions will determine the Class that you receive. As you might expect, this makes Professions exceedingly important." Grey told me seriously.

I leaned back in my chair. "Classes, huh. I saw that my Status didn't have one on it. Just said not applicable. When do those come in?"

"Level ten is the first Class up," Azarus said. "But that's a ways away for you, so don't worry about it for now."

Clearing his throat, Grey said. "Returning to the topic of Professions, you should have an understanding of your options before you choose your two. Let's start with Alchemy, shall we? Alchemy is—"

Azarus cut in. "Alchemy is mixin' shit to get new shit, Enchanting is puttin' magic on things, Smithing is beatin' metal into shape, and Engineering is designin' and buildin' shit."

Grey closed his eyes, pained. "Azarus, please. You know that's only the very surface level."

"We've been jawing enough as it is," Azarus said to him. "Let the man choose already. I bet you want him to just let the System choose his true Professions anyway. We can help him with what he gets afterward."

"Hold up for a second," I said, raising a hand. "What about the other three? Those not an option?"

Grimacing, Azarus nodded. "Well, to start Magnus is the only Artist within leagues of here."

"How do you know?" I asked him.

"Profession info is publicly available—"

"In the Principality, in order to better subjugate you," Grey muttered under his breath.

Azarus carried on like he hadn't heard him. "—so it's not hard to see who has what in a given area. But as for Wildshaping and Fleshcraft, it's probably not a good idea that you try and get those anyhow. Not 'cause you couldn't do them, but because it's a mite suspicious that anyone your age doesn't already have his two Professions. The people in this town are lickspittles that'll run to Magnus and blab to him about the littlest things to try and curry some favor with him. 'sides," He said proudly. "The four we've got here are probably the best you could get if you want to be a serious classer."

Grey sighed. "In some respects, he's correct," he said to me. "But not all. However, he is correct in that the Professions that we possess are likely the best ones you can pursue without raising any suspicion."

I leaned back forward, elbow on the table and chin in my palm. I closed my eyes in thought for a moment.

I was pretty sure I knew what I was going to choose.

I opened my eyes and dropped my hand from my chin. I nodded to both of them, one after the other. "Alright then. Enchanting and Engineering. How do we do this?"

Grey smiled at me. "Simply take my hand and we can get started." He stretched out his right hand.

I raised an eyebrow at him but nonetheless reached out with my right hand and clasped his.

Grey cleared his throat. "It's very simple. Do you wish to learn Enchantment?"

I raised the other eyebrow but answered him. "Yes, I do." As soon as I said that, I could feel a small spark jump between our two palms, as if we had shocked each other with static electricity. Pulling my hand back, I looked down at my palm. Nothing. Looking back up at Grey, I asked. "It's really that simple? How do I know if it worked?"

Grey nodded at me. "It truly is that simple. As for checking it, I believe that's why Azarus brought a mirror with him, correct?" he finished, looking over at Azarus.

"Aye," He nodded. "But first we've gotta do mine. Gimme yer paw," he said, also stretching out his right hand.

I reached over and took it.

Azarus cleared his throat too, exaggeratedly. Out of the corner of my eye, I could see Grey roll his. "Do you wish to learn Engineering?" he said, equally as exaggerated.

I smirked at him, amused. "Yes," I said simply. I again felt a small spark jump between our two palms.

Azarus pulled his hand back to clap it with his other one. "Alright then! Check 'em out and see what you got, 'cause I'm guessing you didn't think too hard on what you wanted," he said, picking up the handheld mirror next to him and handing it to me.

I took it from him before asking them a question. "I'm guessing this is how you check your Status? Like how I did in the washroom mirror?"

Grey nodded. "Indeed. Unfortunately, it's one of the limitations of the System. You may only access or make adjustments to your Status through either a mirror or a reflective surface. Simply focus on the Status boxes in your reflection and concentrate on manipulating them. No verbal element is required."

I nodded back at him before looking down at the mirror and concentrating on the blue boxes that I could see in the upper right-hand corner. They disappeared and new, larger boxes appeared across the center of the mirror.

**You have learned Material Enchantment!**
**You have learned Mechanical Engineering!**
**Would you like to review your Professions?**
**Y/N**

I looked back up at Grey's expectant face. "Looks like I got Material Enchantment and Mechanical Engineering."

Grey raised his eyebrows in surprise. "Material Enchantment is one of the most common forms of Enchantment. It has a long and storied history within the Profession, so congratulations. But Mechanical Engineering? I'm not familiar. Azarus?" he said, glancing over at Azarus.

Azarus stroked his beard for a moment. "Hmm. Sounds like Clockwork. But no, haven't heard of it before. Maybe it's because he's a Precursor?"

I gaped at them. "Seriously? You guys don't have any kind of machines on this planet? Nothing at all? Gears and pistons and ball bearings and all that jazz?"

"Well, well," Grey said, also stroking his beard. "A new profession. It's been some time since that occurred. I take it that you're familiar with the fundamentals, Nathan?"

I leaned back in my chair stunned. No mechanical engineers, huh. In retrospect, I shouldn't be surprised. I'm guessing that magical fantasy land had never had an industrial revolution. "Very, very broadly," I told him. "It's just such a common facet of life back home that it's hard to describe how big it is."

"Hmm," Grey muttered consideringly. "That's generally how a new Profession is introduced. Someone with an existing Profession will begin to experiment and build new knowledge. After a time, there comes a breaking point where knowledge of how a new Profession would work, and it's added to the pool of available Professions. In your case," he said to me. "It's as if so much general knowledge of a Profession was added to the world at once that it instantaneously created a new Profession in a subject that you were inclined towards."

"D'ya think it might've..." Azarus said to Grey, trailing off.

Grey looked at him confusedly for a moment before his eyes lit up. "Oh! Of course! Nathan!" He said, turning back to me. "Does Mechanical Engineering have anything to do with clocks and clockwork mechanisms?!"

"Uh," I said, stunned at his enthusiasm. "Yeah, it does. I'm pretty sure that clocks are just one of the things that fall under mechanical engineering as a field."

Grey smiled wider than I'd seen him do so far. "Then we may well have just witnessed a Profession Shift. Gods, it's been so long since that's happened. It was nearly before my time..." He trailed off. Refocusing, he must have seen the confusion on my face. "Oh, my apologies Nathan. You wouldn't know what that is. Suffice it to say, Clockwork is, possibly *was*, still a relatively new Profession, only about a century old. It's been believed that the Profession was heading towards a Shift, since it's so new. A Shift happens when enough information about a Profession has accumulated among the population that it changes names and begins to encompass a wider field of expertise. It's been long believed that Clockwork Engineers were only scratching the surface of the potential that their Profession could tap into. However, the general belief was that the Shift was centuries of experimentation away. How exciting!" He finished, still smiling widely.

"Okay," I said, nonplussed. "I'm just going to go back and look at my Professions, alright?" Having said that, I looked back down at the mirror and focused on the yes button.

The blue boxes on the mirror rearranged themselves into the familiar heptagram from yesterday, except there were changes this time. On opposite sides of the heptagram, two of the circles were outlined in blue-white light. Inside those circles were symbols now. On the left-hand side of the heptagram, the circle had a small gear symbol in it. On the right-hand side, the circle had a small symbol I didn't recognize in it. I guess those two symbols represented the Professions I had acquired.

"Huh," I said consideringly, looking at the rest of the Profession panel. "Hey Grey, I hate to rain on your parade, but I have a question."

Grey snapped out of it to look back at me. "Hmm? Yes, Nathan?"

"Earlier you said that people can only take two Professions, right? Well, why is that?"

Grey stared at me blankly for a moment. "The answer should be obvious," he said slowly, as if I were a particularly dim child. "It's because once you accept two Professions, the rest of the Profession star closes off."

Out of the corner of my eye, I could see Azarus looking at me pityingly.

I felt an eyebrow twitch. "Yeah? Well, it didn't on mine. The rest of the circles are still open."

Grey froze.

Azarus froze.

"What?" I said, looking between them.

# Chapter 11
# The Eighth

"Nathan, please repeat that," Grey said hoarsely. "Are you saying that you still have open Profession Rings at each of the Professions star's vertices?"

"Uhh," I said. "You mean the circles at the points of the star? Yeah, they're all still open for me."

"Bleeding hells…" Azarus muttered.

Grey looked at me intently for a moment. "I think, Nathan, that it is time you share your racial Talents with us. That is, if you're comfortable doing so."

Azarus snapped his fingers. "Yeah. Yeah! Never heard of something like this, it must be that."

"Okay…" I said, acquiescing. "Um. How do I do that? Can I just show you my Status, or do I have to write it out or something?" I paused for a second. "Wait. Would you even be able to read my handwriting? Did this language skill change the language I write in?"

Grey shook his head. "There are skills to observe another person's base status, but they do not include racial Talents. Nor Talents in general, or Skills. You cannot simply show your Status to another. You'll simply have to relay them to us verbally. As for the intricacies of Language Adaptation," Grey smiled wryly. "We'll save that for another time. Suffice to say, some scholars have spent their lives researching that one, common Talent."

"Alright," I replied. "I have three of them and that language talent. I'm gonna warn you though, they have pretty crappy explanations. The first one is called 'Hidden Amidst the Spheres' and it says 'Veil your Status'. Second is 'The Scintillant Blade' and it says 'Strike the root', whatever that means. The last one is called 'Dream of the Infinite', and it says 'Allows unshackled Aetherial growth." I finished, looking expectantly at Grey.

He stroked his beard thoughtfully for a moment. "It must be the last one that's causing this," he murmured. "The first sounds like a defensive Talent, given to you in order to protect your Precursor status. The second…frankly, the explanation is opaque. Testing will be required in order to determine its effects. But the last…"

"Aetherial growth?" Azarus said, scratching his head. "Okay, so Aether is stuff that souls are made of, and what we absorb to level up. What does it mean by 'unshackled' Aetherial growth?"

"There has long been a theory," Grey murmured distractedly. "That the reason Professions generate Impact is because the act of creation somehow affects the soul. In a positive manner, it is believed. The theory goes that by creating through the use of Professions, you impart some of your own refined Aether into your creations. By doing this, one 'frees up', so to speak, room in your soul for more to fill it. However, the boundaries of the soul are still accustomed to a greater density of Aether, and thus relax, rather than contract. When more Aether is introduced into the soul, the boundaries are more elastic and thus expand until they can tolerate no more. Through this, the theory states that Impact is merely the training of the soul to handle greater amounts and density of Aether. Coincidently, this theory was the life's work of Silvain von Gradon, who penned the seminal work on

Professions. However, to this day it remains only a theory, as it is beyond our ability to observe the inner workings of a soul. Hmm."

Grey looked up from his muttering to see that both Azarus and I were staring at him blankly.

"Ah," he said embarrassedly. "Forgive me. I lost myself for a moment. Suffice it to say, Professions are good for the soul."

"Hells, I could have told you that," Azarus said smugly.

Grey coughed into his fist.

"Returning to the point," Grey said swiftly. "The wording of Nathan's Talent is interesting. When it speaks of 'Aetherial growth', it must be referencing Professions. What is most interesting to me, is that it implies that restriction of only two Professions is a shackle, or perhaps a restriction. Thus, 'unshackled Aetherial growth' must mean that Nathan has no restrictions on the number of Professions that he can take."

"Alright, but what good would that even do? I mean, if that means he could take all seven Professions, that would be splitting his attention too many different ways. It's already hard enough to juggle two Professions." Azarus said doubtfully.

"I have no idea! How exciting." Grey said cheerfully. "Presumably there is some manner of benefit to taking so many Professions, but what it could be is unknown. Nathan told me earlier that his Talents were uncorrupted, despite his late Awakening. It is unlikely to be a detriment."

"Well, okay. I'm down. You guys still have two other Professions, right? Let's test it." I told them.

"Aye." Azarus nodded. "Let's give it a shot." Azarus extended his right hand to me once more.

I took it in my own right hand.

Azarus looked me in the eyes. "Do you wish to learn Smithing?"

"I do." I felt that same spark again. When I did, I let go of his hand. "You're supposed to feel a small spark when you accept a Profession, right? Well, I felt it again."

Grey smiled broadly. "Excellent. My turn then." He extended his right hand to me as well.

I took it.

Grey also looked me in the eyes. "Do you wish to learn Alchemy?"

I returned his stare. "I do."

Spark.

I let go of his hand and nodded at him. "Felt it again."

Azarus piped in. "Well? Don't keep us waiting. See if it worked."

"Alright, alright. Keep your pants on." I told him. I picked the mirror back up again and looked at it. Again, I mentally opened my Status.

**You have learned Blacksmithing!**
**You have learned Medicinal Alchemy!**
**Would you like to review your Professions?**
**Y/N**

Mentally selecting Yes, I brought up my Professions pane. Sure enough, two of the empty circles had been filled in on my Profession star.

But that wasn't the only thing that had changed with it. In the space in the center of the star formed by the intersecting lines, something had appeared. It was hazy, and I couldn't quite make it out, but it appeared to be another symbol written in blue-white light. Whatever it was, it was indistinct. I got the impression that it wasn't finished.

I closed my Status and looked back up at Grey and Azarus.

"Well, it worked," I told them. "I picked up Blacksmithing and Medicinal Alchemy."

Grey smiled widely at me. "Excellent! I've never even—"

"Hold on." I interrupted. "That's not all. Something else is coming through in the middle of the star. It's hazy, but it looks like another symbol. Can't quite make it out though."

Azarus was dumbstruck. "Couldn't be," he said, looking over at Grey. "Could it?"

Grey looked so excited he could explode. "My gods! An eighth Profession! I'm *absolutely* certain something like this has never happened before in the history of Vereden. Well, at the very least in the Post System era, that is," he added offhandedly. "I have no conceivable idea what it could be. We *must* ensure that Nathan acquires it. Presumably, it will fully manifest once he has acquired the other three."

Azarus groaned out loud, drawing our attention to him. "Slight problem with that. We can get him Wildshaping and Fleshcraft if we're careful about it," he said bitterly. "But like I said earlier, that shithead Magnus is the only Artist around for leagues."

Grey paused in his excitement. "Ah…" He said slowly. "That is, indeed, a roadblock."

I looked between them both. "So, what? We give up on the idea?"

We sat in silence for a moment. After being so excited at the idea earlier, Grey looked monumentally disappointed. I'm sure I looked disappointed too. Azarus just looked contemplative.

Noticing the look on his face, Grey said to Azarus. "What is it? Do you have an idea?" he said hopefully.

Azarus didn't say anything for a moment, just staring off into space. After a moment, he leaned forward in his chair.

"There is one thing," he said slowly. "Grey, you know how I have to leave town once a month for Smithing supplies, right? There's shit all for good materials to be found around here."

"Yes?" Grey said. "I believe you go to—" He paused for a moment. "Ah, I believe I see where you're going with this. Do you know someone then?"

Azarus nodded. "Aye, I do. I could probably manage it."

"Hold on," I interjected. "Don't keep me in the dark. What are you talking about?"

Azarus looked over at me. "Well, like I said, I leave for another, larger city every month for crafting materials. Place is called Rhoscara, pretty much the stronghold of one of the other ruling dwarven Houses other than the Savoy."

Grey picked up his glass of water, long gone warm. "Your mother's House, in fact," he muttered into it.

Azarus nodded. "Aye," he said solemnly.

I decided not to ask.

"Well," Azarus continued, looking back at me. "I figure that nobody would care if I took my 'slave' with me to get my supplies."

I raised my eyebrows. "Just like that? No guard is going to try and stop me?"

Azarus nodded. "Just like that. Nobody gives a shit what you do with your legal property, after all."

"Terrible practice," Grey said, shaking his head.

I thought about it for a moment before something came to me. "Wait a second. Hold on." I said, raising a hand. "I'm going to say something right now, and I don't want you two to get pissed about it, alright? It's purely hypothetical."

Grey and Azarus looked at each other for a moment before looking back at me. "Continue, please," Grey said politely.

"Alright," I started. "If me leaving town with Azarus is an option, and I can go with him to this other city, what's stopping me from staying there? I mean, you said I don't have the slave binding because they didn't brand me correctly, right?" I told them. "Don't get me wrong, I'm grateful for what you two have done for me. If you're right, this Magnus guy might have just ordered me killed, and I'm thankful for that. But despite being a Precursor, and despite whatever sick racials I may have, I'm a pretty ordinary guy. I don't know anything about magic, or intrigue, or even how to fight. I can't see how much help I'm going to be to you guys."

Azarus crossed his arms while Grey nodded.

"You are correct in that you do not have a proper slave binding, Nathan," Grey answered me calmly. "But there are two problems with what you say. The first is that although you may not possess a binding, you are still legally a slave within the dwarven Principality. If you decided to stay behind in Rhoscara, someone here would eventually notice your absence and report it to the slave catchers. We would never report you, but it would not be up to us. They would find you eventually, I can assure you. Dwarven slave-catchers are a rightly feared organization for their skill and prowess. They would be able to easily tell that you possess a false brand and would remedy that and then deliver you back here, or to Magnus."

"Not only that," Azarus said gruffly. "But you still have a collar on."

I looked at him. "What's the problem with that? I thought this thing only worked with the right brand? We could just saw it off or something, right?"

Grey winced. "That is an exceedingly bad idea," he said to me. "While you are correct about the relationship between a slave brand and the collar, that is not all that the collars do. Acting as an activation signal for a brand is merely one part."

"Those damn things," Azarus picked up. "Have other enchantments in them as well. First is a standard tracking spell. Doesn't matter where you are, they can find you if you're wearing one. Second, is the death enchantment," he told me. "Whoever holds the control slate that a collar is bound to can activate an enchantment to kill whoever is wearing the collar at any time."

I paled. "T-they can? How?"

Grey coughed into his fist. "Well," he said delicately. "I'm given to understand that different collars have different, ah, functions. Some poison you, while others simply kill you instantly."

"Magnus is a sadistic little shite, so he buys all kinds of collars for the 'variety'. I can tell that yours is an explosion type, though." Azarus told me bluntly, making an explosion with his hands. "Boom."

"So, you're telling me that I'm wearing a literal bomb collar right now," I said, fighting a growing panic.

Grey shot Azarus a disapproving look. Azarus held his hands up in defeat.

Looking back at me, Grey said. "Calm yourself, Nathan. This is not as bad as it seems. I'm given to understand that House Savoy is well aware of Magnus's predilections, and thus ensured that he could not simply execute his slaves with impunity. After all, that would be a waste of good money. Thus, they ensured that the control slate was in the care of the manor Seneschal, Orinbar."

"He's an uptight bastard and doesn't do enough to curb Magnus and his tantrums, but he's made sure that slave deaths were kept to a 'minimum'," Azarus told me.

"Beyond that," Grey piped in. "Physically tampering with a slave collar in any meaningful degree will set off the death enchantment. So no, Nathan, we cannot simply 'saw off your collar', if you don't wish for a premature death."

I took a deep breath, held it for a moment, and then let it rush out of me. "Okay," I said, still anxious. "I guess I'm with you guys. What's the plan then? When do we leave for Rhoscara?"

"Ain't no rush," Azarus said. "We've got a few more days before I'm scheduled to leave again."

"Besides, there are two other Professions you should learn first before you leave, Nathan," Grey said to me. "I believe I have a good idea of how you can acquire Wildshaping. And you, Azarus? Do you know anyone amenable that knows Fleshcraft?"

Azarus smirked. "Oh yeah, I know someone. And they owe me."

# Interlude 1
# Candlelight Liquor

In a darkened room lit only by candlelight, two people sat at a small table nursing drinks. The sun had long set, and the calls of the various wildlife could be heard echoing outside the building. Curtains had been drawn over the window along the far wall to block out the light from the moon.

Azarus stared moodily down into his cup, finding it empty. He reached for the bottle sitting in the middle of the table to pour himself some more, only to find it empty as well. Across from him, Grey had long abandoned his own drink to stare in contemplation off into the distance. He seemed as if he were a million miles away. Azarus sat the empty bottle back down to stare into his cup again.

After a few moments, Azarus spoke up. "So, what's yer take on all this?"

Grey didn't answer him.

Speaking louder this time, Azarus repeated himself. "I *said*, what's your take?" he said. "Oi, Greycton. You there?"

Snapping out of his fugue, Grey directed his gaze back down to Azarus. "Ah," he said slowly, as if he was only now realizing where he was. "Apologies, Azarus. What did you say?"

Pushing his empty cup away from him, Azarus said. "So, what's your take on him? The Precursor guy."

"In what way?" Grey said confusedly.

Throwing his hands in the air in frustration, Azarus answered him. "Pick one! The fact that he even exists, the fact that he might have some kind of eighth bleedin' Profession, or, I don't know. The fact that he somehow made his way here, to you of all bleedin' people, in this bleedin' situation! That don't strike you as suspicious at all!?" he finished, raising his voice.

Grey leaned forward and shushed him. "Lower your voice. He only recently managed to fall asleep."

Azarus relaxed slightly before looking back down at his cup. "My own damn house," he muttered under his breath.

Grey sat back into his wheelchair with a sigh before staring off into the distance again. "I don't know what to think, Azarus. Precursors have no rhyme or reason to the timing or location of their appearance. Some have postulated that the System itself chooses the ideal time for them to appear. Perhaps they're right."

"Don't give me that shite. I know you ain't some kind of Gyreite street preacher, hollering about how we need to trust in the System." Azarus said, looking up at Grey and raising an eyebrow.

Grey made a frustrated sound. "What other explanation could there possibly be? I truly don't believe that Nathan is either malicious or has ill intent. He was *Unawakened*, Azarus. At his age! He has no knowledge of even the most basic knowledge of our world, our society. He's floundering. Frankly, I'm surprised he's holding up as well as he is."

"Holdin' up, huh," Azarus said, unimpressed. "I don't know if we're seeing the same thing. That guy is a mess. He's a tangled-up ball of anxiety and confusion."

Grey leaned forward. "Exactly my point. You know as well as I do the care that Elven slave-takers show to those they capture. I don't know what he saw when he was captured, and I don't intend to ask. Many of those that have undergone what he has simply shut down. I'm thankful that he's not completely broken, at least. He will recover."

Azarus settled down. "Yeah," he said. "Alright, I guess."

"Besides," Grey said confusedly, settling down as well. "Where is this suspicion coming from? What could he have possibly done to bring this on?"

Azarus sighed. "Nothing, I suppose. It's just a damn weird situation. Booze has my hackles up, I'm guessin'."

They sat in silence for a moment.

"An eighth Profession," Grey said wistfully. "I wonder what it could be."

"No bloody idea," Azarus grunted. "The seven we got already cover anything I could think of."

Grey picked up his cup and took a sip of his drink. Grimacing at the taste, he set it back down. He looked back up at Azarus. "The thing is," He began. "The thing is that this is, truly unprecedented. As you well imagine, I've spent a considerable amount of time poring over the Academy's archives, if for no other reason than that I enjoy it. I've never seen even the slightest hint about what an eighth Profession could be. There isn't even any true speculation about the existence of one, beyond academic fringe theories. Why would there be, after all? The Profession page only has seven spots on it, after all." He shook his head. "The Academy likely has the oldest, most intact records still surviving from before Initialization. In all my years, nothing."

Azarus smirked. "All your years, huh? Didn't know you people had records back before dirt was invented."

"Hilarious," Grey said dryly, pushing his drink toward Azarus. With a nod, Azarus took it. Picking up the drink, Azarus mockingly saluted Grey with the cup and then downed what was left in one gulp. Grey grimaced. "Nasty stuff. Don't know how you can stand it."

"It's an acquired taste," Azarus said, finally slurring slightly. "Them Gnolls know how to brew a mean liquor." Setting the empty cup down, he frowned at Grey. "So, we're really doing this then? Putting all our hopes on a freshly Awakened? Man is only level one."

Grey sighed. "What other choice do we have, Azarus?" he said tiredly. "I know people have expectations about my ability, but I'm at a loss. The slave binding is not something I've ever had the time to truly dive into. And now that I've been subjected to it, I find that I've been too crippled by that very binding to be able to truly research it. I have none of my tools, none of my assistants. I do not have my library or the resources I've built up over my long life." His face fell. "I don't have my daughter."

Azarus still retained enough presence of mind to look away uncomfortably.

Visibly gathering himself, Grey continued. "I haven't felt this weak or unprepared in centuries, and I do not appreciate the reminder. But, at this point, yes. I think that the only way I can contribute to our escape is by supporting our new friend. Perhaps he can perform a miracle where I have failed."

"Cheers then," Azarus said grimly, staring back down into the cup Grey gave him. "Here's hoping we're not buggered."

The conversation lulled.

Stirring, Grey spoke hesitantly. "Have you…heard anything new? Perhaps from the new arrivals?"

Azarus shook his head. "Not much. You know I woulda told you if they'd said anything important." He paused. "From what I heard, they were all just members of a fringe farming community eking out a living near the border with the forest. Not important enough to be involved. Supposedly there was a skirmish not far from their home that spooked 'em enough they decided to make a break for it. Poor bastards. They've likely been better off back home than chancing the knife ears."

"I see," Grey said quietly.

Azarus shifted. "They're probably just regrouping right now. Laying low, yeah? They lost a lot of people in the Battle of Helstein. I'm sure the Uprising is doing fine without you," he said awkwardly.

Grey leaned his elbows on the table and put his head in his hands. "I need to be there, Azarus. I *need* to be *there*, instead of here. This is a problem I quite literally created, and it's my responsibility to moderate it. This senseless waste of life will not convince anyone in the House of Lords of the righteousness of their cause, much less the High King. I can only imagine what those vipers are whispering in his ear." He finished bitterly, raising his head from his palms. His eyes were glowing a slight silver.

"Probably why they set this whole thing up," Azarus replied, unperturbed.

Grey settled down. "Indeed," he said morosely.

"Well," Azarus said, raising his empty glass in a mock salute. "Here's to our new friend then. May he miraculously solve all of our problems," he finished, semi-mockingly.

After a moment, Grey reached for the empty bottle still sitting in the middle of the table. He picked it up and clinked it against Azarus's glass. "May he perform a miracle," he whispered.

# Chapter 12
# Gyre?

I was woken up by pounding on the door to my new bedroom.

After our discussion yesterday, we discovered that we had spent all day talking. It had been twilight by the time we had finished, and we had made the decision to turn in early after everything that had happened. I suppose that they were tired from the whole branding procedure, while Azarus also had to go out and speak to his cousin. Personally, I was also bizarrely tired. Maybe from the emotional rollercoaster of everything we had discussed.

With a groan, I sat up in bed. "I'm up! You can stop now!"

I heard a grunt outside the door from what could only be Azarus. "Get dressed and meet me in the kitchen. We have shit to do." I heard, muffled by the door. After that, he tromped away from the door.

Letting my head fall into my hands, I groaned tiredly. I guess we were going to try and get me one of those Professions we had talked about. I did as he said, swinging my legs off the bed and getting dressed. Exiting my room, I decided to check the door at the end of the hallway, hoping it was another washroom to take care of some business. Sure enough, when I opened the door, it was, remarkably similar to the one attached to Grey's room. I entered and did what I had to.

When I finished, I stopped to take a look at myself in the mirror. Honestly, I looked much better than I had yesterday. Some color had returned to my skin, and it looked like I had somehow filled back out a little. My skin didn't seem to be hanging off me as much as it had been. Maybe it was my Status that had helped me recover so quickly? What drew my eyes the most, however, was my collar.

I reached up a hand and laid it tentatively on its black metal surface. Hard to believe that this thing was some kind of magical bomb collar. It wasn't even that large or thick, outside of the loop on the front to attach chains to. I couldn't feel anything magical about it, although I suppose I wouldn't be able to considering how new to this I was.

Remembering something else, I took off my shirt and turned my back to the mirror. Looking over my left shoulder, I tried to look for the brand that they had put on me.

Yup. There it was.

On my left shoulder was the decoy brand they had put on me. It looked like an S turned on its side with a diagonal slash mark through the center of it. It didn't look as deep or as horrifically scarred as I would have assumed a brand to look. It honestly just looked like a neat, stylized burn that had healed over well. I guess that was because they used a healing potion on the mark right after they had placed it.

I wasn't very happy about essentially being branded like cattle, but they'd already told me it didn't have to be permanent. If we ever managed to get out of here, I was going to ask them to heal the brand first thing.

If.

I exited the washroom and went down to the kitchen. Inside, there was only Azarus.

Looking around, I asked him. "Where's Grey?"

Not looking up from his porridge (Porridge? Again? Did they eat anything else?) Azarus said. "He's busy. Everything we did yesterday set him back on the junk he needs to make for the Prince. Just you and me today. Grab a bowl and we'll leave when you're done."

I stood in the doorway for a moment before doing what he said silently. Once I'd gotten a bowl of porridge, I sat down at the table. Azarus and I ate our breakfast in awkward silence.

Finishing my bowl, I set it aside for a moment before looking back at Azarus. "So…where are we going?"

Finally looking back up at me, Azarus answered me. "Going to see a guy named Vandimar. Like I said, this guy owes me a favor. See, he's the nephew of Magnus's Seneschal. A bit of a fuck up, he got in a spot of trouble with the law about a year back. Came running to me, and now I own him. Figuratively," he said, smirking slightly.

I tilted my head in confusion. "If his uncle is such a big shot, why did he come to you?"

Azarus shook his head. "Nah, see. Orin is a bit of a hard ass. Real big on owning up to your mistakes. He would've let Van do the time."

"And this guy can teach me one of the other Professions?" I ask, raising an eyebrow.

"Nope, he doesn't give a rat's arse about leveling or Professions or any of that. But, see, his pa begged Orin to give Van some kind of responsibility, and he did. Set him up as the owner of the only Butcher shop in town. So, he may not have any Professions, but his 'slave' does. We're going to see if we can convince his Butcher to teach you Flesh-craft," he finished, standing up and heading to the front door.

I stood up as well and followed him out the front door. Closing the door behind me, I saw that Azarus was waiting on me. With a jerk of his head, he motioned to the path out of his clearing away from the house. With a nod, I followed him out.

***

We had walked maybe five minutes in silence before we stopped. Or rather, Azarus stopped abruptly.

"Fuck, I forgot," he muttered to himself. Turning to me, he had an awkward look on his face. "Look, there are a few things you should know whenever we're in town, yeah?"

"I'm listening," I told him.

"Okay, so. Legally, you're a slave. That means if you don't want to raise suspicion, you're going to have to act a certain way. Keep your head down, don't stare at people, don't look anyone in the eye. And, well," he said, looking away and rubbing the back of his head. "If anyone talks to you, you have to refer to them as 'Master'. If you don't, they can probably get you punished. I'm telling you; you don't want that."

I frowned slightly. Okay, that sucked, but I guess I could deal. I told Azarus as much.

Nodding, Azarus continued, still awkward. "And uh, don't be surprised if people kind of trip over themselves with me. I'm the only other noble in town, next to Magnus. Dwarves, we're not big on being casual with people that are above us on the ladder, yeah?"

"Alright," I answered him, slightly confused.

Nodding at me, Azarus set off back on the path. I followed him.

***

Maybe ten minutes later of brisk walking, we reached town. I tried to keep my head down, but I could tell that it wasn't quite as busy as it had seemed yesterday when I had been brought here. Could be that it

103

just wasn't that busy in the mornings, could be the new slaves had gotten the town in an uproar. I didn't know, and honestly, I didn't care all that much.

When we exited the path, Azarus's demeanor changed visibly. Straightening his back and lengthening his stride, he seemed like he was walking around like he owned the place. He deliberately schooled his face into a neutral expression and kept his head facing forwards. I kept my head down as best I could.

Out of the corner of my eye, I could see other dwarves stop at the sight of Azarus as we strode through town. Every time, every dwarf that I saw would bow slightly at the waist to him before moving on. Azarus ignored them and just kept walking with purpose.

Finally, Azarus stopped in front of one of the buildings. Looking up slightly to catch a glimpse of it, I couldn't see anything that would necessarily make it a butcher shop. It didn't even really have a sign.

Without turning to me on his left, Azarus whispered. "Watch this."

I didn't have time to question him before Azarus reared up his left leg and kicked the front door of the shop open with a bang. I heard a high-pitched shriek from inside the shop. "Van! Where are ya, ya little sh—" He stopped mid-sentence. "Eh?"

Two people were standing behind the front desk. The first, who was still shrieking slightly, a male dwarf. He was the very image of a fop, with curly blond hair and a powdered face. He was wearing gaudy clothing in reds, blacks, and golds. No beard again, I noticed.

The other was the human woman that I had shared a wagon with that very first night after I had been captured. Raising my head in surprise, I stared at her. Initially, she was gaping at Azarus with wide eyes before noticing me. If anything, she seemed more shocked to see me than the huge dwarf that had kicked in the door.

"Who're you?" Azarus said to the woman confusedly over the shrieks of the dwarf. "Where's Danny? Gods dammit Van, will you shut the hell up? It's just me!"

That seemed to get through to the dwarf, as he finally stopped shrieking and opened his eyes. "M-my lord?" he stuttered. "Oh, my lord, I wish you would stop doing that! It gives me such a fright!"

Behind him, I raised an eyebrow slightly. Now that I understood the language, I had noticed that Azarus had a slight accent, slightly Scottish to my ears. This 'Vandimar' though sounded completely different. If anything, he sounded like he had an Italian accent.

"Yeah, yeah," Azarus said dismissively. "Who's this? Where's Danny?"

The powdered dwarf's face dropped. "Oh, yes. That's right. You haven't been around for some time, my lord. Danny, well." He looked away uncomfortably. "He was chosen for Lord Magnus's little you-know-what. He didn't make it."

Azarus's face darkened like a thundercloud. "That little shite," he growled, clenching his fists. "When is he gonna stop doing that. It's such a fucking waste."

"As you say, my lord," Vandimar answered him, his face lowered.

Azarus sighed, slumping slightly. "I'm sorry Van. I didn't know." He turned to the human woman. "I'm guessing this is his replacement?"

"Yes, my lord. I purchased her just yesterday, in fact. She was with the new arrivals. I tried to run the front desk for a time after losing Danny, but I couldn't quite manage it well." Vandimar said. Noticing me for the first time, he brightened. "Oh! Did you perchance happen upon a new employee as well, my lord?"

"Yeah," Azarus nodded. "Got something to talk to you about. Why don't we do it upstairs? You can stay down here, won't take long," he finished, speaking to me. Afterward, he started walking back to behind the desk, where some stairs to a second floor were set into the right wall. Vandimar scurried after him, leaving us two humans alone.

We stood in silence for a moment, avoiding each other's gaze.

I tugged at my shirt nervously. "So—"

Hearing me speak, the woman jumped before staring at me.

"I can understand ye!" She said in surprise.

"Oh, yeah," I said awkwardly. "I uh. I got Awakened."

"So ye *were* Unawakened then." The woman said, leaning forward. "We thought ye might be. Mighty strange, as old as ye are."

"Yeah..." I said nervously. It just now occurred to me that we hadn't settled on a cover story for why I had only just been Awakened. Shit.

Seeing how nervous I was, the woman dropped the topic. "Well, never did get properly introduced, now did we? The name's Rachel Fergusson," she said briskly, thrusting out a hand.

I stared blankly at her for a moment hurrying forward and taking her hand. She gave it a strong squeeze and shake before dropping it. I let go, shaking my hand. She was one hundred percent stronger than I was.

"Uh, my name is Nathan Hart. Nice to meet you?" I said to her.

"Hart? Like the deer? Nice name, always did like venison." She said in surprise.

"Thank you? My parents gave it to me?" I replied, confused.

"Right, right. So, what's yer story? We," She paused, pain flashing across her face before vanishing. "We were mighty confused about how ye just appeared out of nowhere. Corporal Danvers thought ye might be some kind of rebel spy with the way he couldn't Observe ye."

Rebel. Wonder what that was about?

"Danvers, huh," I said, unimpressed. "Was that the guy who knocked me out?"

"Aye," She nodded. "He was the Army man assigned to our village. He was escorting us through the Barren Forest when, well."

We stood in awkward silence for a moment. We both knew what had happened.

"So, how's Vandimar?" I asked her, desperate to break the silence.

She started, having been lost in thought. "Oh, him? He seems alright, fer a stunty. When the knife ears told us we were going to get sold to some dwarves, I thought fer sure I'd be in bigger trouble. I heard," she said, leaning forward. "That these stuntys really like human women. Thought I might've ended up in a brothel. Butcher shop suits me better."

I raised an eyebrow at her. "Who told you that?"

She paused. "Oh, me brother's wife's cousin, Isabell. She might've been talking out her arse, though. She was a bit of dumb bint, System rest her soul." She finished, making a strange gesture with her hands. First, she held up her right hand with all her fingers together and then brought up her left hand with only her pointer and middle fingers extended across the bottom of her right palm horizontally. It seemed to be representing seven fingers, for some reason.

I stared at her confusedly.

Noticing, she said to me. "Oh, ye don't have the Church of the Gyre where yer from? It's—"

She was cut off by Azarus and Vandimar tromping back down the stairs. At the sight of them, she clammed up.

Still standing behind the counter, Azarus jerked his head in the direction of the door behind him. "Cleared things up with Van. We're good to go." He pushed open the door with his right hand and held it open.

Still standing at the bottom of the stairs, Vandimar was staring at me, fascinated, as if I was a rare animal.

Stepping up awkwardly, aware everyone in the shop was looking at me, I walked through the door Azarus was holding open.

# Chapter 13
# Steak and Surgery

Stepping through the door, I entered what seemed to be a preparation room. It was tiled, with long tables laden with tools and knives along the wall. There were hooks hanging from the ceiling, and a visible drain set into the middle of the room. The room had two other doors in it, other than the one we had entered into, one regular wooden door on the far wall, and one large metal one on the left-hand side.

Azarus had his arms crossed as he looked around the room. He seemed like he was searching for something.

"Ahem," I heard from behind me. "If I could…?"

Turning around, I saw that Vandimar was standing politely behind me. "Ah," I said, realizing. I moved out of the way of the door to let him through.

Smiling at me, Vandimar said. "Thank you, my friend." Having said that, he moved into the room before turning around and addressing Rachel who was staring at us through the door. "We won't require your services for this, my dear. Simply call for me if you need assistance while I'm conducting my business with Lord Azarus and his associate. We'll continue your training when I'm done."

Over the top of him, I could see Rachel silently nod her head.

I guess she only felt like being chatty with me.

Nodding back at her, Vandimar shut the door behind him. Turning back around, he clapped his hands together. "So! On to business!" he said, smiling again. "Lord Azarus says that you need to learn Fleshcrafting? Well, I just so happen to employ a butcher of some skill!"

"Don't see him," Azarus grunted, off to my side.

I started, not having heard him move closer to me. I shot him a side glance, still seeing that he had his arms crossed. Turning back to Van, I started to address him before remembering what Azarus had said earlier. "Ah, 'Master' Vandimar," I said, cringing internally. "You—"

Vandimar interrupted me, chuckling and waving his hand. "Oh, you can dispense with all of that. I don't agree with the practice of modern Luminaran slavery."

Raising both eyebrows, I turned to Azarus. Seeing me looking at him, he nodded back silently.

Turning back to Vandimar, I said to him. "Alright, so you said you employ this person? Is the butcher a dwarf? Is it going to be a problem for them to teach me the Profession?"

Vandimar shook his head. "No, I'm afraid that they too are a human slave. I very much doubt that he'll have a problem with teaching, considering his proclivities," he said, moving past us further into the room. "I say that I employ them, because I pay them a wage. You see, while slaves cannot legally accrue capital and pay to free themselves, nothing is stopping a supportive employer from setting aside a wage for them so they can be freed."

I crossed my arms. "What's stopping you from just freeing Rachel and this butcher right now? Azarus told me you're the nephew of the Seneschal, don't you have the money to do it now?"

Turning back to me, Vandimar had a surprised look on his face. "Is that the impression you had of me? If so, thank you for the compliment," he said, fanning his face dramatically. "But sadly, no. While dear Uncle Orin might be the current Seneschal for Lord Magnus, my family isn't terribly wealthy. We're gentry, after all, not true nobles. My employees are still slaves legally owned by Lord Magnus and thus loaned to me. I set enough aside in the hope that if I present enough to him, he will release them from their servitude."

Azarus scoffed. "Fat chance of that."

"Well, hope springs eternal," Vandimar said to him, smiling forlornly. "It's all I can do. If I'm successful, perhaps I can repeat the process. Despite not being a social equal to Lord Magnus, he doesn't dare dismiss me from his service. He relies on Uncle Orin for all things. Why, I even wonder if his household could function at all without him. He would have to assign me new slaves in order for the town's only butcher shop to continue functioning. Speaking of!" He clapped again. "Bleddyn! Are you around?"

Off to my side, I heard noises coming behind the large metal door set on the left wall. Turning to it, I watched as someone on the other side tried to open it. It seemed to get stuck though.

"Damn thing." I heard someone on the other side of the door mutter through the crack between the door and the frame. With a grunt of effort, the door was fully opened. Striding out of the now-open doorway was another human, a man this time. He was tall, over six feet at the very least, with thick shaggy hair, pitch black in color. Piercing blue eyes were set into a handsome, square-jawed face adorned with a closely cropped beard, as dark as his hair. He was heavily muscled, with scars visible across his mostly bared chest, only blocked by the heavily stained butcher's apron that he was wearing.

Christ, this guy was so good-looking that if I hadn't heard Vandimar call him 'Bleddyn', I would have wondered if his name was Chad. He looked like he had walked right off of the cover of a bodice-ripper novel aimed at lonely housewives.

Vandimar beamed at him. "There you are, my friend! I was wondering where you had wandered off to!"

Picking up a rag from a nearby bench, the man addressed Vandimar while letting his eyes drift over me and Azarus. "I told you that we needed to get the door to the locker replaced, Van. The damned thing is too warped to fit the frame, it's going to cause the meat to spoil," he said, wiping his hand clean on the rag.

Vandimar cringed slightly. "Ah," he said nervously. "I would, but..."

Sighing, the man dropped the rag back on the bench and crossed his arms. "Just take the cost for the replacement out of my 'pay'. Not a big deal, not at this point."

I crossed my arms in puzzlement. There it was again, another new accent. This time, this Bleddyn guy sounded like he had a slight Irish accent. Wasn't this supposed to be an entirely new planet? How the hell did so many people have accents that sounded like they were from Earth?

Catching the movement, the man addressed me. "We have a problem, friend?" he said flatly.

Dropping my arms and raising my palms to face him, I said to him. "Nope. No problem. Just thought you sounded familiar, is all."

"Hmm," he said, noncommittedly. Turning to Azarus, he nodded at him. "Azarus. Been awhile."

Azarus nodded back at him. "Bleddyn. Heard about Danny. Sorry to hear about that."

The man lowered his head. "Yeah. Ain't we all." Raising it back up, he addressed all of us. "So, what's this about?"

I looked at Azarus. He looked at me. We both looked at Vandimar.

Vandimar cleared his throat. "Ah, well. Lord Azarus has brought his new associate here," He gestured to me. "Here to you. He's expressed interest in learning Fleshcrafting."

The man, Bleddyn, sized up Azarus. "'Associate', huh," he said, unimpressed. "Didn't think you were the type."

Azarus stared back at him unflinchingly. "S'complicated. Normally wouldn't, but he was Unawoken when he was brought in. Magnus would have probably thrown him to the dogs. Just trying to do right by him now."

Bleddyn relaxed slightly. "Yeah, okay. I get it." He turned a curious eye my way. "Unawoken, huh. How'd that happen?"

I fidgeted awkwardly. I was reminded *again* about how we hadn't settled on a cover story.

Fuck it, I'll do it myself.

I straightened up and opened my mouth to answer him, but Azarus beat me to it.

"He's from one of those isolated villages from beyond the northern mountains," he said bluntly. "Ventured south, and got caught up in an elven raid. Never heard of the System before in his life. Ain't that right?" Azarus finished, turning an eye on me.

So did everyone else's in the room.

I felt my own twitch slightly. "Yeah, sure. Sounds about right."

"Alright," Bleddyn said, nonplussed. "So, you want to learn Fleshcraftin'? Why?"

This, at least, I had a good reason for. Grey and I'd had a small conversation last night before bed about Fleshcrafting and its options, and I'd made up my mind to actually try and choose which specialization I received.

"Looking to learn Surgery," I answered him. "Healing is a highly respected role in my, uh, village. I always wished I had gone for it when I was younger, but I never had the chance. There was always, uh, someone I wished I could have helped."

Bleddyn and Vandimar exchanged a glance before looking back at me. Bleddyn raised an eyebrow. "Surgery, huh," he said thoughtfully. "Not a bad path."

"Are you fine with this, my friend?" Vandimar asked Bleddyn worriedly.

Azarus raised an eyebrow. "What's to be fine with? Just asking him to teach a Profession. Not asking him to bleeding marry the man."

Bleddyn ignored him. "We didn't get introduced," he said before walking over to me and stretching out a hand. "Names Bleddyn, of Clan Thunderheart."

I took his hand and shook it. "Nathan Hart, of, uh, nowhere in particular."

Couldn't exactly tell him I was from Texas.

"Right," he said, unfazed. "I'll do it. But you have to understand a few things. First, I'm not a Butcher."

I raised an eyebrow and glanced around the room with all the butchering equipment in it that we were standing in.

He waved a hand irritatingly. "This is just the only place that bastard Magnus-" I could see Vandimar wince slightly out of the corner of my eye. "Was willing to stick me. See, I'm actually a Barber."

"So...you cut hair?" I asked him, confused.

He raised his eyebrows in surprise. "Barbers where you're from only do hair? Whatever, doesn't matter. A proper Barber doesn't only do hair, they care for teeth and do some surgery as well. Barbery is related to Surgery, after all. It's an all-rounder version combination Profession of the more specialized Surgeon, Dentist, and Stylist."

"It's useful in more isolated towns and villages that don't have access to big city Professions," Azarus remarked. "Didn't know you weren't a Butcher. Why'd Magnus stick you here?"

"Not like you asked. Who expects a Barber to be doing Butcher's work?" Bleddyn answered. "And like I said, this is the only place he was willing to put me. Too paranoid to let a slave Barber do any work near him. After all, a Barber does a lot of blade work close to some very important bits. Doesn't trust a slave not to slit some throats."

"Aye." Azarus nodded. "That sounds like Magnus. Would ya have done it?"

Bleddyn shrugged. "Hells, I don't know. Maybe? Can't say I'm too happy about being a slave." He paused. "I'd've done Magnus though. In a damn heartbeat."

Vandimar shuddered and wiped his brow. "Can we *please* stop talking about the murder of the legal Lord of this town? You *know* how he is."

"Alright, alright," Bleddyn held up his hands. "But like I said, he didn't want me practicin' Barbery, so he stuck me in a Butcher shop. Accordin' to him, it's all meat in the end. Secondly." He paused and then continued slowly. "Secondly, if I teach you this Profession, you have to understand a few things. Among my people, teaching someone a Profession isn't as casual as it is among you low-landers. If we teach a Profession, we have a responsibility to them. You don't always have to enter into a master-apprentice relationship, but you have to at least show them the ropes. If you're anglin' for Surgeon, I figure I have a few things I can show you. If you're not willing to accept some teachin', I can't help you."

Azarus crossed his arms. "So, you'd want him to come back from time to time, huh?"

"That's right," Bleddyn said, not taking his eyes off me.

I looked between the both of them. "One sec," I told Bleddyn. Afterward, I walked over to Azarus and jerked my head in the direction of a corner away from Bleddyn and Vandimar. Azarus nodded at me and we walked over there. Leaning in, I spoke in a whisper. "Is that fine? You know, considering everything?"

"Should be," Azarus whispered back. "It's not uncommon for slaves to run errands for their masters. Anyone asks, we could just say you were coming down to the shop to get me some meat."

Straightening back up, I turned back around and walked over to Bleddyn.

"Alright?" he asked curiously.

"Yeah, it's fine." I nodded. "I'm willing to accept those terms. I could use a little coaching."

"Gotcha. Remember, if you want Surgery, you have to concentrate on it during the acceptance. Just keep it at the front of your mind, yeah?" Bleddyn said to me before stretching out his right hand for me. "Do you wish to learn Fleshcrafting?"

I scrunched up my face in concentration, trying to think about how much I wanted Surgery. Still concentrating, I took his right hand in my own. I looked him in the eye. "I do."

This one's for you, Dad.

Between our palms, I felt that small electric tingle again.

Letting go of his hand, I nodded at him. "Think it worked? I felt a small shock." I said, playing dumb. Can't exactly tell him I'd done this four times already.

Bleddyn smiled at me. "Aye, if you felt that, then it worked just fine. Don't have a handy mirror on me right now to check it out—"

"Oh!" Vandimar interjected. "I do, in fact! I grabbed one once Lord Azarus told me the reason for his visit. Please, feel free to use it." Having said that, he scurried over to my side. Looking down, I could see him digging out a small handheld mirror that he had hidden in a pocket. Once he got it out, he handed it to me.

"Thanks," I said to him.

He beamed back at me. "You're very welcome!"

Bringing the small mirror up to face level, I looked into it and mentally opened my Status.

## You have learned Fleshcrafting!
## You have learned Surgery!
## Would you like to review your Professions?
## Y/N

Mentally selecting Yes, my Professions page opened up on the mirror. Sure enough, a fifth circle had been filled in at a point on the star, this time with a small scalpel symbol. The symbol in the center of the heptagram in the center of the star was still blurry; however, the only thing that had changed about it though was that the blue-white glow around it was maybe a little stronger? Maybe.

Closing my status, I looked back up at Bleddyn and smiled slightly at him. "Yeah, it worked. Managed to get Surgery, too. Glad I didn't mess that up."

"Good," he said, nodding firmly. "Now we just need to get you out here every once in a while for some lessons." Moving his head in the direction of Azarus, he spoke to him. "Have an idea when that could be?"

Azarus shoved off the wall that he had started leaning on during our conversation. "Hmm," he murmured. "Might be a bit. Got plans for the next few weeks. I'm heading out of town soon. Taking him with me."

"Oh! Is it time for your monthly trip to Rhoscara, my lord?" Vandimar said excitedly. "Do you mind...?"

Azarus rolled his eyes. "Yeah, yeah. I'll get you your pipeweed, as usual."

"Thank you, my lord. I do appreciate you indulging me on this." Vandimar said, bowing slightly.

Bleddyn wrinkled his nose. "Disgustin' habit. Can't stand the smell."

"My friend, I don't smoke for the *smell*, of all things." Vandimar smiled at him.

Azarus coughed into his fist. "Well, that's all we needed. We're heading out, yeah?" He said, looking over at me.

I nodded, having no particular reason to stay.

"Ah, I do have a gift for you, now that I think about it," Vandimar said to Azarus. He hurried over to the large metal door that Bleddyn had come out of earlier and started to tug on it, ineffectually. After a few moments, he looked back over his shoulder at Bleddyn. "Perhaps a little help?"

Rolling his eyes, Bleddyn walked over and yanked the door open enough for Vandimar to enter. Vandimar hurried through the crack. We could hear some rummaging around sounds, and then he came back out carrying a package bound in a waxy cloth tied with twine.

"We recently came into a fine heifer bound for Lord Magnus's dinner table. We kept a few choice slices for ourselves though, and I thought you might like some nice steaks, Lord Azarus." Vandimar said, beaming. He handed the package to Azarus.

"Well, don't mind if I do." Azarus accepted the package happily. He nodded to him and then Bleddyn. "Time for us to head out, I think," he said, before heading to the door we'd entered from and opening it. "'scuse me." I heard, beyond the door.

I looked back over at Vandimar and Bleddyn. "Thanks," I told them. "I guess I'll see you later." Seeing Vandimar smile at me, and Bleddyn nod I hurried out after Azarus. Entering back into the shop I could see Azarus waiting for me at the door, and Rachel looking at me curiously.

"See you later, too," I said to her as I passed her. I saw her blink at that.

Azarus opened the door, and we both stepped through it back into town.

Two more Professions left, then.

# Chapter 14
# Divine History Lesson

We stepped out directly into the sunlight outside Vandimar's butcher shop. Taking a guess based on the intensity of the sun, we might have only been inside for an hour and a half. It must have only been about midday.

Aware that we were out in public again, I tried to adopt a more subservient pose standing behind and to the left of Azarus.

Without turning to face me, Azarus grunted. "Going home." He set off back in the direction we had come into town from.

I followed him without a word, aware of the eyes on us.

Once we reached the secluded path that led back to Azarus's house, I relaxed and sped up until I was walking side by side with him. He glanced at me and nodded.

"So," I said. "Interesting character. Not what I was expecting from what you'd told me about him."

"Hrmm, think I was too harsh. Van isn't a bad guy, just a bit flighty." Azarus mused. "Wasn't some huge crime he committed, anyway. Just got mixed up with bad types and owed some gambling debt."

I nodded. "And that Bleddyn guy? What's your take on this whole mentorship thing?"

"Hill folk," Azarus answered. "They've always been a bit strange. Well, stranger than the rest of you humes, anyway. No offense."

"Hey, I'm not even from around here. *Really* not from around here. Only point of contact I have with the rest of humanity in these parts is Grey, and I guess that Rachel chick," I said to him, unbothered.

Azarus turned his head slightly to look at me. "So, what's the story there? You haven't been around here long enough to really know anyone."

I shook my head. "I don't, not really. Know her, I mean. She was just a member of the caravan that, uh, 'took me in' after I was dumped on this planet. I only saw her a few times after they were raided. None of us could really talk to each other, or even wanted to after what had happened. The raiders didn't want us to, either. Saw a few people get beaten during rest stops for trying."

Azarus shook his head. "Typical knife ears," he muttered darkly.

I was quiet for a moment. "So those were really elves? They seemed so…hateful. Brutal. In stories back home, elves were always depicted as kind, and wise. Not bloodthirsty murderers."

Azarus stopped in the middle of the road. I continued for a moment before realizing and stopping. Turning around, I could see that he had a queer, hesitant look on his face.

Scratching his chin, Azarus spoke. "Answer to that question is complicated, ya know? Grey might be the better person for it."

I looked him in the eye. "Yeah, maybe," I said to him. "But I'm asking you."

Taking a deep breath, Azarus nodded. "Alright, but let's keep walking," he told me. "We still got something I'd like to do after we get home." He set off again, and I followed him.

We walked in silence for a moment while Azarus gathered his thoughts.

"Gods," he started. "The answer to that question lies with the Gods."

"Gods, huh," I said thoughtfully. "So, they're real here? It's hard to tell something like that, back home."

"Aye," Azarus said somberly. "Sometimes we wish they didn't exist either. Now, this all goes back thousands of years. The date wouldn't have meant anything to you before now, but for this it does. We're currently living in the year 2347 SI, or System Initialized. Now before the System, that was really the age of the Gods. Back in those days, there were fourteen of them. Seven Gods of Order, and seven Gods of Chaos. Way I've been told, that didn't always translate to good and evil, but it was a decent guidepost."

He paused to collect his thoughts.

"What history we still have after all the devastation of the war, tells us they were mighty fractious. They'd get into scraps all the time, for thousands of years before the System was even an idea. But something changed between 'em a couple of hundred years before the System. Went rabid, they did. Launched a bloody great war between, well, everyone. All the planets back then were connected in a huge tele-portation network. The fighting stretched across all of 'em, and all the races that lived on 'em. The War in Heaven, it's called now."

"Back up for a second." I interrupted. "Teleportation network?"

"Aye." Azarus nodded. "It's still around today, but we're closed off from all but one of the planets, and relations are strained with who we still have access to. Plenty of people over the years have tried to repair it, but can't make heads or tails of the damn thing. Way they talk, it's not something that can be fixed from our end. But, getting back to it." He shot me a look.

I held up my hands in surrender.

"So, from what I've been taught, the War happens, and Order loses. They lose *hard*. They only manage to take out one of the Chaos gods, while all but two of the Order gods are slaughtered in the fighting. One of those gods rules the planet we're still connected to, Indiqua," he told me. "Set themselves up as the immortal leader of the Orcs. Went bloody great for them, way I hear it. She raised 'em up, and now they're more powerful than the Kingdom and the Principality combined."

I nodded. "Orcs, huh," I murmured.

"Orcs," Azarus confirmed. "Ruled by the bloody Goddess of Prosperity herself."

"So, what happened with the elves then?" I asked. "Are they being led by one of those Chaos gods?"

Azarus sighed. "No, that would have probably been better than what actually happened. See, elves are still attached to their god. They always were. The God of Freedom. Except these days, he's just called the Mad God. Something went wrong with him in the last days of the War. Maybe it was the War itself. Maybe it was something a Chaos God did. We don't know, but we know what happened. The War ended, and he came back to the elves different. More a slavering, bloodthirsty beast than the wild-hearted lover of adventure he was supposed to have been."

Azarus sighed.

"He changed 'em, over time," he told me. "That's what Gods do, apparently. From what I've been told, they were like what you said. Before, they were kind, and wise, and free-spirited. More spirits of nature that walked like you and me than a normal person. They'd grow cities out of a forest that would bring a tear to yer eye. Peacemakers, too. It was them that kept tensions between the humans and the dwarves down. But, after a while, that changed. First, they tried to treat him. Who bloody knows how? How do you fix a God? That didn't work, and then he started to affect them. They got more violent, less kind. They lashed out at other races. Then, they went to war with them, because by then the only thing he wanted was blood."

I nodded to show I was still listening. "So, what about us?" I said, gesturing back and forth between us. "Do humans and dwarves have to worry about a god driving us crazy?"

Azarus shook his head. "Nah, the Gods that humes and dwarves worshipped died in the war. They were two of the Order gods, and they died with the rest of them." He gave me a serious look. "Honestly, after seein' what happened to the elves, good riddance. Don't like the idea of someone or some*thing* that can influence me without even trying. Don't go spreading that around though."

I gave him a curious look. "Why not?"

"Well, even though they're all dead, there are still some people that worship 'em. Don't need some god-botherer getting up in my business 'cause I don't think much of 'em," he said gruffly, making a dismissive gesture.

Azarus went quiet for a moment. I let him, absorbing what he'd told me. Good God gone bad, eh.

"Getting back to it, the years after the elves went nuts were pretty damn bad," he said to me. "Right after the System happened, when things were already bad. Just made things go from bad to worse. Course, it's not like I was there. This all happened in my ancestor's ancestors' times. But we know they didn't last as an Empire after that. They just started fighting until they couldn't fight anymore. Turned to raiding and pillaging when they couldn't muster up a fighting force. You must've came across one of the groups that does slave catching on the side. Bad luck, that."

"Yeah," I muttered. "And right after that caravan captured me too."

"Hmm." Azarus nodded.

124

We walked quietly for a moment. I was digesting what he had told me when thought struck.

"Hey, you said the Chaos Gods won that war, right?" I asked Azarus.

"Yeah? Why?"

"Well, what happened to the rest of them? You said six of them survived, right?"

Azarus snorted. "Hells if I know. It's not like I made a study of this, yeah? It's just common knowledge."

"Oh," I said, disappointed.

"Ah, well," Azarus shrugged. "I do know that none of them are on Vereden though, so there's at least that. Got enough trouble with the Mad God."

I nodded quietly at that.

We spent the rest of the walk home in silence.

Felt more comfortable, though.

***

We arrived back at Azarus's house before long. Couldn't have been more than ten minutes after we'd finished our conversation.

I stood off to the side while Azarus unlocked his door and then followed him inside.

"Grey!" He shouted in the entryway. "We're back! Where are you!"

"In the kitchen!" I heard a weary voice cry from farther in.

We both went farther into the house, Azarus in front of me. Before long, we entered the kitchen. Sitting in his wheelchair at the table, Grey was slumped over a mug of something with steam rising from it. Seeing us come into the kitchen, he flashed a brief, tired smile our way.

"Well? How did it go? Were you able to acquire Fleshcrafting?" He asked me.

I nodded at him, slightly concerned. "Yeah, went fine. I ended up going for Surgery like I said I would. How about you, though? You look worn out."

Grey grimaced. "Ah, well. Let's just say that my work for the Prince is quite exhausting with this collar around my neck."

Azarus leaned up against the wall near the doorway. "You finished then?" He asked awkwardly, crossing his arms.

Grey nodded at him. "Yes, indeed I did. I packed everything into the crate already."

"I'll take it up to the mansion tomorrow then." Azarus sighed.

I looked between the two of them. "What does this guy even have you making?"

"Higher tier items that are difficult to acquire through normal means." Grey sighed as well. "Potions, elixirs, enchantment disks of greater strength, magical tools. With my level of knowledge, I'm capable of producing many things. And unfortunately, under a slave compulsion, I have no choice but to obey."

Azarus grunted, frowning. "Sure he's making a damn fortune hawking all of it, too. The bastard."

"Perhaps, perhaps not," Grey whispered to himself thoughtfully before forcing a smile. "But enough of that! Now that you're home, I believe you told me you had more plans for the evening, Azarus?"

I looked over at Azarus with a raised eyebrow. Seeing me looking at him, he nodded at me.

"Aye, I do," he said, before walking over to the table and sitting down in a chair. "We're going back out in a bit, I reckon."

"Are we going to try and get the other Profession I can still get here? Wildshaping, right?" I asked him.

126

Azarus shook his head. "No, we can do that tomorrow, or even the next day depending on how today goes. No, I'm thinking it's time to get you some levels. We're heading out to the forest to kill some monsters."

I straightened up in my chair. "Wait, seriously? How's that going to work? I don't know how to fight at all."

"It's fine, I'm not expecting you to fight much. We're pretty much going to go out, I'll grab some of the weaker monsters, and you'll kill 'em with a weapon I'll give you." Azarus said dismissively.

"I mean, are you sure?" I said doubtfully.

I wasn't nervous about being around literal monsters that could rip me apart at all. Honest.

Grey cleared his throat. "I assure you, Nathan. You won't be in any true danger, at least at this point. Azarus is more than capable of dealing with the low-tier monsters that spawn on these lands."

"Besides," Azarus interjected. "You're going to have to get over it. If you want to advance at all, you need to get used to fighting monsters."

Grey shot him a look.

Azarus held his hands up defensively. "Hey, I'm just saying. You know I'm right."

I took a deep breath before nodding. "Alright. Okay. I'll give it a shot."

"Good," Azarus said, standing up from his seat. "Follow me to the forge out back. I've got some weapons you can choose from." Having said that, he moved to the door that led outside on the back wall of the kitchen. Opening it, he exited into the backyard, leaving the door open behind him for me to follow.

I exhaled and stood up to follow him as well.

"Nathan, a moment." I heard from Grey.

Turning my head to face him, I saw that he had a comforting smile on his face.

"Truly, it won't be that bad. Although bluntly said, Azarus is correct. Combat is simply a fact of life if you desire any form of strength in this world." Grey said. "It's especially important if you wish to free either of us from our current situation."

"No pressure then," I muttered under my breath. Nodding at Grey, not trusting myself to speak, I followed Azarus out the back door.

# Chapter 15
# Pokey Stabby

When I reached the forge that Azarus had mentioned, I found that he was rummaging around in a large cabinet in the back. Looking around, I could see that the structure was well outfitted, as far as I could tell. There were tables, large metal cabinets, and tools all over. There was also the forging area itself. There was the expected large anvil and a spacious kiln with an oversized bellows resting nearby. Azarus was sorting through the largest cabinet in the room.

He must have heard me come in because he spoke to me without turning around. "Oi, come over here," he said to me, motioning me closer behind his back.

I did as he said without complaint. As I did, I was able to make out the contents of the tall cabinet better. Haphazardly stacked inside were weapons of all shapes and sizes. Swords, daggers, maces, spears. You name it, I could see an example inside. The cabinet seemed to hold much more than its admittedly large size seemed able to hold.

"Is the cabinet enchanted or something?" I asked Azarus curiously.

He turned away from his rummaging to give me an incredulous look. "That's what you have to say? Look at all of this! Ain't you impressed? I made 'em all meself!" he said, slipping deeper into his accent and gesturing to the weapons.

"Cool, I guess?" I said uncertainly. "Dude, I don't know the first thing about weapons. It's the magic that catches my interest the most."

Azarus slumped. "Aye," he said tiredly. "Standard spatial enhancement. Not uncommon. Now enough of that. We need to pick you out a weapon. Now I know this is a long shot, but do you have preferences?"

I shrugged uncertainly. "I mean, I've always thought swords were kinda cool? Doesn't everyone?"

"Hmm." Azarus stepped away from the cabinet to size me up. I shifted awkwardly under his gaze. "A sword, eh. Probably not a good idea."

"Why not?" I asked curiously.

Azarus scratched his chin under his beard. "Well, despite what the stories tell you, swords are bloody difficult to use. You can't just pick one up and start waving it around without practice. You're more likely to hurt yourself than the other guy."

"I mean, you're the expert." I paused. "I assume, anyway. I never did ask you what your Professions are."

Azarus blinked before nodding. "Aye, that's right. I didn't think about it. Well anyway, I'm a Weaponsmith and a Construction Engineer."

"Construction Engineer? If that means the same thing as it does back home, you...design and build, I guess buildings?"

Azarus shrugged before waving his hand back and forth. "Eh, sort of. There's some nuance to it, and it's a bit wider than you'd assume. But that ain't important right now, we're talking *weapons*. You have any other preferences?"

I stared at him flatly. "Dude, I don't know. You're the one who makes them, I'm guessing you have an idea about what I should use."

He scratched the back of his head embarrassedly. "Ah, well. You're right, I do. I just didn't want to hand you something you'd hate if you had something in mind." He cleared his throat. "I'm thinking we start you off with a spear."

"Pointy stick, got it." I nodded.

Azarus rolled his eyes. "A bit more than that," he said sarcastically. Turning back to the cabinet, he groped around inside of it for a moment before grabbing hold of something. Pulling it out, I could see that it was a spear. Plainly decorated, it seemed to be roughly seven feet in length and made of dark brown wood. The actual point of the spear seemed to be leaf-shaped and formed of a shining silver material, probably steel. "Catch." He lightly tossed the weapon in my direction.

I started before fumblingly catching the spear. Holding it in my hands, I was surprised at how light it felt. I guessed it might only weigh somewhere under ten pounds. Looking up at Azarus, I said. "And what am I supposed to do with this?"

Azarus jerked his head in the direction of the doorway. "C'mon, let's get you a little more comfortable with that." He walked past me out of the forge. I followed him, still carrying the spear. Once outside, I saw that Azarus had moved a little bit away from the forge in the open area in front of his house. Coming to stand not far from him, I rested the butt of the spear in the grass.

Azarus crossed his arms. "Now, at your level, a spear ain't too complicated. You pretty much just need to know how to thrust, how to block with it, and how to smack things away from yourself. Give it a go, yeah?"

I stared at him blankly for a moment before glancing around. "What, on you?"

He nodded encouragingly. "Yup."

"What if I hurt you?" I asked nervously.

Azarus uncrossed his arms and stifled a chuckle into his fist. "You won't."

"I mean, are you sure?"

He threw up his hands. "For godsakes, just poke me already!"

"Alright, alright already," I muttered. Taking a deep breath and grabbing the spear with both hands, I set it horizontally. Exhaling, I stabbed the spear forward at Azarus.

The spear point stopped on contact with him. Hell, it didn't even rip his clothes. I stared uncomprehendingly for a moment before realization set in and I felt embarrassed. Of course you weren't going to hurt him, dumbass. He'd kind of alluded to being high-level the other day. I drew the spear back.

"Not bad for a first try," Azarus said, unbothered. "But you're holding it wrong. Get in a stance again."

I did as he said, this time without question. When I did, he moved over to my side. Grabbing my hands, he moved them on the spear.

"More like that. Gotta change your footing, too," he said. He nudged my feet into different directions as well. Taking a step back to look at me, he tsked. "Straighten your back and set your shoulders."

I did as he said. The new stance he had put me into felt a little awkward and I told him so.

Azarus nodded. "Aye, it probably does. You'll get used to it though. Might pick up Spear Proficiency today. Give it another go, yeah?"

I gripped the spear firmly in the new stance and thrust at him. This time, even I could tell that I had delivered more force. Still stopped on contact, though.

"Better," Azarus said, nodding. "Let's try a block next, yeah? Set the spear up across your body."

I set the spear up horizontally around shoulder height with my hands spaced evenly on the haft.

"More outward," Azarus told me.

I did as he said.

"Alright, now I'm going to smack it a little. Try and keep a hold of it." Having said that, he stepped closer and brought his right hand up in an axe shape, and chopped down lightly at the midway point of the spear.

I buckled, not anywhere prepared for the amount of force he'd delivered in that one tiny chop. The spear itself visibly flexed and creaked from the blow as well. I managed to keep my hands on it, though.

"Not bad," Azarus said musingly. "Let's try again, yeah? This time, set your feet a bit more."

He chopped down again. This time, I was better prepared for the blow and handled it much better.

"Alright then. Let's run through those two exercises for about, oh, maybe twenty minutes?" Azarus said, pleased. "Only really got that much time. We don't have all day. I can show you how to fight better another time."

With that, we did as he said. We alternated between practice thrusts and blocks for roughly twenty minutes. Over time, I could tell I was getting better and better at both of them. It was somewhat uncanny how quickly I felt that I was advancing. When we finished, I told Azarus that in between tired breaths.

Azarus smacked his fist into his palm and nodded. "Aye, ya definitely got Spear Handling then. You can check your General Talents later. Picked that up right quick, didn't you?"

I was leaning forward with my hands on my knees at this point. It had been a long time since I'd done so much exercise at one time, and I wasn't used to it anymore. Looking up, I said to Azarus, "Aren't mages supposed to be more about flinging around fireballs and stuff, and not as much about the pokey-stabby? Why'd you learn how to use a spear?"

Azarus tilted his head, puzzled before realization stole across his face. "I never mentioned it, did I?" He scratched his beard again, embarrassed. "I'm not a Magi. I'm a Cultivator. We're exactly the sort to learn how to use weapons. And I didn't just learn how to use a spear, I learned how to use everything. Managed to pick up the General Talent Weapon Handling as well. I'll tell you, that took me a fair bit of time to do."

General Talents, huh. I was too tired to ask him about it now. I figured I'd just ask Grey later. Finally catching my breath, I stood up straight.

Azarus nodded at me. "Good?" He asked. I nodded back at him. "Alright then. Let's get this show on the road, yeah? Hand me the spear. Can't let the guards see you carrying around a weapon or there'll be trouble." After I handed him the spear and he slung it over his shoulder, he set off in the direction of the clearing exit. I jogged to catch up with him.

"What, we don't need armor or something if we're going to fight monsters?" I asked him.

He shook his head, not looking over at me. "Naw, no point. Nothing around here could hurt me, and I ain't going to let anything even touch you."

Alright then.

Once we exited the clearing and reached the side road that ran between the forest and the mansion, we didn't turn right like we usually did. We turned left. I asked Azarus about it.

"Entrance to the forest is around back of Magnus's bloody huge house," Azarus answered, unbothered. "Nothing for us in town. Just fields beyond the walls in that direction."

I nodded quietly. We proceeded along the path for maybe ten minutes in comfortable silence before I could see an exit up ahead. Not turning to face me, Azarus muttered loud enough for me to hear. "There'll be guards up ahead."

I said nothing, falling back behind him and adopting a similar posture to the one I had used in town earlier. I guessed I was going to call this slave mode, as morbid as that sounded.

When we passed through the exit at the end of the path, I could see that another clearing lay on the other side. Risking small glances to the other side, I could see that the forest ran all the way up to a wall along the back of the clearing on my left. The wrought iron fence that surrounded the mansion continued along the back of it with only a small gate sitting alone to my right. Across the small, empty clearing, I could see a gate set into the large wooden wall, not quite as big as the gate at the entrance of the town. Slouching on either side of the gate were two more of the guards-dwarves that I had seen patrolling down.

As we entered the clearing and started making our way over to the two guards, they caught sight of us. Straightening up, I could tell they were trying to look more professional. We stopped right in front of the gate. Azarus addressed the guard on the left.

"Heading out," he grunted at him before reaching for the lock on the gate. The guard on the right cleared his throat.

"Taking a slave with you this time, Lord Azarus?" He asked nervously.

Azarus turned a gimlet eye on him. "Got a problem with that?" He glowered.

The guard held up his hands. I could tell he was sweating slightly. "No! No problem, my lord!"

Azarus turned back to the gate. "Good," he said roughly. He finished unlocking the gate and shoved the large wooden doors open with one hand and stepped through. I followed him, keeping my head down. Once I was through, Azarus turned around. "Going to be out for about three hours. Don't," he said warningly. "Lock it."

I could see that both guards nodded vigorously. Azarus grunted again and then shoved the gate closed behind us. As the gate was closing, I could hear the left guard furiously whispering at the guard that had been on the right.

With the gate closed, we both turned around and stepped away from it. Relaxing somewhat now that we were away from prying eyes, I could make out what was outside the walls. It was a much larger clearing than either the one Azarus's house lay in, or the one we had just left. It was filled with curiously cut short grass with a tree line on the far side of the clearing, this time with no discernable path that I could see.

Azarus had relaxed somewhat as well. Turning to me, he handed me back the spear. I took it from him.

"Alright," he said to me before nodding in the direction of the tree line on the far side of the clearing. "We're heading over there."

We started marching across the clearing. As we did so, I was able to make out some curious marks that had been left in it. Sometimes I would see a large, brown stain left in the grass. Others, I would see a patch of burnt grass extending in a star-burst pattern. All over though, the ground seemed curiously churned up.

It gave me a bad feeling.

When we reached the far side of the clearing and were standing right in front of the tree line, Azarus turned to me. "Now, I ain't going to let you be in any real danger in there," he started seriously. "But you have to listen to me, alright? Stick close, don't wander away, and do what I tell ya. You'll be fine."

"Alright," I said, my voice breaking slightly. I cleared my throat. "Alright, I got you," I repeated.

Azarus clapped my shoulder reassuringly with one hand before turning around and striding into the forest.

I followed him nervously.

# Chapter 16
# Check A Look

Despite how I had thought this was going to go, Azarus made no effort to move quietly through the forest. In fact, he seemed to be doing the opposite. He was loudly stomping through the underbrush without a care in the world. I followed behind him, nervously clutching the spear that he had given me earlier. I only lasted five minutes before asking him why. Scurrying up to walk beside him, I cleared my throat.

"Uh, hey," I asked hesitantly. "Is it a good idea to be making so much noise?"

Azarus snorted without turning to face me. "It's fine. We're not here to avoid monsters, we're here to kill some. If making a racket draws 'em here quicker, all the better." He stopped for a moment. "Speaking of."

I tensed up, wildly whipping my head around me in a circle. Despite what he'd said, I didn't see anything.

"Is something here?" I furiously whispered to him.

Azarus was still relaxed. "Yup," he said in a normal volume, still not turning to face me. "Nothing big, which is good. This will be a proper first monster for ya. Just give him a bit to work up the guts to attack us."

I grew tenser now that I knew that some kind of monster attack was about to happen. Intellectually, I knew that both Grey and Azarus had reassured me that I wasn't in any danger. That Azarus was more than strong enough to protect me. But knowing something wasn't the same as believing it. What was about to try and kill us? What kind of monsters did this planet have? I tried to think of fantasy monsters I'd heard of before.

Suddenly, behind me, I heard a snarl and a whooshing noise. In a motion too fast for me to track, Azarus spun around and thrust a hand out over my shoulder, grabbing something. Belatedly, I yelped and jumped forward a step before spinning around.

Clutched in Azarus's right hand was the snout of some kind of fucked up looking dog creature. It looked like a stretched-out hybrid of a wolf and a bear, with bulky limbs and a thinner body. It had the more rounded face of a wolf, but the larger blockier snout of a bear. Its proportions were all over the place.

The wolf-bear creature was snarling and clawing at Azarus, trying to dislodge his hand from its snout. However, the blows of the creature didn't affect Azarus at all. They just bounced off him like my own spear had earlier. Unbothered and unharmed, he grabbed the body of the wolf with his other hand and slammed the creature down onto the earth. Once he'd done so, he leaned his body weight down onto the creature, immobilizing it. Azarus looked back up at me calmly.

I was stunned at how fast the entire encounter had gone. If I had been in here alone, I'd have been fucked. That thing would have killed me before I'd even seen it. The electrifying feeling of adrenaline was still pumping through my veins.

"Oi," I heard Azarus say. Snapping out of it, I focused on Azarus. "Lesson time, yeah? Time to get you your first General Skill."

I let out a shaky breath and nodded at him. "Yeah. Yeah, okay."

Azarus nodded back at me. "Alright then. First, we're gonna get you Observe. It's probably the most basic skill you can have and one of the most useful," he told me over the muffled snarls of the creature. I tried to ignore it. "It ain't hard to get. Literally everybody does, ya know? It's just easier and faster to get it from trying with a monster instead of a person. That's why we didn't try before now. All you have to do is concentrate on the beastie, really."

I opened my mouth before closing it again. I'd had a thought.

"How do you activate a skill?" I asked him.

Azarus raised an eyebrow from where he was laying on the creature. "You focus on the target and either say the skill out loud or in your head. You should be able to feel it activate."

I nodded thoughtfully before giving it a try. I focused on the creature that Azarus was pinning and concentrated. "Observe. Observe!" I grew slightly frustrated. "**Observe.**" I was startled when information started streaming into my head. It was like I suddenly had a memory of looking at a unique Status window. Changing my focus, I tried to decipher it.

| Name | Mangy Warg Runt |
|------|-----------------|
| Level | 5 |
| Age | ?? |
| Species | Monster |
| Abilities | ?? |

Snapping out of it, I blinked rapidly.

"That was fast." I heard Azarus say. Re-focusing on him, I could see that he had a surprised look on his face. "I'm guessing it worked? Didn't take you more than a second to get the skill."

Taking a breath, I said to him. "I'm pretty sure that I got it before you even said anything. It just came too easily to me."

"Aye, that sounds likely." Azarus nodded. "It's a damn easy skill to get."

I shifted from one foot to the other. "But, uh. It didn't seem very helpful." I told him. "The skill didn't tell me much. Most things on the window had question marks on them. I could only see its name, level, and species."

Azarus shrugged. "I mean, yeah. It's a new skill. It's low-level right now. Your gonna have to practice with it if you want it to show more."

"So, what. Just use it on things? Can you use it on anything?"

"Why ask me? Give it a shot, yeah?"

I did as he said, first on him. This time, I tried to use the skill mentally like he'd said I could. **Observe.**

??

I got nothing from him. Guess I was just too low-level to make anything out. I tried it again on a tree to my right. **Observe.**

| **Name** | **Oak** |
| --- | --- |
| **Age** | **53 Years** |
| **Species** | **Tree** |

That was all it said. Curious, I asked Azarus about it.

"Well, the way I understand it, you can Observe anything. But only things with a Status that can be represented by the System are gonna have anything more than a name, age, and species. Well, except for artifacts," he amended himself. "Don't worry about that for now though. We don't have any around."

Artifacts, huh. Whatever, I put it out of my mind like he said. "Did you try and Observe me when we first met? Did I have anything?" I asked him curiously.

He shook his head. "Nah, it's considered rude to Observe people you don't know. If you're Awakened, you can always tell when someone is doing it. I felt it a second ago, for example. Guessing you didn't get anything from me."

"Ah," I said awkwardly. "Sorry?"

"Don't worry about it. Anyway, we got something else to do, yeah? Still need to deal with the beastie," he told me, leaning harder on the monster.

I started. Somehow, the monster that had tried to eat me had completely slipped my mind and attention while I had been testing Observe. Focusing back on it, it seemed to be struggling against Azarus in a weaker fashion. It was still struggling, however. The look in its eyes hadn't changed from earlier. It was still feral and rabid as if bloodshed was all it desired. Nevertheless, it was still slightly uncomfortable for me to see Azarus treating it so roughly.

"We didn't talk about monsters much," I asked him, uneasy. "But, uh, they're not like animals, right?"

"What? No. 'Course not." Azarus told me, bewildered. "Low-level monster like this? Only thing on its mind is ripping people apart. He don't even need to eat what he kills. Now, it's time to put him down. Take that spear of yours and give him a good stickin'.'"

I took note of what he said. 'Low level', huh. Taking a deep breath, I grasped my spear more firmly and got into the stance that Azarus had shown me earlier. I paused. "Does it matter where I stab it?"

"Nope. This thing doesn't have organs. More Aether shaped like a monster than flesh and blood. Now quit delaying and just stab the bloody thing." Azarus answered, irritated.

I did what he said. I thrust the spear forward at a spot on its chest that Azarus wasn't covering. I didn't quite hit the spot I had targeted, but the spear still slid into its chest fairly deeply. The monster nearly instantaneously stopped struggling and snarling, growing unnaturally still with startling swiftness. After a moment, the creature burst into a puff of greasy black smoke, completely dissipating its form.

Turning away, I vomited off to the side. I didn't do so because I was bothered by killing something. No, I did it because the smoke smelled fucking *terrible*. God, I'd never smelled something so vile in my life. It was like someone had mixed rotten meat and waste together.

The moment that the creature grew still, Azarus jumped off it from where it lay. He'd moved far enough away from the Warg that he'd completely dodged the smoke. Walking over to me with a cheery grin, he slapped my back with one huge hand. "Ye'll never forget your first whiff of Miasma. Breathe it in. Savor it. That's the smell of *progress*, my friend."

I glowered up at him, my hands on my knees. "Couldn't have warned me about it?"

He just grinned down at me. "Nope. Time-honored tradition. Gotta let the greenhorns really *experience* the smell, you know?" He paused to look at me speculatively. "Surprised, though. Didn't think you'd kill it in one blow. I thought for sure you'd have to poke it a good three or four times. What are your Virtues like?"

Wiping my mouth with the back of my hand, I straightened up. "You mean my stats, right? Well, I've got ten in everything. Is that good?"

Azarus drew his head back in surprise. "You're fucking with me. You're only level one and you've got ten in each of your Virtues?"

I blinked at him. "Yeah?"

He shook his head. "Gotta be a Precursor thing. Having that many at level one is downright bizarre. I sure as hell didn't have that many when I was Awoken. More like ones, twos, and threes in everything. Guess that explains it." He paused to give me a considering look. "If you've got that many points now, I'm wondering how many free points you'll get when ya level up."

"Free points?" I asked him.

"Yeah, when you level up you get a certain amount of Virtue points that you can put where ya like. Amount ya get is based on what race you are, yeah? Dwarves and Humans both get six. Who knows what you'll have? Guess we'll see later. Plan is to get ya at least two levels out here. But never mind that. Take a look there." Azarus told me, pointing to where the monster had been laying.

I gave him a puzzled look but did what he said. I moved over to where the smoke had dissipated, set my spear down, and crouched. I was about to ask him what I was looking for when a glint caught my eye. Focusing on it, I reach for the glint with my right hand. Scooping up a small pile of dirt and leaves I sorted through it, revealing a small gem, no bigger than a bead. Wiping it off, I held it up to the light. It was mostly opaque, but I could see a small wisp of rainbow light floating in the perfectly spherical gem. I stood up and gave Azarus a questioning look. "What's up with this?"

"That," he said. "Is a monster core. It's a small one, cause the monster was weak, but it's still a core. Monsters leave them behind when they die every time, and they're damn useful. They're mostly used in Professions. Keep it, yeah? We'll do something special with it when we get back since it's your first."

I gazed back down at it. Monster cores, huh.

"Well, time to get a move on." I heard Azarus say. "Gonna do that a bunch more, yeah? We didn't come out here to kill only one monster." Looking back up, I saw Azarus had turned back around and started to tromp back through the forest. Scrambling, I picked up my spear and hurried after him.

# Chapter 17
# Racked

Our trip through the forest would continue in a similar fashion for the next several hours. Azarus would stomp through the forest, making as much noise as he possibly could. The racket that he made would draw various monsters to us in droves. Then, he would grab them, pin them, and get me to kill them. Sometimes I would manage to kill them in one strike like I had with the Warg. Sometimes it took a few pokes with my pointy stick. While the monsters would always target me first, somehow instinctively recognizing me as the weaker link, they never got to touch me though. Honestly, after a while, the process started to bore me. It had finally sunk in that I wasn't in any danger.

During our trip, I took to using Observe as much as I could. Azarus had mentioned that using the skill would increase the effectiveness as it leveled. I used the skill on the trees, the grass, the bushes, and of course the monsters as much as I could.

Something interesting he mentioned though, was there was only so far things like Observe could go. According to Azarus, General Skills, and General Talents were fairly limited by the System. They could only level up to seven, and then they capped out. Apparently, you could do something with them afterward, but Azarus just waved me off when I asked about whatever that was and told me to concentrate on the hunting.

One thing about the monsters especially piqued my interest, though. We ended up being attacked by more than just Wargs. We encountered a variety of different monster types during our trek. However, they all seemed to be variations of general forest creatures. Everything that we encountered seemed to be some kind of fucked up version of a regular animal that you could find in any regular forest. From Deer with two sets of bladed horns, to knee-high rats, to even a disturbingly buff squirrel the size of a German Shepard. I was curious, so I asked Azarus about it.

"Oh, these?" he answered me. "Well, we might have mentioned it, but monsters are affected by where they form. Since this is a forest, you get forest creatures. Ugly buggers, but generally recognizable."

"Huh," I said. "Do they care about the regular animals?" During our trip, I hadn't really seen anything but monsters.

Azarus shook his head. "Nah, they don't. They'll leave the wildlife alone. For some reason, monsters only care about people that are Awakened. Hell, if you were still Unawakened, they'd just ignore you like they do a deer or something. Well, if you didn't try and attack 'em, I mean."

I scratched the back of my head with the hand not holding onto my spear. "So, I guess we're just making too much noise to see anything else but monsters, huh."

Azarus grunted in agreement. Our conversation died after that.

***

We continued for maybe another half an hour before Azarus suddenly stopped. I nearly walked into his back; I was following so closely

145

behind him. Stumbling to a stop I opened my mouth to ask him what he was doing before closing it. Azarus was staring intently into the trees before us. I tensed in anticipation. He'd done this many times before over the last few hours. It usually meant that he'd sensed a monster.

I was startled though when he did something different than usual, though. Instead of readying himself, he turned back around to give me a speculative look.

I stared back at him blankly. "What? What's up?"

Azarus tapped his chin in thought, still staring at me. "Well," he said, drawing out the word with a grin. "I'm thinking maybe it's time to get you some real combat practice."

I gripped my spear till my knuckles turned white. "What do you mean?" I said uneasily.

I knew what he meant, I was just scared of it.

"I'm thinking that I'll let you take care of this next one by yourself," he confirmed for me. "It's getting about time to start heading back, and I think it'd be useful for ya."

I took a deep breath in an attempt to calm my nerves. It didn't help much. "Are you sure I can do it?"

Azarus scoffed. "Course ya can. If you've got ten in everything like ye said, then these beasties won't be able to put up much of a fight for ya. We haven't gone deep enough to find anything that's a real threat."

I was silent for a moment. Azarus had mentioned it a few times, but from what I understood, fighting monsters was the best way to level up in this world. With this System. He wasn't always going to be around to hold my hand. I was eventually going to have to learn to fight monsters by myself if I wanted to survive. At least it was better to do it for the first time with someone to supervise me.

Wait.

He was going to supervise, right?

"Oh, aye," Azarus said airily. "I'll be around," he told me when I asked. Having said that, I watched dumbfounded as Azarus casually started to saunter off into the woods to our right. Once he reached one of the trees, he stepped behind it and didn't emerge around the other side. Forgetting my nervousness for a moment, I walked over to the tree bemusedly that he had stepped behind, to see if he was just hiding behind it. Looking behind, I could see that he wasn't. He'd vanished.

Stepping back from the tree, I looked back in the direction that he'd been staring in before he left. I didn't see anything right now, but I believed that something was coming this way from how he had acted. Moving back into the center of the small clearing we had stopped in, I set my spear in the way Azarus had taught me. I set in to wait for whatever was coming.

After maybe three minutes of trying not to hyperventilate, and mostly succeeding, I heard a rustling in the bushes in the direction I was staring. With a snort, the monster emerged from the bushes perhaps fifty feet in front of me. I relaxed somewhat when I saw it.

It was one of the weird deer that we had encountered earlier. From the way that Azarus had manhandled it earlier, I wasn't terribly frightened. If it had been one of those freaky squirrels though, then I would have been more nervous. It wasn't even that big, as well. Sure, it was slightly larger than the one that I'd killed earlier, but not by much. This one came up to roughly mid-chest on me, while the one from earlier only came up to about my waist from the floor to the tip of its antlers. With a reddish coat, the only thing that distinguished it from a normal deer was its small, underdeveloped antlers. They were metallic, with the tips shaped more like knives than a normal deer's horns. I used Observe on it curiously.

| Name | Young Blade-Rack Hart |
|------|------------------------|
| Level | 6 |
| Age | 2 weeks |
| Species | Monster |
| Abilities | ?? |

Ha ha, Azarus. I could see why you wanted me to solo this one.

Feeling more confident and firming my resolve, I reset my stance and waited for the monster. I may have decided to fight it, but I wasn't confident enough to make the first move.

Only a few seconds had passed since the deer had exited the bush, and it was already eyeing me with malice. Huffing, snorting, and pawing at the dirt, the deer gave me a baleful, red-eyed glare before throwing back its head and opening its mouth. A strange, hissing scream echoed around us as the deer bayed.

I froze. For some reason, it felt like I couldn't move my body. I couldn't even blink or move my eyes. With a sense of mounting panic, I was only able to watch motionlessly as the deer lowered its head and entered into a charging stance. Springing forward with its back legs, the deer rushed in my direction, antlers first.

Mentally, I kept trying to struggle my way out of whatever the deer had done to me. I didn't know what to do, and all I could do was watch in dread as the deer approached me with speed. When the deer had cleared perhaps thirty feet, whatever it had done to me wore off. Stumbling, I tried to get the spear up in a block position between me and the deer hastily. But in my panic, I didn't use the blocking stance that Azarus had shown me. With a tremendous bang, the deer connected with my clumsy block and blew me straight off my feet.

Flying back several feet, I landed on my back, still somehow holding onto the spear despite the impact. I lay stunned for a moment before snapping out of it and trying to find the deer.

It was charging directly at my downed form, antlers lowered.

Throwing the spear up across my body, I somehow managed to interpose the spear between myself and the deer's horns. It collided with the spear again with another bang. Grunting, I managed to keep my arms from buckling.

But the deer wasn't done.

It stayed locked onto my spear, trying to reach me with its bladed horns in order to gore me. It kept pushing and shoving its horns so wildly against the spear that I could feel the razor-sharp tips cutting into the flesh of my arms. With a snort of effort, the deer managed to push its horns far enough forward that I could feel a gash open up on my left cheek.

Wild with panic, I found a well of strength within and brought my legs up underneath me. With a hoarse scream, I kicked out with both feet and sent the deer flying. Blood pumping loudly in my ears. I scrambled to my feet. Looking around wildly for a moment, I tried to find the deer. It had only flown a few feet off from me and was lying dazed on the ground.

Instinctively realizing that I didn't have long before it was going to try and gore me again, I set the spear in a sloppy stance and charged it with another scream. It had tried to kill me when I had been on the ground, and I was going to return the favor. I managed to reach the deer in time before it recovered and thrust down at it with all of my strength.

I hit it. My spear slid all the way through the flesh of the deer and pinned it to the forest floor. With a shrill cry, the deer went wild and tried to dislodge my weapon from its body. Flailing its head around, the deer tried to reach me with its horns. I kicked the deer as hard as I could with my right foot in its bottom jaw, stunning it. I withdrew the spear from its body and thrust it down with my full body weight, lodging it even deeper into the forest floor.

I held on desperately to the spear, kicking its head again. When it started trying to flail after recovering, I would thrust downwards after a kick so the monster couldn't escape.

"Just. Fucking. Die already!" I bellowed between kicks to the deer's head.

After a few rounds of this routine, the struggles of the deer started to weaken. Gradually, the deer lost strength. It stopped moving.

I stared down at the monster suspiciously. Was it dead? I decided to give it one more kick to be sure. But when I reared my foot back and did so, it passed straight through the head of the deer. It had exploded into that same, greasy black smoke that all monsters did on death. With my kick not connecting to anything, I overextended and slipped. I fell straight onto my back, right where the greatest concentration of the weapons-grade stench of the smoke curled on the ground.

I vomited directly into the air from a combination of the sink and the adrenaline of the fight. It fell right back down onto my chest. I lay there for a moment, soaking in my own vomit and blood, staring blankly up at the canopy of trees above me.

"Well." I heard foggily, somewhere off my right. "That could've gone better."

I blacked out.

# Chapter 18
# Scars

I jerked awake with a gasp.

Lurching forward into a sitting position, I looked around wildly only to slow down in confusion. The last thing I remembered, I had just succeeded in killing that monster deer and laid down on the forest floor. I definitely wasn't in the forest anymore. Calming down, I could tell that I was back in my room in Azarus's house.

Laying back down with a groan, I settled my right forearm over my eyes. I must have passed out after winning the fight. Azarus must have carried me back, maybe because I had been too injured to continue.

Shit, that was right. My injuries.

Sitting back up and dragging the cover that had been laid over me off, I tried to inspect myself. I didn't appear to have any bandages on me. It was too dark in my room to see anything, though. Running my hands over my body wasn't really telling me anything. Looking back up at the window, I could tell that it was near sunset. I decided to get up and go check in the mirror.

Throwing my legs over the side of the bed, I stood up and walked out of the room. Making my way down the hall, I opened the door to the washroom. Stepping in and closing it behind me, I was startled by a lamp I had never noticed before flaring to life. I guess it reacted to how dark it was or something? Shaking it off, I looked into the mirror and was startled again.

Stepping closer to the mirror, I touched my left cheek. Starting from next to my nose and continuing backward diagonally was a scar on my face. It was long, but not terribly wide. It wasn't even finger-width. Tracing it, I could feel the scar tissue.

Huh, I thought calmly. It had cut right through the only freckle I'd had on my face. I'd always hated it. Gone now, I suppose.

It had the feeling of a fresh scar, which I supposed I shouldn't be surprised about. Azarus must have brought me back here to get healed by Grey. Having a thought, I tugged my shirt over my head and looked back in the mirror. Sure enough, I could see a number of other new scars on my body. Primarily on my arms, but I had a few on my chest as well. They all resembled the one that I had on my cheek.

Stepping back from the mirror, I tried to twist around to see how they felt. I quickly put a stop to that when I felt several of them give a sharp sting. Guess they were too new to be trying to be moving sharply. Gazing at the mirror for a moment at all the new additions to my body, I frowned.

I'd never been a particularly active type of person, in the past. I didn't have many scars on my body, and those I did have were from things that had happened to me as a child. Seeing so many scars on my body was new for me. I guess that fucking deer had really given it to me.

Grabbing my shirt from where I had thrown it, I tugged it back on. I guess I should go find Grey or Azarus to ask them what had happened, then. Giving one last look at the scar on my face, I exited the washroom.

*\*\*\**

I didn't find Grey in the kitchen like I had lately, so I tried his room. Knocking on his door, I didn't get a response either. Opening it anyway to take a peek, I saw that there was no one in there either.

Closing the door and stepping back from it, I crossed my arms. Where was everyone? Now that I thought about it, I couldn't hear anyone in the house. Maybe they were outside? Heading back to the kitchen, I stepped through the back door and closed it behind me. I didn't see anyone off the bat, but now that I was outside, I thought I could hear something coming from the right side of the house. Guess they were in the forge, I thought to myself.

Walking over to the forge, I could make out both Grey and Azarus's voices. They were too muffled for me to make out what they were saying, though. Once I got close enough to the forge, I called out a subdued, "Hey."

The voices stopped talking, and I entered the forge. Inside, I could see that Azarus had his arms crossed and was leaning against his anvil. Grey was in there too, sitting in his wheelchair with his hands clasped. When I entered, they both looked up at me. Azarus looked away after a second, however.

"Ah, Nathan," Grey said calmly. "Good to see you awake. How are you feeling?"

I shrugged and then winced at the movement. "Mostly alright, I guess. If I move too quickly, I feel it. Otherwise, it seems mostly fine." I paused. "I'm guessing you healed me then, Grey?"

Grey inclined his head slightly. "In a manner of speaking. Even if this infernal collar wasn't blocking my skills and magic, I've never possessed any ability in Healing magic. No, what I used to help you was potions."

I nodded at him. "Yeah. Okay. Well, thanks for using them on me."

"It's no trouble. You weren't in any true danger when Azarus," He shifted at the mention of his name, I saw. "Brought you to me. Simply…banged up, so to speak. I do apologize for the scars, however. If you had been healed by an actual Healer, they wouldn't be a concern. Rather than true healing, potions accelerate the body's natural healing process and thus leave a scar behind. If you wish, you will be able to contract the services of a healer to remove them. Well," He paused for a moment. "When we're free of this place, of course."

I brought a hand up to my left cheek to trace the scar there. "Good to know, I suppose," I murmured.

Azarus cleared his throat. Both Grey and I looked over at him, with me crossing my arms. "I, uh, wanted to apologize for not stepping in. I was watching the whole time and was planning to if it looked like you were in mortal danger. And you weren't," he said hurriedly. "You weren't ever in mortal danger, even if it might not seem that way. But, uh, I haven't fought with anyone as low level as you for a long time. I forgot how fragile you can be, that low on the path," he finished awkwardly.

I frowned at him. "What do you mean I wasn't in any mortal danger? Sure as hell seemed like it to me."

Azarus grimaced. "Look, I would've been able to react fast enough to stop the beastie if he was about to land a fatal blow. He wasn't ever in a position to do that before you killed 'him, yeah? You had it handled. Sorta."

"Handled?" I asked him skeptically, before throwing up my hands in frustration. "After that damn deer froze me, I just panicked and acted on instinct. Dude, I don't know what I'm doing when it comes to fighting! Especially bloodthirsty monsters! I swear I told you this!"

Azarus looked away, scratching the back of his head. "I, uh. I guess you did. I just didn't…"

Grey cleared his throat. "Nathan, if I may?" I looked over at him, still angry. "It seems to me, that the problem here is a cultural one."

"A cultural problem?" I asked him incredulously. "A cultural problem is what nearly got me killed?"

"Indeed," Grey replied calmly. "If I understand correctly, your world possesses neither monsters or the System, correct?" At my nod, he continued. "Please understand then, Nathan. Our societies have *always* lived under the threat of monster attacks. Even before the advent of the System. They developed with the knowledge that sometime in our lives, we would likely need to defend ourselves from a monster that would seek our life. Thus, we are educated with this knowledge beginning from the earliest periods in our lives. Children are taught simple games of how to identify and escape from a monster attack. Once they reach a certain age, they are taught, for years at a time, basic weapon skills to defend themselves. Once they've unlocked their Status, everyone is advised to take at least one combat-related Skill. All of us, from the lowliest peasant farmer to the highest noble in the land, have internalized this fact."

Maybe it was his calm, even tone that did it, but I gradually relaxed from my tense stance during Grey's explanation.

I uncrossed my arms. "So, what you're saying is…" I said thoughtfully, furrowing my brow.

"That Azarus most likely never even considered the fact that you would be ill-suited to confronting a monster as you are." Grey picked up. "I confess, the possibility is so alien to our unified culture that I only considered it when you returned, ravaged by a simple low-level monster. The Hart," He smiled slightly. "That injured you is considered such a small threat to many, that it's common for rural communities to bring children with them to cull such a beast. If only to introduce them to monster fighting in a controlled environment. They're no more physically powerful than a regular deer, simply more aggressive. Now, I do not tell you this to excuse Azarus's mistake."

I could see Azarus wince.

"In truth, this is as much my mistake as his, and thus I apologize as well," Grey told me, bowing slightly in his wheelchair. "I should have realized how strange the practice of monster hunting would be to you and insisted on more instruction before you ventured out. Azarus showed you some simple spear forms before you left, yes?" At my nod, he continued. "What he likely showed you were refresher forms, the most basic of basic forms to show someone that are meant to remind the pupil of what they already learned. What you *need* is a full course on combat, including both the full weapon forms and combat knowledge and tactics in monster hunting. I assure you, before you are taken into the forest once more, we will ensure you have received them. *Won't* we, Azarus," he finished with a pointed look at Azarus.

Azarus straightened up and gave me a firm nod. "Yeah. And I'll stick closer next time, yeah?"

I looked between the two of them for a second before sighing. "Okay. I guess that's all I can hope for in the end." I leaned against the inside wall of the forge before sliding down it to sit on the dirt floor.

Grey raised an eyebrow. "Are you sure you're alright, Nathan?"

I grunted from where I sat on the floor. "Yeah, I'm fine. Just…tired, you know?" I let out a breath, resting my arms on my upraised knees. "So, where do we go from here?"

Grey and Azarus exchanged a look before Azarus motioned for him to speak. Grey cleared his throat and smiled. "Well, reviewing your gains, of course! That was the whole point of this exercise, was it not? Azarus, if you would?"

Oh, I guess it was. Time to see what nearly getting gored by a deer gave me on my Status. Yay.

"Oh, yeah. I got one around here somewhere." Azarus said, moving over to a desk and rummaging around on it. "Where are ya, where are ya…" He muttered. "Ah, found it!" He held up a small, soot-covered object. Taking out a rag and polishing it, Azarus revealed it to be a small handheld mirror.

I raised an eyebrow. "Just have a mirror laying around, huh."

"Course I do." Azarus scoffed, walking over to me and handing me the small mirror. "Gotta be able to check your gains once you're done working, don't ya?"

I took it from him with a wry smile. "I guess so."

Looking down at the small mirror, I mentally opened up my Status.

# Chapter 19
# Bio Spheres

Mentally selecting the yes button, the small mirror exploded with little blue boxes.

**You have gained four levels!**
**You have gained the General Talent, Spear Proficiency!**
**Spear Proficiency has reached level 3!**
**You have gained the General Skill, Observe!**
**Observe has reached level 2!**
**You have forty unspent Virtue points**

"Hmm," I said thoughtfully, gazing down at the prompts. I looked up at Azarus after a moment. "Looks like we found out how many free points I get."

Azarus grinned at me. "Yeah? Out with it then."

I grinned back at him. "Looks like ten per level. I got four levels out there, and I have forty now."

His grin shifted to a scowl. "Ten bleeding points? Talk about bloody unfair."

"Are you quite sure about the amount, Nathan?" Grey sputtered.

I raised an eyebrow at him from my position on the floor. "Yeah? I mean, I'm just telling you what my Status says. What's the big deal?" Azarus was looking at Grey curiously, too, I could see.

Grey pinched the bridge of his nose. "What's the big deal, he says," he muttered to himself. "Nathan, that is an absolutely unprecedented number of free points to gain for every level. *Nobody* gains that many points."

"Nobody, huh," I said, curious. "Azarus already told me that Humans and Dwarves get six. Who else is there?"

Grey took a deep breath. "In truth, there are many races known to us. However, there are only six races of any relevance to us, with the collapse of the interplanetary network. Obviously, there are the Humans and the Dwarves. I believe that I have also mentioned the Orcs, as well?" At my nod, he continued. "They receive the highest number of free points of the known races, at eight per level. The other three races that we have knowledge of since the advent of the System, are the Gnolls, the Goblins, and the Antium."

He paused for a moment, looking around the forge. He grimaced.

"Ah, perhaps first a change of scenery is in order. No offense to your lovely forge, Azarus." Grey said to Azarus delicately. "But it is not exactly a place of relaxed conversation."

Azarus snorted, hopping down off his anvil. "It's not meant to be. Go on, git. We'll be along in a bit."

Grey raised an eyebrow at him for a moment before nodding at both him and I. Placing his hands on the wheels of his chair, he began wheeling out of the forge back to the house. I watched him go for a moment before turning back to face Azarus. While I had been watching Grey, Azarus had moved to stand in front of me. His right hand was outstretched in front of him in my direction. Taking it, I used it to lever myself to my feet with a grunt. From the effort I'd needed to even do that, I must have been more tired than I thought.

"Thanks," I muttered to him. I started to turn around before Azarus cleared his throat. Looking back over at him, I raised my eyebrows in question. I could see that he had an awkward look on his face.

Azarus brought his fist up and coughed into it before speaking. "We good?" He asked gruffly.

Ah.

I turned back around fully and stared at him for a moment. I sighed. "Yeah," I said to him tiredly. "Water under the bridge." At his slightly confused expression, I clarified. "It means we're good."

His expression clearing up, Azarus nodded at me. "C'mon," he said, moving towards the entrance to the forge. "Got more to talk about. Still gotta make dinner too. Might as well make those steaks Van gave us, yeah? Celebrate your first few levels."

I felt my spirits lift somewhat. God, some steaks sounded great.

I followed him.

***

Once we got back into the house, Azarus stuck to his words. We made the steaks for dinner, frying them up in a cast iron pan over his oven. One thing that stuck out to me while he was cooking that I found neat was he never took his hand off of the panhandle while cooking, even though it must have been ripping hot. When I asked him about it, he laughed and told me that heat this low wasn't able to affect him after learning the general skill Fire Resistance from his time in the forge.

The steaks were great. Azarus had seasoned them with a local blend of herbs and spices that reminded me of Montreal steak seasoning, somehow. Except spicier, with a slightly sweet taste to it as well. Honestly, it was better than it sounds.

By the time he had finished, the sun had fully set outside, and some lanterns strategically placed around the room came alight. We ate our dinner in peaceful quiet, lit by firelight.

Leaning back into his wheelchair with a sigh, Grey patted his stomach. "Excellent job, Azarus. You may be a poor cook with anything else, but you certainly know your meats," he finished with a playful smile.

Azarus smirked back at him. "I know what I'm good at, old man. That's why I let you handle the other stuff."

I had laid my head down on my arms after finishing my steak, feeling drowsy. I sighed contentedly into my arms. Hearing someone clear their voice, I lifted my head. Grey was staring at me with a raised eyebrow. I stared back at him blankly for a moment before I remembered that we were going to resume our conversation after dinner. Flushing slightly, I straightened back up in my chair.

"Where were we? Ah, don't tell me. The other races, yes?" Grey said thoughtfully. At my nod, he continued. "Let us start with the Goblins, yes? They're the only other race that is native to either Vereden or Indiqua. Truthfully, not much is known about them, as they're very insular. But relevant to our conversation, it is known that they receive five points per level, from past investigations into the subject. The other two races, the Gnolls, and the Antium, are both known to receive seven points per level." He heaved a sigh. "At the very least, those poor people deserve that much."

I laid my chin in my hand with my elbow on the table. "What's their deal then?"

Grey grimaced slightly. "Ah, well. Both races are essentially refugees upon Vereden and Indiqua. The Gnolls upon Vereden, and the Antium upon Indiqua. They're non-native, you see. After the collapse of the interplanetary network, there was a sizable enough population remaining on each planet that they were able to establish a healthy enough population, if not small ones. History tells us that there were some very unfortunate members of other races that did not have that luxury."

I made an interested noise. "How did that happen? That there was enough for the Gnolls and the Antium to breed true if they're non-native?"

"In the case of the Gnolls, nobody knows," Grey answered me. "Not even the Gnolls themselves are aware. The answer has been lost to history, unfortunately. As it is, they're very careful with their marriage and breeding rights to this day in order to maintain a stable population. This is made somewhat difficult by the fact they're nomadic, by nature. Their clans roam the continent, caring little for borders. They own no property nor land. In fact, they disdain the ownership of land in general."

Azarus cleared his throat. Grey paused, realizing that he had slipped into his 'enthusiastic teacher' voice, as I'd taken to referring to it mentally.

"On the other hand," Grey continued, switching tracks. "We know well why the Antium were upon Indiqua at the time of the collapse. During the war, the Antium were servants of the Chaos Gods. The Queen of the Antium people at the time had sent one of her daughters to launch an offensive from their home planet. However, upon the collapse and the initialization of the System, it is said that the Antium survivors, including the Princess that was sent to lead the campaign, were freed from the control of the Dark Ones. At the urging of their Princess, they surrendered. Afterward, they settled within the jungles of Indiqua."

"Huh," I said. "You know, I never asked. Judging from their name, I'm guessing the Antium are pretty much Ant people. What about the Gnolls, though? What are they?"

Azarus spoke up. "Eh, imagine a really fuzzy hume with the head of a fox. That's pretty much a Gnoll."

Grey closed his eyes briefly in frustration. He let out a breath. "Azarus is...somewhat correct. The Gnolls are a bestial race, vaguely reminiscent of various breeds of fox. It is my understanding that the survivors upon Vereden are merely a subset of their people. Supposedly, there are other breeds of Gnoll upon their home planet that are evocative of other animals. However, that is not our focus here. I was merely introducing you to the other races you may expect upon Vereden."

"Point of all this jawing was," Azarus butted in. "Is that you've got a downright unfair number of free points."

I looked between the two of them for a second. "I'm guessing that's good? I mean, since I get so many points per level, am I just going to get stronger than other people as time goes on?"

Grey smiled at me kindly. "Ah, somewhat. While it is true that having so many points is a boon, you will only truly notice the difference in comparison to others at lower levels. Once you begin to reach past the breakpoints, Virtues are considered more of a...foundation, so to speak. The pillars upon which you've built."

"Low levels, he says," Azarus muttered into his mug. "You mean the levels most people reach."

I leaned back in my chair a little. "So, is that why I didn't get really tired earlier? I mean, I haven't exactly made a habit of tromping through the woods like that."

Azarus sat his drink down and snorted, waving his hand dismissively. "You've got ten in everything. A little trek like that ain't gonna stress ya."

I nodded at him. "Point taken."

Grey cleared his throat. "Getting back to the important matter of Nathan's points, he now needs to decide how to allocate them. Which means he needs to choose his Path." Catching my eyes with his own, Grey spoke in a serious tone. "This is exceedingly important, Nathan. We've told you before about Magi and Cultivators, and the time has come for you to decide which you wish to become. You must make a decision before you begin allocating points to your Virtues, as they heavily influence what you are capable of as either."

I straightened up in my chair. "Okay then. What's the actual difference? And not," I interrupted Azarus before he could open his mouth. "Just the fact that one is more likely to hit people than the other."

Azarus smirked.

Grey laughed slightly. "Very well. There are essentially three main differences between Magi and Cultivators. One practical, one methodology-wise, and one that is more...philosophical. The first, practical difference, is that yes, Magi tend to receive skills and talents that are more likely to lend themselves well to ranged combat, while Cultivators are more likely to receive abilities more suited to melee. This isn't an ironclad rule, as either can drive their advancement in any direction they wish. The second, practical difference is that in general, Magi generally take more talents than activated skills with their level ups, as compared to Cultivators, who take more skills."

"Why is that?" I asked curiously.

"Because of the disciplines themselves," Grey answered me. "What you actually learn to be considered either a Magi or a Cultivator. You see, there is more to being either than simply making a choice and investing in the correct Virtues. There exist entire fields of study that are generally referred to as Magecraft for the Magi, and Arts for the Cultivators. This is one of the, frankly bizarre, blind spots of the System. You see, the System does not track either of them. They are influenced by it, yes, but only because you as an individual are."

Grey paused for a moment to take a drink from the glass that he'd had with his dinner.

"So, Cultivators like myself." Azarus picked up while Grey was drinking. "Learn Arts from the four Schools. Sealing, Flow, Purification, and Might. Anything else we need; we get from skills."

I raised an eyebrow at him. "Doesn't seem like a bunch to pick from."

Azarus shrugged. "Eh, they're broader than you'd think."

Grey had finished his glass while we were talking. "And in general, Cultivators can receive some truly unique skills from the System. On the other hand, Magi like myself choose talents over skills more often than not, when offered by the System. This is because Magecraft is a far more expansive discipline than Arts. There are many schools of Magecraft, and sometimes it seems like more are being pioneered every day. But currently, there exist thirteen recognized schools of Magecraft. These are," He cleared his throat. "Evocation, Mind, Thaumaturgy, Spatial, Abjuration, Divination, Illusion, Shapeshifting, Animation, Healing, Ritual, Chronomancy, and least of all Necromancy," he finished with a distasteful look on his face.

"That's a lot," I said, nonplussed.

"Oh indeed." Grey nodded. "The field is very broad. You can see why most Magi focus upon talents that can passively empower them, over taking a skill. Most likely, you would be able to find an equivalent within one of the Schools of Magecraft." When he finished speaking, Grey leaned back in his chair and settled his hands in his lap. He had a far-off, thoughtful look in his eye.

We sat in silence for a moment while Grey gathered his thoughts.

"The final difference between Magi and Cultivators is, as I said, somewhat…philosophical," he said starting slowly. "It has been said in the past that the true goal of advancement upon your chosen Path is the search for…truth."

"Truth?" I asked incredulously.

"Indeed," Grey answered, still not looking at me. "Truth. For Cultivators, this is a search for inner truth. What drives you? What do you value? Who do you ultimately wish to become? What are you willing to sacrifice, in your search for power? These are merely some of the questions that a Cultivator must confront."

I was silent. I didn't know the answer to any of those questions concretely. Thinking about them made me uncomfortable, to be honest. I didn't know what the fuck I was doing, on this magic alien planet. I didn't know what drove me. I didn't know what I even wanted these days, other than to survive another day. Grey and Azarus had talked before about wanting to be free, either from slavery or from their family. Being free sounded great, but I had no idea what I would even do with that freedom. I chanced a look over at Azarus only to see him with an unusually solemn look on his face. I looked away before he could catch me staring. I forcefully put it out of my head when Grey started talking again.

"On the other hand," Grey said with more enthusiasm in his tone. "Magecraft is the search for external truth. It is the joy of discovery. Of adventure into the unknown! Magi chart their own course through life with a hunger for knowledge, and a deep desire to uncover the secrets of both the universe and the System itself. Well, they're supposed to at least," he finished wryly

I perked up at that. That sure as hell didn't sound as heavy to me.

Grey smiled at the sight of me paying more attention. Azarus rolled his eyes, dropping the intense look on his face.

"And now I ask you, Nathan. Which Path are you more interested in pursuing? Be aware, you must commit to one of them fully. You cannot be both in this world." Grey said expectantly.

I opened my mouth to answer him.

# Chapter 20
# To Be a Magi

"I'm pretty sure I'd prefer to be a Magi," I told them.

Azarus rolled his eyes. "Saw that one coming."

I raised an eyebrow at him. "What, was I that obvious?"

"Oh, only somewhat." Grey smiled broadly at me. "It was noticeable that you were visibly more interested in the subject when Magecraft was mentioned."

"Thought about betting on it, but I didn't want to lose me money on a sucker's bet," Azarus smirked at me.

I rolled my eyes back at him. "All right, all right. So, if I want to try and become a Magi, what sta— I mean Virtues do I have to put points into?"

"Ah, well. The two main stats that you should be investing in are Intelligence and Wisdom. Now, that doesn't mean you should simply put five points each into either." Grey cautioned me. "Rather, I recommend spreading a few of your points into the neutral virtues as your main."

"Neutral Virtues?" I asked him curiously.

"Indeed. While Intelligence and Wisdom are the primary Virtues of the Magi, and Strength and Spirit are the Virtues of the Cultivator,

Vitality, Dexterity and Perception are Virtues that either can take. In fact, it is highly recommended that you do so." Grey told me.

I tapped my fingers on the table in thought. "Let's back up a second, yeah? What do each of the Virtues actually *do*?"

"An excellent question, Nathan." Grey praised me. "Let us start with Intelligence and Strength then, shall we?"

I could see Azarus cross his arms and roll his eyes again. He leaned back in his chair, visibly bored of the coming lecture. Whatever, *I* was interested.

"As the two primary Virtues of Magi and Cultivators, they are deemed 'Power' Virtues. Simply, these two Virtues determine the overall capability and power of your Spells, Arts, or Skills. Additionally, they enhance you physically. For Strength, it is rather obvious. The Virtue increases your physical ability, leading to greater bodily might. On the other hand, Intelligence enhances you *mentally*. Progressively higher levels of Magecraft require greater mental ability and flexibility in order to accomplish them. Quite simply, if your Intelligence score is too low, you will be unable to mentally visualize the thought forms required." Grey explained.

"Huh," I said. "So, Intelligence makes you smarter and Strength makes you swole. What about Wisdom and Spirit?"

Grey cocked an eyebrow at me while Azarus screwed up his face in confusion.

"What the bleeding hell is 'swole'?" He muttered to himself

I restrained a smirk.

Grey let it pass without comment. "Wisdom and Spirit are termed as 'Well' Virtues. Vitality is included in the category," he told me. "Wisdom increases the pool of Mana that you can draw from, while Spirit does the same for Ki. There are some esoteric side effects to increasing your Wisdom or Spirit values as well, but that will not be relevant to you for quite some time indeed."

"And Vitality? You said that was a 'Well' Virtue." I asked Grey.

"Hmm, how to put this," Grey said thoughtfully. "You have noticed that both your Status and the Observe Skill track what is termed as 'HP', correct?" At my nod, he continued. "The abbreviation is short for 'Health Points'—"

One hundred percent just an RPG term, as I thought.

"—but what *is* 'Health', in the context of the System?" Grey asked me.

Oh, he wanted an actual answer. "Uh, I'm guessing how much damage you can take before you cark it?"

"Yes, but *how?*" Grey coaxed me patiently. "How does the System measure something as nebulous as overall health? Why does one's 'Health Points' only diminish from a direct attack, but *not* from illness, or overall age? How can it be that when an elderly person passes peacefully in their bed, surrounded by family members, their HP has not diminished until the very moment of death?"

"Well, that's all news to me. Interesting news, but still news." I said to him, nonplussed.

Grey paused for a moment in realization. "Ah, forgive me, Nathan. I'm simply too used to giving this lecture to, ah, 'regular' students. The answer is that what the System is measuring as 'Health', is ones Vitality. Vitality is the Virtue that determines ones HP. The greater the amount of Vitality, the larger your pool of HP and the more damage you can take in battle before you 'cark' it, as you so eloquently put it."

"Well, okay. But that doesn't actually answer the question of what System is tracking as 'Health' for 'Health Points." I said to Grey.

He beamed at me. "We don't know!" he said cheerfully.

I stared at him blankly. "You…don't know?"

"Oh, indeed. Even with centuries and centuries of testing and hypothesizing. With the libraries of books that have been written on the

169

subject. Make no mistake, there are many things we simply cannot say for certain in regard to the System, even something as foundational as the intricacies of one of the Virtues. Isn't it exciting?!" Grey told me animatedly.

I cut my eyes to Azarus for a moment. He shrugged at me. I looked back at Grey.

"You don't have theories about it?" I asked him skeptically.

Grey waved a hand dismissively. "Oh, of course, there are theories. There are dozens and dozens of them! Everything ranging from 'Vitality is the Virtue of the Soul', to 'Vitality is a measure of how much time you have left to live'. Why, I even heard a theory once about how it's a measure of a secret barrier we all have that deflects damage." He wiggled his fingers at me in a 'spooky' manner and laughed. Putting his hands down and clearing his throat, he continued. "Truly, we don't know for certain. If anyone attempts to say what it is that Vitality is affecting with certainty, they're a charlatan. We only know the practical effects. More Vitality equals more HP equals it's harder for you to die in combat."

"Uh, alright then," I said, at a loss. I shook my head slightly to reorient myself. "And the last two? Perception and Dexterity, right?"

"Mmm, yes. The least common of the Virtues." Grey nodded. "Perception and Dexterity are, at best, considered secondary. They can be invested in by either Magi or Cultivators, but neither is advised to invest too heavily. They simply do not give enough of an advantage."

"Alright, but what do they do then?" I asked him.

"Perception affects the senses," Grey explained to me patiently. "It enhances them with every point invested. Sight, sound, hearing, smell. Even your senses of taste and touch are enhanced by Perception. At least, to a degree. On the other hand, Dexterity increases your reaction speed and physical acuity. A person that has invested in Dexterity will find that they are quicker to react in combat and able to control themselves bodily in a more precise manner. These two are often termed 'Defense' Virtues. Indeed, you could consider Perception as a form of active defense, and Dexterity as a reactive defense."

I absorbed what he had told me in silence for a moment. After a bit, I spoke back up. "Alright, so I guess I invest most of my points into Intelligence and Wisdom and then spread the rest around between Vitality, Perception, and Dexterity?" I asked Grey.

He nodded at me. "Indeed."

When he didn't elaborate any further, I looked at him confusedly. I glanced at Azarus as well, only to see him raise an eyebrow at me silently. I looked back at Grey. "And that's it?"

Grey shrugged at me. "What else could there be? Allocate your Virtue points as you see fit, now that you are aware of their function." He sighed. "Ultimately Nathan, I cannot make decisions for you on your specialty. I can only educate you. It's considered somewhat of a faux pas to dictate to another how they build themselves."

I flushed slightly. "Uh, alright. I'll just...do that then."

Picking up the mirror that I had brought in from the forge, I focused on it and brought up my Status. Touching the surface of the mirror so that it focused on my Virtues, I could see that next to them each had a small plus sign next to them. After Grey's explanation, I had a pretty good idea of how I wanted to distribute my points. Fiddling with the mirror, I did so. When I was done, I looked at my decision.

| | |
|---|---|
| **Name** | **Nathaniel Eugene Hart** |
| **Titles** | **N/A** |
| **Level** | **5** |
| **Age** | **24 Sol** |
| **Race** | **Human (Precursor)** |
| **Affinity** | **Terrestrial** |
| **Classes** | **N/A** |
| **Professions** | **Material Enchantment, Mechanical Engineering, Blacksmithing, Medicinal Alchemy, Surgery** |
| **Health** | **240/240** |
| **Stamina** | **100/100** |
| **Vitality** | **14** |
| **Strength** | **10** |
| **Spirit** | **10** |
| **Dexterity** | **18** |
| **Perception** | **14** |
| **Intelligence** | **22** |
| **Wisdom** | **22** |
| **Free Points** | **0** |
| **Options** | **Talent Page, Skill Page, Professions Page** |

When I used all my free points, a new blue dialogue box popped up.

### Would you like to commit to these Virtues?
### Y/N

I mentally selected yes. In the end, of the forty points I'd gotten from four level up's, I'd decided to put twelve points into intelligence and wisdom both, eight points into Dexterity, and finally four points into Vitality and Perception each. That sounded like a Mage build to me.

When I finished, I looked back up at Grey and Azarus. I nodded at them. "Well, I'm done."

Grey met my eyes and nodded back at me. "So you are."

Azarus clapped his hands together. I jumped.

"Well, now that that's over with," he said cheerfully. "Probably time for us to hit the hay. Got more stuff to do tomorrow."

"In—" Grey interrupted himself with a yawn. "Indeed. It's been a long day for us all. Time for some rest."

Azarus stood up from the table and I followed suit.

"Goodnight, gentlemen," Grey said to both of us. "I'll see you in the morn." He wheeled out of the room towards his room by the stairs. After a moment, I could hear his door open and shut.

I looked at Azarus and then down at the plates that all of us had left from dinner. "We just going to leave them, or…?"

Azarus waved dismissively with a grunt. "Deal with it tomorrow. G'night." He left the kitchen as well, tromping up the stairs to the master bedroom.

I sighed. I spent a few moments picking up the dirty plates and utensils on the table before putting them in the washbasin that was sitting in the corner of the room. Exiting the kitchen myself, I headed up the stairs as well and entered the room that had been given to me. Kicking my shoes and pants off, I sat on the edge of the bed. Leaning over to put my face in my hands, I groaned quietly.

God, what a day.

It didn't feel like it, but only this morning I'd gotten another Profession in Surgery. We'd almost immediately left after that to the forest. We must have been in there all afternoon. I was exhausted in a way that I hadn't been in a very long time. Not since…

Well, at least this was a good exhausted. I slipped under the covers and lay my head down. Despite my still unfamiliar surroundings, I fell asleep near immediately.

The screech of tires.

Flames.

A man and a woman screaming in agony.

Beeping.

Sobbing.

Oppressive silence.

Steel on steel.

A whooshing noise, and then screaming.

Hooves pounding in the dirt.

The crack of a whip.

A horrible smile.

A finger lifting my chin.

"You want to know why?"

***

I jerked awake with a strangled cry. Sitting upright violently I stared off into space with a blank, unseeing stare. Slowly, I started to be able to focus. I was hyperventilating and soaked in sweat, even though I had just woken up. I slowly put my head down in my hands and struggled to hold tears back.

God.

That had been similar, but it wasn't the same. I hadn't had that nightmare in some time, but it was different this time. Longer.

That only made it worse.

Please, please don't let those start up again. I don't know if I can take my nightmares coming back on top of everything else that was happening to me now. I didn't need that on top of being on a magic alien planet.

Gradually, I was able to get ahold of myself. Raising my head and rubbing my eyes, I glanced at the window. At the very least, it looked like I had gotten enough sleep. It was clearly morning. I lay back down for a moment with a sigh.

I let myself gaze blankly at the ceiling for a few more moments. Before long, I leveraged myself back up into a seating position and swung my legs off of the bed with a grunt. I picked out a different set of clothes that Azarus had left for me in the dresser. Still looked the same though.

I opened the door to my room and stepped out. Before closing the door, I paused and looked back at the bed.

I shuddered slightly, and closed the door behind me.

# Chapter 21
# Aurora

I made my way downstairs, still somber from my nightmare. I was trying not to let it affect me too much, but it was difficult considering my past experiences with them. Luckily, it didn't seem like anyone else was up yet to see me in this state. For once, it looked like I had been the first person to wake up in this house. Making my way into the silent kitchen, I opened the curtains to the small window set in the far wall to let in some morning light. I sat down at the kitchen table afterward, at a bit of a loss.

I might have woken up slightly early, but I was still hungry. Problem was, I didn't exactly know how to cook around here. I could cook back home though, I'd had to. But I was used to modern meals, with modern appliances. I decided to get up and look around the kitchen and see what was available. Making my way over to the large wooden cabinet and opening the left door, I was surprised to find a large amount of perishable goods inside it, lying there. Vegetables, meats, grains, and even what looked like fruit of a kind that I didn't recognize. Hell, there were even more steaks that Vandimar had given us yesterday, laying open carelessly on a middle shelf.

I gazed at the contents of the cabinet in confusion. Nothing in there looked spoiled at all. In fact, all of it looked exceedingly fresh, as if it had either just been slaughtered or picked today. A moment later, I felt dumb. Of course, it was magic keeping everything fresh, you idiot. Looking around the inside of the cabinet again, I found what I expected. On the inside of the door I had opened, I found another one of those small discs with a symbol inscribed on it. Didn't recognize this one, though.

"Oi." I heard from behind me. I jumped in startlement, banging my head loudly on the top of the cabinet. Clutching my head and hissing in pain, I drew back and turned around. I found Azarus staring at me bemusedly from the doorway of the kitchen.

I stared back at him, awkwardly clutching the top of my head. "Uh, hey," I said to him. "Morning."

"Mornin'," he said back to me, amusedly.

I stopped rubbing my head, the pain fading. I moved away from the cabinet to lean against the table awkwardly. "So, uh. What's the plan for today?"

Azarus moved out of the doorway and over to the cabinet I had just banged my head on. "Hmm, well. We got three days before we're heading to Rhoscara, so I figure we'll just do a bit of practice today. We'll leave trying to get ya another Profession till tomorrow. We, uh, didn't get the chance to try and test your racials with everything that happened yesterday." He turned back around to face me, holding a loaf of bread in my direction. "Ya want some toast?"

"Sure, I'll take some toast." I nodded at him. I sat down at the table.

Azarus nodded back before moving over to one of the preparation tables. Setting the loaf down on it, he started to slice it up. Once he'd finished, he moved over to the large cast iron oven, starting it by putting a finger on one of those small enchantment discs. Moving back over to the prep table, he opened a drawer on it and pulled out some kind of wire contraption. Opening it up, I saw him start to put pieces of sliced bread inside of it, before closing it back up. He picked it back up, and moved back over to the oven. He opened the secondary door on the front of it above the fuel door, and shoved the wire rack full of bread inside.

I just watched all of this curiously. I guess this was how people made something as mundane as toast in magic fantasy land. Some of the steps weren't unusual to me, as I'd watched Azarus cook the steaks from last night, but it was interesting nonetheless. The way that magic was used to mirror some conveniences and appliances from back home was fascinating to me. Honestly, I'd thought that living on this planet would be rife with discomfort, considering the level of comfort I'd been born into on modern-day Earth. But it hadn't been bad so far. Sure, it didn't measure up, but ironically my standard of living on Vereden had risen dramatically since I'd been 'sold' to Azarus.

Azarus finished up and turned back around. He paused when he saw me watching him. "What?" he asked me.

I shook my head, somewhat embarrassed. "Ah, it's nothing."

He shrugged and moved back over to the cabinet. Opening it, he pulled out a jar of something and a few blunt knives before heading over to the table and setting them down. He sat down at the table as well.

We sat in silence for a moment before I broke it.

"Should we wake up Grey?" I asked Azarus.

He shook his head. "Nah, old man needs his sleep." He paused before leaning over the table. I copied him curiously. "Don't let him know I said this, but the brand is rougher on him than it is on others. His level is so much higher that it's suppressing more, and that means he overestimates himself. All that work yesterday tired him out." He leaned back out. "I'll wake him in a few hours. Sides, it's not like I didn't make some for him. I'll just put it in the cabinet for when he wakes up."

I nodded to show I understood. "So." I began, curiously. "Speaking of the cabinet, what kind of enchantment does it have?"

"Hmm? Oh, it just has a standard stasis disc in it. Makes it so nothing ever spoils in there." Azarus answered me distractedly. I followed his gaze and saw that he was watching the oven. What, could he see through it to the toast or something? Who knows, maybe he could.

"Is that common?" I asked him. "You know, for most people to have one of those?"

He looked over at me. "Eh, sorta," he answered me, wiggling one huge hand back and forth. "Discs are a relatively new thing, yeah? They've made enchanted items much cheaper than they used to be. Before that, ya had to get everything custom enchanted, and that could be mighty pricy. They're still not cheap, but I just got a bunch of them 'cause I'm, uh…"

Because he was a noble, got it.

I nodded to show I understood and Azarus nodded back at me, somewhat embarrassed. He looked back over at the oven.

"Toasts done," Azarus grunted. He got up from the table and moved back over to the oven. Opening up the door he'd put the bread in, he pulled the wire toast maker out and closed it afterward. With his free hand, he put his thumb on the second enchantment disc on the oven. I remembered from last night that this one doused the fire inside. Shuffling back over to the table, he opened the rack, revealing the toast. "Dig in," he said. Opening the glass jar he'd gotten from the cabinet; he revealed it to be some kind of jam. He slathered a piece of toast using one of the knives.

I copied him, and we ate in silence. The jam turned out to be made from some kind of berry that I couldn't place.

When we finished, Azarus stood up from the table, uncaring of the crumbs we'd left on the table. He closed the rack of toast back up and put it in the cabinet. Turning back around to face me, he said. "All right, time to get to work. Meet me in the backyard, I'll fetch the trainin' weapons."

I stood up as well. "Right now?" I asked in surprise. "Shouldn't we let the food settle first?"

Azarus looked at me weirdly for a moment realization flashed across his face. "Ah, right. You're not an Unawoken anymore, that's not an issue. Ya ain't gonna blow chunks if ya work hard after eating now."

I raised my eyebrows in surprise. Good to know, I guess.

With a final nod to me, Azarus exited the kitchen via the back door.

Looking around the kitchen and how dirty it was, I sighed. Guess it was up to me again.

I got to work.

\*\*\*

I cleaned up in the kitchen only a little, just enough so that it wasn't disgusting. When I finished, I exited the same door that Azarus had. I found him waiting impatiently in the yard with two spears in hand.

"Finally," he grunted at me. "What took ya so long?"

I rolled my eyes at him. "Don't worry about it. We gonna do this or not?"

He answered me by tossing one of the spears at me haft first. Surprisingly, I caught it just fine without even blinking. I guess those new stats were good for something after all. I set the butt of the spear in the dirt.

"All right then," Azarus said, nodding. "We'll start with testing your Racials. Sounded like ya had two active ones, yeah?"

"Yeah." I nodded back at him. "Hidden Amidst the Spheres, and The Scintillant Blade."

"Yeah, those. Now, Racials shouldn't be too hard to activate. That's not the point of them. We just got to figure out what they do. Why don't ya try the second one you mentioned first? Sounds more suited to combat than the other."

"Okay," I said, nonplussed. "Do I just try and activate it like a Skill? Like Observe?"

"Yup," Azarus answered simply.

I nodded at him, and then concentrated.

Surprisingly, it came to me even easier than Observe did.

### The Scintillant Blade.

The blade of my spear erupted with ethereal, rainbow-colored fire. I jumped, holding my spear away from me in alarm. After a moment, I calmed down. The fire wasn't giving off any actual heat when I brought my hand closer to it. I hesitated for a moment, before touching it. I watched in fascination as the rainbow fire curled around my hand like water. It was warm, but not the warmth of a fire. If anything, it reminded me of the sensation of gentle sunlight on my skin. It was...comforting.

"Neat." I heard Azarus say. Jerking back to reality, I felt my cheeks grow warm. Looking back at him, I could see that he was watching me with patient amusement. He spoke up again. "Now, let's see what it can do." Having said that, he motioned for me to attack him.

For some reason, I felt uneasy. I well-remembered yesterday's training, and how I wasn't able to even pierce Azarus's clothes with my spear. I didn't expect the few levels I'd gotten to have made much of a difference, so why did I feel reluctant to attack him with this ability? I voiced my concerns.

"I dunno man, I don't know if I should," I told him uneasily.

Azarus sighed noisily. "Look, Nate. Ya ain't gonna hurt me. I haven't mentioned it yet, but I'm over a hundred levels above ya. It'd take a damn miracle for ya to do actual damage to me. I appreciate it, but we're just trying to see what effects that stuff has. Now, come on. Get in your stance."

I didn't feel reassured, but I did what he told me. Getting into the spear stance he'd taught me yesterday, I nodded at Azarus to show I was about to attack him. He just raised an eyebrow at me. With a shout, I charged at him and thrust, scintillant spear point first.

The spear blade slid into Azarus's flesh with no problem, stopping only when the blade disappeared. I stared at the point of entry, around where a liver would be on a human, horrified. Azarus slowly looked down at the spear lodged in his stomach with a blank look on his face. He looked back up at me.

"Well, damn," he said faintly.

# Chapter 22
# Paper Cut

I panicked.

I let go of the spear still lodged in Azarus and sprang away from him clumsily.

"Oh shit, oh fuck, oh shit, oh fuck." I chattered uselessly, staring at the point that the spear had pierced Azarus's flesh. My ears were ringing and my world was narrowing. Vaguely, distantly, I was aware that I was having a panic attack. I was familiar enough with them at this point in my life to recognize the symptoms. I was violently knocked out of my fugue when Azarus nonchalantly, seeming without a care in the world, firmly grasped the spear with one huge hand and yanked it out of himself in one smooth motion. He didn't even wince.

I gaped at him, horrified.

"But, blood…" I said incoherently, raising one limp hand to point at his wound. I think I was trying to point out how he was going to bleed out now that the wound was unobstructed.

Except, that didn't happen.

The large stab wound on Azarus's belly, visible through the tear in his shirt, wasn't bleeding at all. It was clearly visible, and I could even see individual severed muscle fibers around the entrance, to my horror. But the wound was, disturbingly, clean and blood free.

Azarus reached up to scratch his chin, uncaring about the seeming mortal wound. "Interesting. It's like your spear didn't care a whit about me defenses." He directed his gaze at me finally. "What?"

I was still staring at him aghast. But at least I wasn't panicking anymore. The way that Azarus clearly didn't seem to care overmuch about his injury was keeping the panic at bay. I was still concerned, however. I cleared my throat roughly, aware of how dry my mouth had gotten over the last few minutes.

"Are...are you okay?" I asked Azarus hesitantly.

"Yeah?" he said confusingly. "Why wouldn't I be?"

I opened and closed my mouth in increasing astonishment. "I just stabbed you!" I near shouted at him. "You have a huge fucking hole in your stomach! Why the fuck else would I be asking if you're okay?!"

Okay, I was actually shouting at him at the end of that.

Azarus looked down at himself for a moment, puzzled. He stuck his index finger into the wound on his stomach and wiggled it around briefly. I nearly vomited. "What, this? It'll take more than this to take out ol'Azarus," he said boastfully. He looked back up at me to see the sickened look on my face. After a moment, realization stole across his own. "Ohhhh, I get it." He let out a chortle.

I stared at him, aghast.

"Welcome to life as an Awakened, Nate," Azarus told me cheerfully. "This is what it's like, yeah? Things like your itsy bitsy poke ain't a real danger to someone like me."

I just grew more confused. "But..." I muttered helplessly. "When the deer attacked me, I was *definitely* bleeding all over the place."

Azarus nodded. "Yeah, 'cause you're not even past your first threshold. For someone like me, who is? I don't got to worry about bleeding all over the place anymore." He paused for a second. "Well, not unless I get hurt way, way worse than this."

I was calming down significantly now. Azarus genuinely didn't seem to care about his wound, and the unaffected way that he was speaking was helping me more than he seemed to realize. I dragged a hand down my face, suddenly exhausted again, even though I had only woken up from a full night's sleep maybe an hour and a half ago.

"All right, I'll bite," I muttered tiredly into my hand. "What's a threshold?"

Azarus had no trouble understanding my muffled words. "None of your beeswax," he rebuked me cheerfully.

I took my hand off my face to give him a gimlet stare, unimpressed with his dodging the question. He smirked and raised his hands in a placating manner.

"Seriously, it's not something ya should worry about just now. You're a long ways away from *that*. Plus, you're not supposed to talk about it with people before they're ready, yeah? Ya can influence 'em too much and fuck it all up," he told me, semi-seriously. "For now, pay it no mind. Just know, this little pin-prick will heal on its own right quick. See? Already happening."

I paid closer attention to the wound again, even though it made me queasy to do so. To my astonishment, he was correct. The stab wound that I had left on Azarus was visibly already healing. It wasn't healing like he had some kind of comic book healing factor. No, this seemed more like vastly sped-up natural healing. The wound itself was visibly smaller than it had been a few moments ago, and it already had some scab tissue growing on it.

I relaxed even further, now that I knew Azarus was truly in no danger. "Still," I said hesitantly. "I can't imagine that was pleasant. I'm...sorry for hurting you." I told him sincerely, if not also awkwardly.

He literally waved it off. "Eh, I got a talent for that. Barely felt it," he grunted before visibly brightening. "Now, what I'm more

185

interested in is that skill of yours." He tossed my spear back to me like he had only moments ago. I caught it again. "Try it again. Only this, I just want ya to come over here and try and cut me arm. We ain't gonna try and fight with the skill again yet."

I took a deep breath and let it out slowly. I then did the process again a second time, to try and clear out any residual panic adrenaline. Okay, Nate. Your fantasy dwarf friend (?) wants you to use the skill you thought had killed him again. You can do this.

I concentrated.

### The Scintillant Blade.

That same rainbow flame appeared around the blade of my spear again. I eyed it warily for a moment. Shaking it off, I walked over to Azarus as he'd said to and stood in front of him. He wordlessly held up his right hand in front of him in an invitation. Hesitantly, I brought the flaming head of my spear closer to his arm. Just like it had with me, when the flame touched his skin, it didn't burn him. It just kind of rolled and twisted around the surface of his skin. I looked up at Azarus to make sure he still wanted to do this. He just raised an eyebrow at me. Looking back down, I pressed the spear's blade to his skin.

A gash immediately opened up on Azarus's arm, even though I hadn't put any force behind the blade.

I instantly moved the spear blade away from Azarus and took a step back. I was trembling faintly. I tried to steady myself, or at the very least hide it. I needn't have bothered, Azarus was looking down at his arm in shock.

"Well, I'll be damned," he muttered in amazement. "Never even heard of something like this." Lifting his head to look at me, Azarus firmed his expression. "Time to wake the old man. He'll want to know."

***

After stomping back through the house, with me following quietly behind him, Azarus pounded on Grey's door until a groggy voice told us to come in. After following Azarus in, I stood awkwardly off to one side as Azarus started whispering something to a still-sleepy Grey. Whatever Azarus was saying to Grey seemed to wake him up fast, however. I was able to watch as Grey went from tired to instantly awake and focusing on me in the blink of an eye. The assessing gaze that Grey was giving me was making me a tad uneasy. I shifted nervously from one foot to another. Grey blinked.

"Ah, how rude of me," Grey said, smiling disarmingly. "Please, pull up a chair Nathan. I believe we have a few small tests to run." He gestured to a familiar wooden chair sitting in the corner. Azarus just leaned against an open spot on the wall.

I shuffled over to the chair and moved it to where Grey had leveraged himself into his wheelchair. I sat down in it, aware that both Grey and Azarus had their eyes fixed on me. "So…" I said nervously. "What's up?"

"Well," Grey said calmly. "Azarus was telling me about how you two were testing your racial skill, yes? However, he mentioned that you were able to injure him quite easily. Which, frankly, is highly, *highly* unusual."

I cleared my throat. "Uh, yeah. I guess that's what happened."

"Fascinating," Grey murmured to himself.

187

Coughing into his fist to get attention, Azarus spoke. "Why don't ya show it to him, yeah? Maybe he'll have a better idea of what we're looking at."

I stared at Azarus blankly for a moment before looking around. I looked back at him. "With what?" I said, somewhat exasperated. "I need a weapon to use it." I paused. "Wait, how do I know that? Somehow, I just *know* I need something with an edge on it to use the skill."

Grey had wheeled over to his desk while I was talking and started to rummage around through a drawer. After a moment of searching, he withdrew a small paring knife. Wheeling back over to me, he handed it over while speaking. "That's not uncommon at all. Instinctual knowledge of what is required to use a skill is a fundamental facet of the System. There you go. Why don't you try using the skill on the knife?"

Taking the knife and a deep breath at the same time, I concentrated and activated my skill for the third time today.

### The Scintillant Blade.

The blade of the knife in my hand erupted into now familiar rainbow flames.

Grey stared at the flames in fascination. "Well, if nothing else it's quite visually striking," he hummed to himself for a moment. "This manifestation reminds me of the auroras of the far north. It's been some time since I've seen them, but I've never forgotten the sight."

I paused to take a closer look at the flames myself. Yeah, now that he mentioned it, I could see what he was talking about. The rainbow flames I could conjure did remind me of the aurora borealis back home. Shaking it off, I addressed Grey. "So, how do you want to test this? Do you want me to just cut Azarus or something again?"

"If you could." Grey nodded. "I wish to observe this phenomenon in action myself. Perhaps I'll be able to glean something from it. Azarus, if you would?"

Azarus shoved off the wall he had been leaning on silently while Grey and I were speaking. Walking over to where I was sitting, Azarus held out the same arm that I had cut earlier. He cleared his throat and smiled at me. "If ya don't mind, could ya lay the next cut over the other one, in a kinda cross pattern?"

Grey and I both stared at him, Grey in consternation and myself in horrified amazement.

Grey sighed and pinched the bridge of his nose. "Really, Azarus? Really?"

"What?" Azarus said, smirking and shrugging. "Ladies love a wicked-lookin' scar."

I shook my head, wide-eyed. "Whatever you say, man." I brought the knife up to his arm and laid the blade perpendicular to the other cut. Pressing the blade down on his arm lightly, another gash opened up on his arm just as swiftly as it had earlier. Pulling the blade away quickly, before he could get any more injured, I looked over at Grey.

For the first time since I had met him, Grey had a truly confused look on his face. Leaning back in his chair, Grey rubbed his chin. "I...have absolutely no idea what just happened," he said wonderingly. "I cannot even sense the flames themselves, much less whatever method they're using to bypass Azarus's defenses."

Azarus's eyebrows shot up. "Yeah? I mean, I wasn't too surprised when I couldn't feel 'em, but you? You of all people can't feel 'em?"

Grey shook his head. "Indeed, no. Truthfully, I'm as shocked as you are. These flames," he said, gesturing to the knife that was still roiling with rainbow fire. "Might as well not exist to my senses."

Crossing his arms, uncaring of the wounds on his right, Azarus frowned. "Huh."

Looking between the two of them, I spoke. "Is...that a problem?"

Grey hummed. "Not truly, I suppose. The only problem comes from the fact that we'll have difficulty analyzing what your flames are capable of. We'll need to base any conclusions on them purely from observational data. At least for the moment." Grey sighed. "If we had access to my lab, it would be a different story. I'm sure I would be able to detect something with some of my more specialized equipment."

"Best I can tell," Azarus interjected. "Those flames just completely ignore most defenses. They don't seem to do any damage themselves, though."

Grey gazed thoughtfully at the knife in my hand at those words. "I wonder..." He whispered.

Azarus raised an eyebrow at Grey. "Ya got an idea?"

Grey nodded absent-mindedly, staring into the distance. After a moment, Grey turned his gaze to me. "Nathan, I have a request. Would you mind testing your skill on me in the same way that you did Azarus?"

Azarus laughed disbelievingly before I could answer. "You're joking, ya gotta be. It's one thing for the skill to hurt me, it's a whole other for it to hurt *you*. Doesn't matter how bound your Status is, you just got more *weight* to ya."

Grey ignored his words, gazing at me patiently.

I took a deep breath for a moment to steady my nerves. Fuck it, why not. Apparently, knife wounds didn't mean much to these people anyway. I nodded at Grey, not trusting myself to speak.

Grey nodded back at me and silently rolled up his right sleeve. Apprehensively, I brought my still flame-covered knife closer to his arm. Taking a deep breath and holding it (while noticing that Azarus did the same, despite his words) I brought the knife down on Grey's arm.

Nothing.

Unlike Azarus, the knife didn't immediately wound him.

Letting out the breath I had been holding in a sigh of relief, I withdrew my knife from Grey's arm and mentally canceled the skill. The flames on my knife winked out.

Azarus let out a breath as well. "What'd I tell ya," he said, crossing his arms. "It's ridiculous to thi—"

"No," Grey said, interrupting him. Directing my gaze back at Grey, I could see that he was staring unblinkingly at the point that the blade had rested on his skin. I felt a shiver run up my spine at the intensity of his gaze. After a moment, Grey pinned both Azarus and me with a stare. "Look closer."

The both of us leaned closer his arm unquestioningly at the authority in Grey's voice. At first, I couldn't see anything on his arm. But after a moment, I could see what Grey had at about the same time that Azarus did, based on his intake of breath.

On Grey's arm was a small incision, no bigger or deeper than a shallow paper cut.

# Chapter 23
# Assassin's Potential

For the first time since I'd met him, Azarus looked genuinely uneasy. "Tha's not good. Tha's not good at all," he said, his accent thickening in his distress.

I looked over at Azarus, furrowing my brow at the blatant agitation written across his face. "What do you mean? I'm not a fan of hurting you guys, but isn't it good that I have a strong racial?"

Grey spoke before Azarus could, drawing my attention back to him. "Indeed, it is," he said evenly, his gaze steely. "In some regards. However, what Azarus is referring to is the…overall picture, not merely the potency of your racial."

At this point, I was truly confused by their reaction. "What do you mean?"

Sighing heavily, Grey ran a hand over his smooth head. "The problem Nathan, is the interest that your talent will attract if its capabilities are leaked to the general public. You must understand, the ability of your racial talent to affect those far above your level in such a manner is not only unusual, it's unheard of. In all my years…" He shook his head. "I can only conclude that this is due to your Precursor nature. However, you must make all attempts possible to conceal the depths of its potential."

Azarus shifted uneasily. "Don't let anyone know ya can punch so far above your weight if ya can help it. If ya do, you're gonna get taken and turned into a weapon for some uppity noble. That's an assassin's skill if I've ever seen one."

"Yes." Grey nodded. "Do not hesitate to use the skill. It bodes well for our purposes and our current circumstances. However, if you must use it against an opponent, give them no chance to report it." He fixed me with his gaze. "Do you understand?"

It was my turn to be unsettled. I did understand what he was saying, I was just deeply uncomfortable with it. Jesus Christ, I wasn't a murderer. I'd grown up in modern America and had never gotten into anything more serious than an elementary school fistfight. It was one thing to kill mostly mindless monsters that resembled animals, but it was an entirely other matter to kill another person. Nevertheless, I nodded jerkily at Grey's words.

Grey's expression softened slightly. "Well," he murmured. "If we cannot sense the mechanism by which Nathan's skill functions, it might well be too dangerous to continue testing it. Continue to use it in combat, for now, and we will try again once we escape."

"If. If we escape." Azarus said grimly.

"If," Grey affirmed quietly. He shook his head slightly. "On the other hand, there is also Nathan's second skill to test, no? The Status concealment one? Have either of you tested that one?" he asked us in a forcibly cheerful tone.

"Ah, no." Azarus answered, shaking his head. I did the same.

"Well, give it a go I'd say," Grey said, motioning to me. "From what I recall, it certainly sounded less...portentous, in application. Afterward, you can continue your martial training with Azarus."

I nodded quietly. I guess. Not like I had anything better to do.

I closed my eyes and concentrated.

## Hidden Amidst the Spheres.

I felt a clicking sensation deep inside me, somewhere I couldn't quite put my finger on, but nothing else happened. However, I felt a sense of…potential, I guess? It was hard to explain. It was like I could reach out to my Status in some way. Instinctively, I tried. I was surprised at what happened.

In my mind's eye, my Status expanded before me.

| | |
|---|---|
| Name | Nathaniel Eugene Hart |
| Titles | N/A |
| Level | 5 |
| Age | 24 Sol |
| Race | Human (Precursor) |
| Affinity | Terrestrial |
| Classes | N/A |
| Professions | Material Enchantment, Mechanical Engineering, Blacksmithing, Medicinal Alchemy, Surgery |
| Health | 240/240 |
| Stamina | 100/100 |
| Vitality | 14 |
| Strength | 10 |
| Spirit 10 | |
| Dexterity | 18 |
| Perception | 14 |
| Intelligence | 22 |
| Wisdom | 22 |
| Free Points | 0 |
| Options | Talent Page, Skill Page, Profession Page |

My eyebrows shot up in surprise.

"Nathan?" I heard Grey ask curiously.

I waved one hand absentmindedly. "One sec," I said, not opening my eyes.

Okay, so my Racial allowed me to view my Status without using a mirror, but I could tell that wasn't all to it. My Status looked different from how it usually did on a mirror. There was something about the text that looked…impermanent, somehow. Like it could drift away with the wind. I reached out to my Status mentally, raising a hand as well to help focus. I mentally tapped one of the entries and received an impression of possibility. Of change. Mentally shrugging, I tried it out.

I opened my eyes to the expectant looks of both Grey and Azarus. Feeling self-conscious, I spoke. "Well, can you guys try and Observe me, then? I want to see if what I did reflected outwards."

"Of course," Grey said absentmindedly. As soon as the word Observe had left my lips, Grey had gotten that focused look in his eyes that I knew to be an indication of Observe use, Azarus following him. Shortly after, I felt two small tingles on the back of my neck.

Grey must have spotted what I did first because an amused smile crossed his face. He met my eyes, nodded at me, and sat back to watch Azarus's reaction. It didn't take long.

Azarus snorted, obviously canceling his skill and focusing on me. "You *wish*," he told me. "You're not handsome enough to be a dwarf."

I smirked back at him. "Oh, I don't know. I think I get by," I said modestly, buffing my nails on my shirt.

Azarus rolled his eyes at me. "So, is that it? Ya can change your Status to show what ya want it to?" he asked curiously.

I shook my head. "No, that's not all. It uh, lets me mentally view my Status as well. I mean, I need to be able to see it to change it, right?" I said, laughing nervously. Mentally, I braced myself. After everything else that had happened, I was ready for them to go all doom and gloom and act like this was the end of the world.

They didn't.

"Not bad." Azarus nodded, impressed. "Don't got one of those meself."

Grey rubbed his chin. "I do wish we had tested this before you had committed your free points. That way, we would be able to test which version of a Status viewing skill you have."

I was taken aback, but not in a bad way. I relaxed somewhat. "So, something like this isn't super rare."

Grey waved a hand dismissively. "Oh no, not at all. Skills that allow you to bypass the usage of a mirror are not *common*, but they're not unknown. It's merely down to personal preference whether you choose to pursue one. It depends on how much you value the convenience factor. I myself have one," he told me.

"Cool," I said, relieved. "So, what was it you were saying about skill versions?"

"Oh, there are generally two versions of Status viewing skills. The first merely allows you to view your status as it is through a medium of your choice, usually mental, but affect no changes to it. In those cases, you still need a reflective surface to interact with your Status. The second merely allows you to work mental changes on your Status, without visualization. Things such as free point allocation, or skill selection. It typically depends on the quality of the skill. I suspect that since yours is a racial, it will be the active changes version." Grey explained to me happily. I could tell that he was happy to be back in his element, teaching me things.

Azarus rubbed his chin. "Though, ya know," he said musingly. "Never heard of a skill that lets ya view and change your status at the same time."

"Hmm." Grey nodded. "Yes, neither have I. But it's not altogether unusual. Thematically, it makes sense to be able to see and change your Status when you'd like. I suspect there might have been similar skills for others in the past if the Skill was of an unusually high quality.

However, it makes sense for a Racial to be so flexible, as well. Congratulations, Nathan."

I shrugged, mildly uncomfortable. "Thanks, I guess".

Azarus grew uncomfortable for a moment himself. "But, ah. Both of those Racials, they kinda got a theme, don't they? They both seem like skills for an assassin."

Grey paused for a moment before speaking. "Technically, yes," he said delicately. "I do believe they would suit that skill set the best. However, don't let our musings influence you over much, Nathan. You are free to develop in whichever direction you see fit."

"What the hell do you mean?" I asked them, baffled. "I kinda get my veiling skill, but the flames? How is a skill that conjures brightly glowing rainbow flames supposed to be an assassin skill?"

Azarus rolled his eyes at me. "You'll get better at using it. I wouldn't be surprised if ya can dim them down enough that the light is barely seen."

"Azarus is correct." Grey nodded. "Racials are often highly versatile, and their usage is dependent on the skill of the wielder."

Oh.

We sat in silence for a moment before Grey broke it again.

"There are a few things I suggest that you change on your Status," he told me. "Normally, your Status displays your race as a Precursor, correct?" At my nod, he continued. "I suggest changing it to simply display yourself as a human. Furthermore, you should conceal your additional Professions. If someone Observed you and noticed that you had more than the standard two, I suspect that would bring trouble."

"All right." I nodded. "But…which two do you think I should leave up?"

"Leave Surgery," Azarus suggested. "Bleddyn already wants ya to be coming by the shop, so you'll need that reason if a guard asks ya."

"Indeed, and I would recommend that the second profession that you leave be your Alchemy." Grey picked up. "To those in the know, they will already be aware of my presence in this house, thus easily explaining how you acquired it."

"Sounds fine to me. I'll just, uh, do that then." I said awkwardly. I closed my eyes and concentrated on my skill again. Once my Status was back up, I mentally made the changes we had talked about. Once I was done, I went over my Status again critically.

| | |
|---|---|
| Name | Nathaniel Eugene Hart |
| Titles | N/A |
| Level | 5 |
| Age | 24 Sol |
| Race | ~~Human~~ (Precursor) |
| Affinity | Terrestrial |
| Classes | N/A |
| Professions | Material Enchantment, ~~Mechanical Engineering,~~ Blacksmithing, ~~Medicinal Alchemy, Surgery~~ |
| Health | 240/240 |
| Stamina | 100/100 |
| Vitality | 14 |
| Strength | 10 |
| Spirit | 10 |
| Dexterity | 18 |
| Perception | 14 |
| Intelligence | 22 |
| Wisdom | 22 |
| Free Points | 0 |
| Options | Talent Page, Skill Page, Profession Page |

I could still see the items I had hidden on my Status, but they seemed, well, veiled. I opened my eyes and looked at Grey and Azarus again. I'd had a thought while working on my Status.

"What about my Virtues?" I asked them. "Wouldn't the amount I have seem suspicious? Should I hide those too?"

Grey smiled patiently at me. "That will not be an issue, Nathan. Observe type skills do not display Virtue distribution."

"Oh. All right then, give it a go," I said to them.

They both got that look in their eyes again, and I felt that same tingle. After a moment, they stopped and Grey nodded at me in satisfaction.

"All appears well to me. Azarus?" Grey said, turning his head to Azarus.

Azarus just grunted, nodding.

Grey turned back to me and clapped his hands. "Well then! I believe that's all we needed to discuss for now, yes? I remind you gentlemen that you woke me to have this conversation, and at this point, I'm quite hungry. You two," he said, pointing from me to Azarus. "Also have some training to get back to, no?"

"Oh, joy," I said sarcastically.

Azarus shoved off of the wall he had been leaning on. "Oh, quit your bitchin'. It won't be that bad."

\*\*\*

I flopped down on my bed with a groan.

Yeah, it had been pretty bad.

After our conversation in Grey's room about my Racials, Grey had left to make some breakfast for himself, while Azarus and I had left for more training. Once there, we had spent the rest of the fucking day out in the sun, 'training'. More like torture, to me. He'd started by showing me more spear forms, than having me run through them over and over and over again. Once he'd been satisfied that I was starting to get the hang of them, he'd moved on to actual fighting. Of course, once I'd started to fight Azarus, those forms broke down. I was clearly not ready for actual combat yet. Whenever I'd screw up like that, Azarus would make me go through everything that he'd taught me all over again before we could fight again.

I didn't end up fighting all that much today.

It was exhausting. The only real breaks that we took were either for water or for lunch and dinner. I'd just gotten back from dinner. When we were done with dinner, Grey had told me that he had an idea about how to get me the last Profession available in town, Wildshaping. He told me to prepare myself for tomorrow morning. Turning my head to my window, I could see that it was fully dark by now. I guess I should be getting to sleep soon.

I knew that I should take a bath after all that exertion today, but I was too tired to move from my surprisingly comfy bed. I'd do it in the morning.

Curious, I decided to check my Status to see if my Spear Talent had grown from everything I'd done today. Too lazy to reach for the mirror that I knew was inside my bedside table, I used Hidden Amidst the Spheres to check mentally.

Yup, Spear Proficiency had grown again. This time to level four.

I guess I wasn't too surprised to see that it had grown a level today. Azarus had worked me hard.

I relaxed my mental hold on my Status, letting it dissipate. For a bit, I just stared blankly at the ceiling in peaceful silence. After a few minutes of zoning out, I mentally reached for Hidden Amidst the Spheres again.

But this time, I just held the skill activated without pulling up my Status. I hadn't been completely honest with Grey and Azarus that my skill could only view and change my Status. I don't know why I hadn't told them; they'd been extremely forthright with me since they literally saved my life. I had no reason to distrust them.

But…

Something in me said that I needed to keep this on the down low. I don't know why, I hadn't even gotten that feeling about my apparent super-assassin skill.

Every time that I activated the skill, there was a sense of…potential that built up before I opened my Status. Intuitively, I knew there was more to that feeling, but I didn't know what to do with it. Sitting up and forgetting my exhaustion for a moment, I just held the skill in its activated state without opening my Status with bated breath. The potential just kept building and building until some kind of reservoir built into the skill felt like it would burst. And then…

It just dissipated without doing anything.

Letting out a sigh and flopping back on my bed again, I put my arm over my eyes.

Whatever, I'd figure it out later.

# Interlude 2
# Weird Guy

Walter Meyers tried to keep his head down while he followed his new dwarven master through the markets. This wasn't difficult for him, as he had already gotten a harsh lesson about staring from the dwarf that had purchased him. In the scant few days since he'd been a slave, he'd learned. Master Horsoun had no pity for him.

Walter was slowly becoming numb to it all. Only sixteen years old, and his life was already over. He'd been forced to flee the war by his frantic father, along with the rest of his family. What little life and prospects that he'd had were gone now, no doubt burned down by those damn dolls. His family were all dead as well, killed in an elven raid while trying to seek a more peaceful life in dwarven lands. Everyone knew that the rebels didn't dare try and strike into the Principality.

He supposed it didn't matter much for him, at this point. He was just property now, no better than old Matilda, the family milk cow.

Walter didn't know what he and his master were doing in the markets today and didn't much care to find out. He'd learned another lesson from Master Horsoun about curiosity, after all. He just quietly walked behind his master, dull eyes down and fixed on his master's feet as he trudged along.

Slowly, as he and his master trudged down the main thoroughfare of the small dwarven town he'd found himself enslaved in, he began to hear a commotion. He still didn't dare look up, not until his master stopped as well. Risking a glance up at his master's back, he could see from behind that the dwarf had stopped to rubberneck the source of the noise. He followed his master's gaze.

The commotion was coming from another pair of dwarven master and human slave. The dwarf was yelling at his slave for dropping what looked to be a large amount of cutlery. The utensils were sprawled out all over the hard-packed dirt road.

Walter didn't recognize the dwarf, which also didn't surprise him. He was huge frankly, the largest dwarf he'd ever personally seen. With blazing red hair and a surprisingly long beard, he was nearly the average height of a human man. Something about the beard tickled his memory, but he felt like he'd forgotten most of the lessons he'd had with Brother Franklin after everything that had happened to him. On the other hand, he did recognize the human that was being yelled at.

It was that weird guy the caravan had picked up the day of the raid.

Walter was somewhat surprised to see him. He figured the stunty's would have put him down by now. After the guy had just shown up on the edge of camp and gotten Corporal Danvers all up in a tizzy, word had gotten around that he might be Unawakened. His best friend Paul had been the first person to find him, and had excitedly told him the story. From what he'd said, the weird guy had just appeared out of thin air, like a mage or something. Walter ignored the pang in his heart at the reminder of Paul, dead at the end of an elven spear.

The yelling of the dwarven master had drawn the attention of one of the guardsmen, who had sidled up to the huge dwarf. He was too far away to hear what they were saying to one another. Master

Horsoun must have been too far away as well, as he sauntered over closer in order to eavesdrop. Walter followed dutifully.

"…untrained…" He heard as heard in snippets as he and his master got closer. "…ungrateful…night…barracks…" Whatever the huge dwarf was saying to the compliant guard, it probably didn't bode well for the weird guy. When the master was done speaking to the guard, the guard saluted the large dwarf. The guard strode over to the strange man and grabbed him roughly by the arm and wrenched it behind him. The human let out a strangled noise of pain at the movement. Holding the arm of the man behind his back in a bar, the guard began force-marching the slave out of the market in the direction of the gate. Despite everything that had happened to him so far, Walter felt an ounce of pity for the man.

"Hmph. Good on you, My Lord." Walter heard Master Horsoun say with approval in his voice. "Come along, boy."

Walter followed dutifully as his master began to walk towards his destination again. As he left the scene of the accident, he caught sight of the huge dwarf's face. It was twisted strangely, gazing in the direction that the slave had been taken in.

Walter tried not to think too deeply on it. Like most things, these days.

Better to just be numb to it all.

***

Later that day, Walter stumbled into the slave barracks, exhausted. His master had driven him hard. He'd been hauling goods and packages for Master Horsoun to and from the post office all day. He had no idea why his master needed so much junk, and he didn't dare ask.

Flopping onto his patchy woolen bunk in the barracks, he let out a sigh. He hadn't eaten since his meager breakfast at first bell, and he was starving. It was near sundown, and he knew that the next meal would be as meager. At least it would be soon, he'd learned that they typically served dinner around this time. He just needed to wait for the rest of the field slaves to come in, and then the overseers would ring the dinner bell. He closed his eyes to rest until then.

As he was dozing, a hand shook his shoulder. Groggily opening his eyes, Walter followed the hand up to its owner. It was Mr. Matheson, one of the only other survivors from his caravan.

"Up, boy." Mr. Matheson said gruffly. Henry Matheson was a large man, built from a lifetime of labor on a farm back home. Walter supposed his size was what had saved his life in the end. A large, strong-looking slave was more likely to sell, after all. "You slept right through the dinner bell."

Fully awake now, Walter sat up in his bunk. He looked up at Mr. Matheson. "When did you get in?" he asked him. As far as he knew, Mr. Matheson had been assigned to work the fields.

Mr. Matheson scowled slightly, reaching up to fiddle with his slave collar absentmindedly. "Not long ago. I figured a green boy like you couldn't handle a real day's work, and came to find you," he said gruffly. Walter didn't take it personally. Mr. Matheson had tried to look out for him as best he could since they'd been sold. "Foods ready," he told Walter, turning around and striding to the entrance of the barracks they'd been assigned to.

With a groan, Walter sat up and followed him. Exiting the barracks, he found most of the slaves standing in line for their bowl of thin stew. Shuffling into line, Walter settled in to wait for his turn. Before long, he'd received his meal for the night and bowed his head in thanks for the food, as his mother had taught him. The overseer didn't acknowledge him at all.

Holding his stew close to his chest protectively, Walter searched for a place to eat it safely. He found that Mr. Matheson had saved a spot for him near the bonfire that was in the middle of the circle of slave barracks. He made his way over to Mr. Matheson and dug into his food without a word. Mr. Matheson didn't acknowledge him either.

When he was finished with his dinner, Walter merely stared blankly into his empty wooden food bowl. He didn't know how long he sat there next to Mr. Matheson, as blissfully numb to the world as he was. Walter jerked out of his empty-mindedness when he felt a nudge on his shoulder. Turning to face it, he found it had been Mr. Matheson.

"Look at that." Mr. Matheson said, pointing. Walter followed his finger. With a start, he saw that Mr. Matheson was pointing at the weird guy from earlier that morning.

The guy looked rough. He had a large, visible bruise across half of his face, overlaying the fresh-looking scar on his left cheek. He was visibly dirty and looked nearly dead on his feet. Despite that, the weird guy was going from person to person and asking something. Everyone that the guy spoke to either ignored him or was telling him to fuck off. Walter understood. Everyone was tired. They just wanted to eat their food and relax as much as they could, before they had to exhaust themselves again tomorrow.

"What does he want?" Walter asked Mr. Matheson, curious despite himself.

Mr. Matheson grunted. "He was put in the fields with us today. Damn near worthless, he was. He kept going around and askin' if anyone would be willin' to teach him Wildshaping."

Walter was surprised. He studied the man again before turning back to Mr. Matheson. "He doesn't have his Professions?" Walter was only sixteen, and he already had both of his Professions. That guy was definitely older than him.

Mr. Matheson shrugged. "Guess not. Danvers was probably wrong. That guy ain't no spy." He paused a moment before continuing. "Might've been Unawakened after all." There was naked pity in his voice.

Walter turned back to study the stranger. Slowly, he became aware that a feeling had made its way past his wall of numbness. "What's his name?" he asked Mr. Matheson, still watching the weird guy.

"Said it was Nathan." Mr. Matheson said, off to his right.

Slowly getting to his feet, Walter set his empty food bowl on the log that he had been sitting on. Before he could go anywhere, he felt a large hand grab his wrist. Turning to face it, he found that Mr. Matheson was looking at him with an unreadable expression on his face.

"Don't know if that's a good idea, boy." The large man said softly. "Best not to get mixed up with his business."

Walter felt angry despite himself. "He's not going to last long if he doesn't have his Professions," he whispered furiously to Mr. Matheson.

Mr. Matheson sighed. "Are any of us?" he asked under his voice. He let go of Walter's wrist abruptly. "Go on then. I'm not your father."

Walter staggered slightly, before getting his feet under himself steadily. He turned in the direction of the weird guy, Nathan, and started making his way over to him without another word.

The guy had taken a seat on one of the logs in between one of the barracks and put his head in his hands. Walking over to him, Walter sat next to him with a thump. The man jerked upright and turned to face Walter with a wild look on his face. However, when his eyes met Walters, a look of recognition spread across his face.

"You…" the man said slowly. "Were you…?"

Walter looked away from the man and down at his clasped hands. "Yes," he said simply. He didn't need to say anything else. The man clearly understood. With a sigh, the man dragged a hand down his face, before wincing when his motion upset the bruise upon it.

"Can I help you?" the man said tiredly.

Walter looked back up at the man. "Um. I heard you were looking for someone to teach you Wildshaping?" he asked hesitantly.

The man's eyebrows shot up in surprise. "Are you offering?" he asked, shocked.

Walter nodded nonverbally.

The man took a breath and let it out, clearly relieved. "What's your name?" he asked Walter, extending a hand.

Walter looked at the hand for a few moments before slowly taking it in his own. "Walter Meyers," he said softly, not looking the man in the eye.

The man shook hands with him once before letting go. "Nathan Hart. It's nice to meet you, Walter."

Walter mumbled something in response. Even he wasn't sure what he said.

Mr. Hart nodded as if he understood, nonetheless.

The two sat in awkward silence for a moment before Walter broke it. He limply extended his hand again. "Do you want to…?" he asked questioningly.

"Yeah," Mr. Hart said firmly. "I do." He took Walter's hand in his again.

Walter looked up at the man finally and met his eyes. Absentmindedly, he noted that they were green. Walter took a deep breath before speaking again. "Do you-" His voice broke. Walter cleared his throat, embarrassed. Mr. Hart just waited patiently. "Do you wish to learn Wildshaping?"

"I do," Mr. Hart said decisively.

A brief spark in between their clasped hands.

Mr. Hart visibly relaxed once they'd dropped their hands. "Thank you, Walter," he said sincerely. "I won't forget this."

"It's fine," Walter mumbled, looking down to study his feet.

"No," Mr. Hart said resolutely. Walter jerked his head up at that. He saw that Mr. Hart had clenched his jaw. "I mean it when I say, I will not forget this. You were the only one to give me the time of day, and I didn't even have to come to you." Mr. Hart stretched out a hand to lay on Walter's shoulder. "You're a good man, Walter."

Walter's eyes welled up, against his will. Not even his father had acknowledged him as a man before he'd died trying to negotiate with the elves. Desperately, he wiped at his eyes with the back of his hand.

"Despite the situation we find ourselves in." Mr. Hart said soothingly to Walter. "I really believe that we can't let ourselves sink to their level. They're trying to beat the empathy out of us. It's what all of this," he said, waving an arm around himself at the slave grounds. "Is about. They want us to become something less than human. Nothing but unthinking, unfeeling machines to do their labor for them. Don't let them turn you into that, Walter," he finished, before losing some of his confidence and flushing. "At least, that's what I think."

Walter got his emotions under control. He looked back up at Mr. Hart with eyes red from tears. "Thank you. I-I'll try."

Mr. Hart nodded back at him with a smile. He got to his feet with a groan, twisting back and forth to let several audible cracks sound from the small of his back. He extended a hand down to Walter. "I don't know about you, but I'm exhausted. I'm about ready to hit the hay," he told Walter.

Walter nodded and then hesitated. "Do you...? Know where you're going to sleep tonight? Did they assign you a bunk?"

Mr. Hart shook his head. "No, they didn't. And I was being literal about that hay, anyway. The guard told me to just sleep in the hay pile near the overseer's barracks," he said, pointing a thumb at the visibly nicer building off to the side of the circle of slave barracks. He paused a moment, before bringing a hand up to his bruised cheek. "Well, after he gave me this. Anyway, I'm not sticking around here. The guards are going to be taking me back to my 'master'," His face twisted slightly at the word. "In the morning."

"Oh," Walter said, slightly disappointed. He couldn't help but feel that he had connected with Mr. Hart, and had been looking forward to maybe having a new friend.

Mr. Hart must have sensed this because he put a hand on Walter's shoulder again. "Don't worry about it. I'm sure we'll see each other again. Like I said, I won't forget what you did for me."

Walter nodded, embarrassed that Mr. Hart had seen right through him.

"Well, goodnight, Walter." Mr. Hart said. With a final nod at him, Mr. Hart started walking in the direction of the overseer's barracks.

Walter watched him go for a moment, before deciding to copy him and go to sleep. He walked past the bonfire that Mr. Matheson was still sitting at and gave him a nod. Mr. Matheson nodded back. Reaching the barracks that he'd been assigned to, Walter meandered over to his bunk and flopped into it, just as he had earlier. This time, however, he got under the paper-thin sheets. Settling down in his bunk to go to sleep, Walter felt better than he had in days. At least, mentally.

Don't lose his empathy, huh. Walter felt that his mother would have approved of Mr. Hart.

Father would have probably hated him, though.

With that comforting thought, Walter fell asleep.

# Chapter 24
# Shape of the Wild

I stumbled my way into the clearing that Azarus's house sat in, pushed from behind by a bored dwarven guard. I didn't say anything in response to the shove, I just got my feet back under me. No use getting mad at these guard assholes, I was starting to get used to their shit. The bored guard behind me nudged me in the middle of the back with his truncheon.

Yeah, yeah. I get it.

I got moving, making sure I was still mentally and physically in 'slave mode'. I trudged up the dirt path leading up to the house with both my head and shoulders lowered. Once we got to the door, the guard stepped in front of me. He visibly puffed himself up before, honest to God, taking out a small handheld mirror from a pouch belted to his waist. With one hand, he wiped a smudge of dirt from his cheek and adjusted his hair.

Any embarrassment I might have felt for this asshole was preemptively smacked right out of me yesterday when he had casually backhanded me. Even with how fast I healed now with my new Status, I still had a fading bruise the next day.

With one last adjustment of his armor, the guard knocked on the door of Azarus's house and waited anxiously. I stifled a laugh behind him, aware that it would probably get me another backhand. Thumping boot noises from inside the house heralded the opening of the door.

Taking up most of the space in the doorway, Azarus stood holding a mug of something in one hand. The guard saluted when he saw Azarus, standing straight and bringing his right arm standing straight up with a clenched fist. Azarus just took a sip from his mug, visibly unimpressed.

"Lord Azarus!" the guard nearly shouted. "As you requested, your slave spent the night in the barracks, in order to better appreciate your magnanimity! I'm certain he will carry your burdens with better care in the future!"

I rolled my eyes at Azarus from behind the guard. Azarus didn't bother being so discrete, as he visibly rolled his own eyes at the guard. "Yeah, whatever. Thanks, or something," he said dismissively. He jerked his head in the direction of further inside the house at me from over the top of the guard. Sidling past the guard, careful not to show him my face lest he see my barely hidden smirk, I slipped inside the house. Without another word, Azarus shut the door in the face of the guard.

"Oh." I heard a crestfallen voice say through the door. Azarus didn't pay it any mind, but I just barely managed to keep myself from bursting out laughing. Whatever, fuck that guy.

Azarus turned interested eyes my way once he'd shut the door. "So, did it work? Did ya get it?" he asked me.

I nodded at him. "Yup. I got it. I mean, just barely, but I got it." I held up a hand to forestall any more questions. "Can it wait, man? What he didn't say is that I worked the fields yesterday too, and as you can see, I'm filthy. I need a bath."

Azarus closed his mouth and nodded at me. I stepped past him and made my way upstairs.

"Oh, and Grey's got some breakfast ready in the kitchen when you're done." I heard Azarus say from behind me. I just waved a hand over my shoulder in acknowledgment as I was walking up the staircase. Once I was upstairs, I grabbed a change of clothes from my room before heading to the bathroom.

*** 

I spent a good amount of time in the bath after scrubbing myself clean. Honestly, I needed the relaxation after all the hard labor I'd done yesterday. I might have lazed around in the tub for half an hour before I reluctantly picked myself out of the tub. Catching a glimpse of myself in the mirror, I could see I was pink all over. One good thing I could say about these magical bathtubs is that the water never got cold. Those enchantment discs kept it at a steady temperature the whole time.

I got dressed before exiting the bathroom and heading down the stairs. Hearing voices from the kitchen, I walked over in that direction. I guess even with all the time I spent in the bath, Grey and Azarus were still idling in there. Entering the kitchen, I could see that both were sitting at the table and sipping something from mugs. There was a kettle steaming on the still-burning oven behind them.

"Ah, Nathan!" Grey perked up at my appearance. Azarus turned around in his chair as well and nodded at me. I nodded back at both of them. "I trust you're feeling better?"

"Yeah, but I'm pretty hungry. I didn't get much to eat yesterday. Azarus said something about food?" I asked Grey. He just inclined his head to the stasis cabinet. Oh, yeah. That made sense. Making my way over to it, I opened the cabinet. Inside, I found a large plate of eggs and what looked like bacon, still steaming. I happily took it out and closed the cabinet behind me and went to sit at the table. While I'd had my back turned, Grey had grabbed the kettle and prepared me a cup of whatever they were drinking as well. Murmuring my thanks to him, I accepted the mug and took a sip to try it. I was surprised to find that it tasted exactly like peppermint tea, but I wasn't complaining. I sat down to eat my breakfast, uncaring about how Grey and Azarus were going to watch me. I was too hungry to be self-conscious.

Once I was done with my breakfast, I sat back with a sigh. After having such a full meal, I expected to be tired again, but I surprisingly wasn't. Maybe it was the tea? I turned my attention to Grey when he cleared his throat.

"So, Azarus tells me you were successful in finding someone to teach you Wildshaping? I must confess, I'm glad that my haphazard plan worked." Grey told me, visibly relieved.

Yesterday morning, Grey had sat down with Azarus and I and told us his longshot plan for me to get Wildshaping without arousing even the slightest bit of suspicion. He'd told us how with so many slaves working out in the fields, it was a guarantee that at least one of them knew the Profession and would be willing to teach it to me. In my experience, it was true that most of the slaves had known some variant of Wildshaping, but not that they were willing to teach me. Nearly all of them had been unfriendly to some degree, with a few showing outright hostility at me approaching them. I tried not to hold it against them. They had all been consigned to a fate that many would find worse than death.

I was lucky to meet Walter.

I relayed my experiences with the slaves and at the barracks to Grey and Azarus. When I was done, I took a drink of my cooling tea to soothe my throat.

"I see," Grey said thoughtfully. "As you say, you were lucky to meet young Mr. Meyers. It is a tragedy that someone so young is now consigned to such a cruel fate. To Mr. Meyers, and his generosity," he said solemnly, raising his mug in the air. Azarus and I copied him, clinking our three mugs together wordlessly. Setting his mug down, Grey continued. "Now then. I'm sure we're all curious to see which variant of Wildshaping you acquired Nathan. I don't believe you had anything in mind when you accepted the Profession, yes?"

I shook my head. "No, I didn't think of anything. I was too tired at the time to even consider it, even if I'd had an idea of what I wanted. Thanks, but I'm going to try the racial this time, yeah?" I said to Azarus, who had just handed me one of the small mirrors he kept in the kitchen.

"Oh yeah," Azarus muttered, embarrassed. "Forgot about that."

I shrugged and called up my skill.

Hidden Amidst the Spheres.

I immediately opened my Status without bothering to play around with that sense of potential. Sure enough, I could see the notification for learning Wildshaping.

**You have learned Wildshaping!**
**You have learned Woodworking!**
**Would you like to review your Professions?**
**Y/N**

I guess that answered the question of whether or not my skill could manipulate my Status or not. Opening up my Professions pane, I saw that one of the last two blank circles on the spiral had been filled in. This time, by a small stylized image of a tree. And the center...

I hummed to myself in thought.

"I assume you received the Profession correctly?" Grey asked me curiously.

"Yeah," I said distractedly. I was still pondering what had shown up in the middle space of the Professions panel. "I got Woodworking, which is fine I guess."

Out of the corner of my eye, I could see Grey and Azarus exchange a glance at my preoccupation. Grey cleared his throat. Snapping out of it, I directed my gaze over to him. I flushed slightly at his raised eyebrow.

"Ah, sorry." I apologized to him sheepishly. "It's just, you know that image I told you about in the center of the Professions page? The one that was too fuzzy to make out. I can kinda, sorta see what it is now. A little."

That perked Grey right up. I could visibly see him restraining his enthusiasm as he leaned forward. "What is it?" he asked me excitedly.

"Uhh," I said, tilting my head to the side. "I think it's a fist?"

That gave Grey pause. "What? A hand? That's it?" he asked me, confused.

"I mean, it's still blurry, but I can kinda make some of it out?" At the look on Grey's face, I smiled sheepishly at him. "Sorry."

Azarus scratched his chin through his beard. "The bleedin' hells does that mean? What kinda Profession does a fist represent?"

Grey slumped back in his chair. He sighed. "I don't know. The symbology of a fist, in relation to Professions in general, is too broad. I was hoping that the mark of the Profession would give us a clue as to what it does, but that's too vague." He sighed again. "We'll simply have to pursue the last Profession that Nathan requires to unlock it. Speaking of, Azarus?"

At Grey's prompting, Azarus snapped out of his musing. Looking up, he found both Grey and I looking at him. "Ah, right." Turning to me, he said. "While you were out, I went and spoke to the caravan master. Something came up for him, and now he's intending to head out to Rhoscara earlier than scheduled."

216

"What does that mean for us?" I asked Azarus, raising an eyebrow at him.

"What'dya think it means? It means we're heading out earlier than I'd planned on, too. A cart is the only real way we're going to be making our way there, so we're going with him," Azarus said decisively.

"All right, I guess," I told Azarus, strangely unconcerned about venturing to another city. "What do I need to do?"

"Ah." Grey piped in. "At Azarus's behest, I went to the trouble of preparing a travel pack for you, Nathan. It will contain everything you require for the journey. I have it stashed in my room, for when you leave."

"Journey, huh," I said, leaning my chin on my fist. "How long do you expect that to take?"

"Eh." Azarus waggled a hand back and forth. "With this driver, should take us about four days travel. Honestly, Rhoscara isn't that far from here. S'why I head there for supplies. And, uh. Why I go there, considering everything, ya know?" he finished, visibly uncomfortable.

Ah.

I remember now, either he or Grey had mentioned that he had family there. From the other side of the family. You know, the ones who apparently weren't slaving assholes.

Awkward.

I shrugged, not making a big deal of it. "When are we heading out, then?"

"Tomorrow," Azarus told me, relaxing slightly. "We're leaving for Rhoscara tomorrow."

# Chapter 25
# Justifying Trouble

The next morning found Azarus and I walking down the path to town again, this time wearing packs. Azarus had woken me up much earlier than the usual time that we did. I had no idea what time it was of course, because Azarus didn't own a clock. Apparently, they were hard to come by, with how new the Profession that made them was. All I knew was that the sun had only finished coming over the horizon when I woke up.

As Grey had told me, he'd had a pack ready for me sitting in his room. Honestly, it was smaller than I'd expected for a pack meant to last me over a week. It looked more like a small rucksack, to me. When I'd mentioned that to Grey, he'd just chuckled and told me that it had a small spatial expansion enchantment on it. Apparently, I could keep the bag after my trip.

After a quick breakfast, Azarus and I left his house after saying our goodbyes to Grey. I'd been a little worried about how a disabled man, much less a disabled slave, would survive by themselves. However, Grey had assured me that this was far from the first time that he'd been left alone to fend for himself while Azarus was in Rhoscara.

We spent the trip to town in silence, both of us too tired to carry on a conversation. Before long, we'd exited the side path alongside the manor and reached the town proper. Slouching into 'slave mode', I slipped behind Azarus without a word. Azarus didn't miss a stride, used to this as well. He just straightened up as well, slipping into his more 'noble' bearing.

He led us through the marketplace without stopping and near the gate that led out of town. As we got closer to the gate, I could see that the guards that normally stood at either side of it were dozing on their feet as well. Azarus veered left when we got to the gate, walking alongside it. After a short walk alongside the wall, we reached one of the larger buildings that I had seen in this small town. It had multiple floors to it, and it even had a small stable off to the side. But I suspect what was out in front was what we were here for.

It was larger and had a slightly different shape to it, but at this point, I could recognize a wagon when I saw one., It was so large it reminded me of a train car, if not quite as long. Mostly made of dark wood with what appeared to be steel wheels, it had a canvas hood that stretched from one side to another. Honestly, the construction of it seemed more sophisticated than the wagon I had been transported in. Maybe in magical, pre-industrial fantasy land, wagon construction was bizarrely advanced. Hitched to the wagon were four of the largest draft horses I'd ever seen, patiently waiting to get underway. A team of dwarves were loading crates into the back of the wagon, while a different dwarf was supervising them. Azarus walked right up to the supervising dwarf, calling a greeting as he got closer.

The supervisor turned to face Azarus as we neared him. I tried to keep my head down, unsure of this dwarf's temperament.

"There you are." I heard an unfamiliar voice say. The voice had an aged lilt to it, with a similar accent that I had heard from every other dwarf but Azarus. "I was starting to wonder if you were coming at all, with how late you are."

Late? I thought to myself. This was still the ass-crack of dawn, as far as I was concerned.

"Ah, sorry about that," Azarus said to the other dwarf, running a hand down the back of his head. I was startled, personally. From my experience, Azarus was pretty standoffish with most other people. The only other person I'd seen him let his guard down with, aside from Grey and I, was Vandimar. I took it to mean that Azarus was more comfortable around this guy. I decided to risk a glance at him discreetly, still aware of the other unvetted dwarven laborers in the background.

Flicking my eyes up, I took him in. Yup, that's an old dwarf all right. Clean-shaven with craggy cheeks, he nonetheless had long, steel gray hair done up in elaborate braids. The dwarf had a long, hawkish nose and a keen gaze, as evidenced by the fact he immediately noticed when I looked up at him. I hurriedly looked down. Azarus might know this guy, he might even trust him. I didn't yet.

"Hmm." I heard from the dwarf. "You said you were taking another along with you, but you didn't mention they were a slave." Disapproval was thick in the dwarf's voice.

I could visibly see Azarus wince from behind him. "Look, it's complicated, yeah? We can talk about it once we hit the road."

The other dwarf grunted in assent. "As you say. The boys are just about done, so go ahead and put your sacks inside too. We'll be heading out in about ten minutes."

Azarus agreed and walked over to the back of the wagon, with me following. Passing by a few of the workers that were loading crates, he carelessly tossed his own pack inside, hitting the far wall. Conscious of the dwarves surrounding me, I instead carefully set the drawstring of my bag on one of the dull hooks embedded into the walls of the wagon. Azarus stepped away from it afterward, with me following.

Azarus walked out of hearing range of the wagon and leaned against the wall of a nearby building. I simply stood next to him, trying not to look too conspicuous.

"So, what's his deal?" I whispered to Azarus, careful to keep my head down in order to mask my lips.

"That's Gren," Azarus whispered back to me out of the corner of his mouth. "Don't worry about him, alright? He's done good by me plenty of times. Once we're on the road, you can act normally. He ain't gonna care."

I made a small noise of assent. "And the others?"

"What? Who?" Azarus said slightly louder, nearly turning his head to me. I saw a few of the worker's heads turn slightly before getting back to work.

I let a breath out of my nose in frustration. "The other dwarves, dammit. The ones that are loading the wagon."

Azarus snorted slightly. "Ya don't got to worry about them. They're just part of Gren's crew in town. It'll just be you, me, and Gren on the road," he told me under his voice.

I relaxed slightly and kept quiet after that. Azarus did too. After maybe another twelve minutes of waiting while the dwarven workers loaded the wagon, they finally seemed to finish. I was trying not to stare too much, but I saw 'Gren' walk over to the workers and have a conversation with them. After a bit of back and forth, Gren deposited a sack of something in the hands of what must have been the lead worker. With mutual nods to each other, the workers started trundling off, some simply heading back into the building that the wagon was sitting in front of. Turning to face our direction, Gren waved Azarus and me closer.

Pushing off the wall, we walked closer. When we were in earshot, the aged dwarf addressed us. "Az, you hop up on the bench with me. You," he said, pointing to me. "Hop in the back. Got a cot you can sit on near the front." Before either Azarus or I could say or do anything in return, Gren walked over to the horses and began to inspect them. Since we were standing side by side, I looked over at Azarus and raised an eyebrow slightly. He just shrugged at me and followed the dwarf's directions, hopping up into the passenger seat on the driver's bench. I rolled my eyes and walked around to the back of the wagon and hauled myself in.

Despite the number of crates I had seen piled into this wagon, it didn't seem too cramped inside. With the way that the wagon was built, there was a small gap between the front wall and the driver's seat where you could see out the front. There was still plenty of room inside to maneuver, with even more room up near the front. Noticing the cot that Gren had mentioned sitting in the left-hand far corner, I shuffled my way over to it and sat down, facing the back of the wagon and resting my back on the front. After a few minutes, I heard Gren climb up into the driver's seat with a grunt.

"All good?" I heard him say to Azarus. Azarus grunted in agreement. "What about you in there?" Gren asked from the driver's seat above me and outside the wagon. I started in surprise. "All good?"

I cleared my throat. "Uh, yeah! I'm fine!" I hurriedly answered him.

"All right then." I heard Gren say. A moment later, I heard what must be a crack from the reins of the wagon. With a few whinnies from the horses, the wagon started moving under their combined might. The wagon was only moving for a few minutes before it stopped again. From the sound of the voices outside, we must have been at the gate. One of the guards began speaking to Gren, and after a short conversation, I heard the guard give an order to someone else. I heard a groan as the large wooden gate began opening. Shortly thereafter, the wagon began moving once more.

Away from the slave town.

We must have been traveling down the road for maybe fifteen minutes before Gren broke the silence we had been traveling in.

"All right, we're far enough away. Now, what's going on Azarus? You know the trouble we could face for bringing a slave to Rhoscara." I heard Gren say to Azarus.

Azarus sighed. "Alright, alright. I get it. But there's something he needs from there, I figured I'd bring him along for my regular trip."

"What is it then? He sick? You sick, boy?" Gren said to me.

I sat up from where I had been listening to them speak. "No, uh, I'm not sick. It's more complicated than that."

Gren growled in frustration. "You two keep saying that! Well, un-complicate it for me. Look, Azarus, I've known you for years and I like you; I truly do. But I'm going to need a more compelling reason than 'it's complicated' to risk my business like this."

"Ah…" Azarus hesitated.

I piped in. "It's because before about a week ago I'd never even heard of the System. I was Unawakened."

There was a shocked silence outside the wagon for a moment.

"Truly?" I heard Gren say, baffled. "How can you have never heard of the System? What kind of hole have you been living in?"

"He's from beyond the northern mountains." Azarus butted in. "Got caught up in an elf raid, and was shipped here. I found him and realized what he was before Magnus," I heard him spit off to the side. "Could have him executed for being a 'waste of money'. I took him in and have been trying to do right by him since."

"Huh," Gren said thoughtfully. "Alright then, but why does he need to go to Rhoscara? I'm not without sympathy, mind," he said in my direction. "It's just that the Florens don't take too kindly to slaves in their walls. They may not be able to do anything about it, since slavery is legal, but they'll make life damn difficult for us while we're there. You know this, Azarus."

"Yeah, I do," Azarus said somberly. "But I know people there. Not just, you know, the obvious. They'll kick up a stink at the gate, and I can ask to talk to someone I know. I'll try and explain things, and hopefully, we won't have a problem."

"Hopefully," Gren said doubtfully.

Azarus sighed. "Yeah."

Gren was silent for a moment. "So, I ask again," he said skeptically. "What's in Rhoscara that you need so desperately, boy? Can't be trying to send a message, nobody really has contact with the northern tribes. No messenger worth their salt would risk it."

"He-" Azarus began.

"I need a second Profession, and we can't get it back in…" I interrupted him again. I paused a moment in confusion. "You know, I just realized I never asked what the town we just left is called?"

Gren made a sound of amusement. "It's named Addersfield. Go on then, you were saying something about Professions?"

I coughed into my fist briefly. "Right. Like I was saying, I learned Alchemy from another slave for my first Profession once I was Awakened, but we checked and there was nobody that I could ask to teach me the second one I wanted." I paused. "Well, at least nobody that wouldn't kill me for asking."

Gren hummed. "All right, but, and I don't mean to be rude boy, you're a slave now. I understand wanting the Professions you desire the most, but…" He trailed off.

"You see-" Azarus started awkwardly.

I cut him off again. "My mother might not have been Awakened to have the actual Profession, but she was an artist by trade among my, ah, 'people'." I wasn't even lying this time. "I want to be an Artist like her, and Azarus said he knew an Artist in Rhoscara. I asked if I could come with him, and he said yes."

Gren was quiet for a moment, digesting what I'd said. "I see," he said quietly. "She *was* an artist?"

"Yeah," I replied, just as quietly.

"My condolences, then."

I shook my head, even though he couldn't see it. "D-don't worry about it." I took a breath. "It was a long time ago."

"I see," Gren answered simply.

Azarus remained quiet.

After a moment, Gren sighed. "All right," he said. "We'll give it a shot. It might be Rhoscara, but people are unlikely to kick up too big of a stink over this. People haven't forgotten your own mother, Azarus."

Azarus just grunted.

All three of us sat in silence for a moment.

"Well," Gren said, breaking it. "Nothing for it but to continue, then."

# Chapter 26
# Breathtaking Beards

Azarus was right for once when he said the trip to Rhoscara would take about four days. The trip itself wasn't that bad, however. I'd had certain expectations for the journey, after my last in a wagon. When we were moving, Azarus, Gren and I were either chatting idly or sitting in companionable silence, listening to the creak of the wagon and the gait of the horses. It's not like I spent the entire trip hanging out in the back of the wagon, either. There was no point in keeping me out of sight with nobody around. I alternated spots with Azarus up on the bench whenever he got sick of being up there. Gren never relinquished his position as driver though.

Gren didn't drive us through the nights. When the sun began to go down, he would pull the wagon over to the side of the dirt road and we would set up camp there. Camp was never anything elaborate for us, just a campfire to cook on and sit around. We didn't use tents or anything like that, either. We would just roll out a few bedrolls inside the wagon and sleep there. When I asked them about the possibility of being attacked by monsters or something and suggested a watch, Gren laughed at me. He said that the wagon was warded against monster attacks, similar to the walls of Addersfield.

Neither he nor Azarus seemed to care about getting attacked by anything other than monsters.

I did learn a few things about dwarven culture, speaking with Gren.

"So, with dwarves, a beard makes you a noble?" I said skeptically, rubbing my own rough chin. It'd been a while since I'd had a chance to shave, out on the road. It had been four days since we'd been on the road, and Gren had told me that we'd probably reach Rhoscara sometime that evening. I was up on the driver's bench with him, as Azarus had wanted to lay down in the back.

Gren grimaced. "Ehhh, no. Doesn't work like that. It's more like, the only ones that are legally allowed to grow a beard are nobles."

I leaned back on the bench, resting against the padded cushion there. "Why? I mean, is it just a way to pick them out of a crowd or something?"

"Well, the answer to that has a long and complicated history." Gren sighed. "And even then, it's viewed as antiquated nonsense. It has a great deal to do with the bad years after System Initialization."

I shrugged nonchalantly. "Not like I'm going anywhere," I said, gesturing with a hand for him to continue.

"Hmm. Well, all right then." Gren mused. "During the War in Heaven, my people lost their god. And good riddance, too." He spit off the side of the wagon. "Ours was the God of War, and while he was a Light God, he wasn't kind. He wasn't a tyrant, but he had certain ideas about what it meant to be a dwarf, and how we were meant to live. See, back in those days the Principality didn't exist. All of us, every living dwarf, lived in one of the mountain holds. It was a sin to live upon the surface, according to him. History tells us that the years after the War and his death were turbulent for everyone. The dwarves were no different."

Gren sighed and stared off into the distance for a moment before continuing. I just sat in silence, listening to the creaking of the wagon.

"The old mountain Jarls tried to hold onto power and continue to govern my people under His rules. The people didn't like that. With the coming of the System, the common people saw a chance for anyone to grow strong, and throw off the chains of tradition that bound them. They chafed under what they saw as outdated and rotten religious dogma from a dead god. And so, the dwarven civil war began. To make a long story short, the Jarls lost." Gren glanced at me. "You can still feel the effects of the civil war to this day, you know?"

I raised my eyebrows at him in interest. "Yeah?"

Gren nodded at me. "Yeah. These days in the Principality, we're still ruled by the families of the five heroes of the resistance against the Jarls. The Orsini, soldiers all. The Luminarans, keepers of law. The Venier, masters of the sea. The Florens, the great builders. And, uh. The Savoy, who feed us." He hesitated, before gesturing towards my collar. "They're the ones who deal in the flesh trade."

I put a hand up to the collar around my neck for a moment before letting it drop. I didn't say anything

Gren cleared his throat uncomfortably. "Well, to make a long story short, the resistance won. Most of dwarven kind followed the Five Families out into the wider world, and found the Principality."

I interrupted him. "*Most* of dwarven kind?"

Gren's face twisted slightly. "Yes. Most."

I dropped the subject.

"I won't beat around the bush." Gren continued, ignoring the mood my question had caused. "After the civil war, the Principality was founded in ways to spite everything the Jarls and the God of War stood for. Where before we lived beneath the earth, afterward we built towards the heavens. Where before our greatest strength was in our warriors, now it's our trade." His face fell. "Where before we were bound by foolish tradition, now again are we bound. By traditions that are just as foolish."

Gren glowered off into the distance.

"Beards. Bah. It's such a silly thing to be resentful over. But in the holds, all dwarven males were required to grow a beard or else face imprisonment. And now, all dwarven males are required to shave or else face imprisonment. It's just another way to exercise control over the rabble." He looked over at me. "Don't tell anyone I said that. I don't want to catch a slander charge."

I shrugged, gesturing towards my collar. "Who am I gonna tell, even if I wanted to? But, what's the, like, actual reason they ban beards for anyone that's not a noble? You know, on paper?"

Gren waved dismissively. "Changes from dynasty to dynasty. Doesn't actually matter anymore what the reason is, I think. It's tradition as much as law now." He sighed again, tiredly. "Nothing to be done about it."

\*\*\*

Gren and I rode mostly in silence for the next few hours. Perhaps around midday, Gren started and picked up the reins from where they'd been resting. He snapped them once and shouted a command at the horses. They gradually slowed, along with the wagon. Before long, we were at a full stop.

I sat up from the slouch I'd fallen into. "What's up?" I asked Gren, concerned.

Gren ignored me and banged against the wall behind him. "Wake up, you big oaf! It's time!"

From within, I heard a sleepy grumble followed by some shuffling noises. After a moment, Azarus poked his face into the gap between the wall and the roof of the wagon.

"Whazzat?" Azarus asked groggily.

Gren tsked. "I *said*, it's time! Get up here, we're almost there."

"Yeah, yeah," Azarus grumbled, waking up more. His face disappeared from the opening and I heard thumping noises as he maneuvered his way out of the wagon.

I looked at the horizon, puzzled. It was clear of anything that seemed like civilization, to me. "We're almost at Rhoscara? I don't see anything." I said, looking back at Gren.

Gren shook his head. "You wouldn't. Look over there, instead," he told me, pointing off to the side. I squinted in the direction of his finger, trying to find what he was looking at. After a moment, I saw it. There was a small stone menhir, almost hidden by the underbrush. Carved onto it was a five-pointed star, with the upper right arm painted a vivid scarlet.

"Oh," I said in understanding. "I'm guessing it's some kind of way-marker? Like, 'you're almost at Rhoscara', I'm guessing? What's with the red, though?"

"Got it in one," Gren told me with a smile. "As for the color, you'll see."

By that point, Azarus had made his way over to the front of the stopped wagon and was looking up at me expectantly. I flushed slightly and jumped down from the bench so that Azarus could climb up. Once he'd sat down on the bench, he looked back down at me.

"Ya remember what we talked about?" Azarus asked gruffly.

I rolled my eyes at him. "Yeah, yeah. I'm not a child with the memory of a gnat, dude."

Yesterday, Azarus and Gren had told me how they expected entering the city to go. The guards would probably be pissed to see a slave if they found me, but they couldn't do anything about it legally. They'd told me to cooperate with them if they wanted to pull me aside, but that Azarus was going to talk to a friend of his and get it sorted out. Apparently, I didn't have to act very deferentially to the Rhoscaran guards, so no 'slave mode'.

Azarus yawned and scratched his chin. "Good, good. Get going, then."

I flipped him the bird, which seemed to confuse him slightly, and headed around to the back of the wagon and made my way into the back.

Gren cracked the reigns and got us moving again, once I'd gotten settled.

***

We'd only been traveling down the road about another half hour before Gren banged on the separating wall, startling me.

"We're in sight distance now," Gren told me. "Might as well get a good look at the city, eh?"

I did as he suggested, lifting myself off the cot and getting on my knees. Shuffling forward, I stuck my head out of the opening and caught my first glimpse of Rhoscara.

It took my breath away.

Over the top of the large crimson stone walls that ran the length of my view, I could see an enormous city. The city seemed to be built on top of a large slope. At the very top of the slope, far in the distance, I could see an honest-to-God palace. Made of some kind of brilliant red stone polished to a sheen, it was massive. There were spires, and flying buttresses, and arches, and massive stained-glass windows built everywhere into it. Every feature of note seemed like it was gilded in shining gold, as well. From the tips of the spires to the spines of the buttresses, it was everywhere. God, I couldn't even imagine the amount of wealth on display here. Beyond even the elaborate stonework, the amount of gold just sitting around on display beggared belief. It far and away blew anything I'd even heard about back home, in both scale and beauty. The palace looked like it was big enough to be a city alone.

Which barely scratched the surface of the city's breadth itself.

Massive, as big as a notable city from back home, it seemed as if it had been artfully arranged to flow from the palace in neat lines. From where I was sitting, I could make out that even the simplest building in Rhoscara was made to grow upwards, and not outwards. But it wasn't cramped, as I could see plenty of greenery carefully planted among the buildings. That wasn't even getting into the various manors and estates that I could see throughout the city. Everything was built in similar shades of red stone, even if it wasn't polished to a sheen like the palace. Scattered all through the city were towers, spires, and monuments galore. While the regular buildings and homes weren't built to the same extravagance as the palace and the manors, these were. To round out the genuinely picturesque scene, there was a large river that was visible in the distance, seeming to flow along the back half of the palace slope. Ships of all shapes and sizes could be seen coming and going from the barely visible, but massive dockyard.

The entire city seemed as if it had been designed for the view that I was seeing right now. As if someone had stood in my exact spot, and dreamed of a city that you could see stretching out far into the distance.

It was breathtaking. Literally.

I hadn't realized it, but I'd been holding my breath the entire time that I was drinking in the sight of Rhoscara. With a wheeze, I let out the breath and took another deep one. Hearing laughter, I looked up at the driver's bench to see Gren looking back down at me.

"Quite a sight, eh?" he said to me, with a twinkle in his eye.

"Yeah," I answered faintly, still taking in the city.

Azarus snorted. "S'bit gaudy."

# Chapter 27
# The Good Captain

As our wagon slowly trundled its way toward the gates of Rhoscara, the spectacular view of the city faded. It was replaced by the less dazzling view of the walls that surrounded the city. The walls themselves were still made of the red stone that seemed to be so common in this city, from what I could recall of the view from earlier. The stone wasn't quite as polished or as beautiful, however. Even from a distance, I could see that they were meant to be utilitarian and formidable. They were tall, reaching maybe thirty feet into the air, which seemed to me to be a nearly excessive height.

The road led directly to the gates of the city, which lay open and inviting. Standing guard outside of those gates were numerous well-armed dwarven soldiers, all of them adorned in shining silver plate mail and carrying spears. Over the top of their plate, each of the soldiers had a crimson red, gold-edged tabard, which was belted at the waist. On the tabard was the image of a black bird of some kind, captured in mid-flight. Clasped in the talons of the bird was a flower of some kind. Whoever had stitched the bird into the tabards had left the eyes the same color as the tabard itself, lending it an intimidating stare.

Visible past the gate guarded by the soldiers, I could make out a checkpoint of some kind. And beyond that?

The massive, sprawling, dazzling city.

I heard Azarus cough lightly. Turning my attention to him, I saw that he wasn't paying attention to me and was intently watching the line of soldiers that blocked the way into the city ahead of us. "Better get down for now," he muttered under his voice, presumably speaking to me. "We'll tell 'em about ya when they ask to inspect the goods and go from there."

I let out a breath and decided to heed his advice. Nodding slightly, even though I knew nobody could see it, I slid down from where I had been crouching. Laying my back against the wall I had just been looking over, I made sure I was sitting in the center of it. Better to be fully visible when they came for me, I guess.

Before long, the wagon must have reached within shouting distance of the gates.

"Halt!" I heard a loud, commanding voice shout.

Seemingly complying, I heard Gren give the command he used to stop the wagon to his horses. Slowly, the wagon lumbered to a halt, creaking and groaning.

I heard Gren clear his throat before calling out. "Greetings!"

Loud metal-clad footsteps were slowly moving in our direction. From what I could tell, there might be three of the soldiers approaching the wagon.

"Is that you, Gren?" I heard the voice from earlier say, growing louder as it grew closer. "Oh! And Lord Azarus too! Guess it's around that time, eh?" The voice was markedly friendlier at that.

"It is indeed," Gren said to the voice with a smile of his own. "How fare you on this fine evening, Sergeant?"

"Oh, not too bad, not too bad." The voice said in a relaxed manner. "You're the first wagon we've gotten so far today." The soldiers must have reached the wagon by now because their voices were coming from right next to Gren's side of the driving bench.

"Hmm, well, you know how it is. Most people, and even most goods come by boat." Gren said to the voice casually.

"True, true." I heard a shifting metal noise. "And how fare you, Lord Azarus? Safe journeys, I hope?"

I heard Azarus take a deep breath. "Aye. Wasn't too bad." He let out his breath. "But, I'm sorry to say that I'm going to have to make your day harder on you, Sergeant Hulisse. I've got some...sensitive cargo in the back that I'm going to have to speak to Captain Gastone about before we go any further."

I directed a weird gaze in Azarus's direction through the wall, even though nobody could see it. Azarus was speaking differently than I had ever heard from him before. He was enunciating clearer, and his accent was noticeably more neutral. It wasn't as clipped as it was with the towns-dwarves from back in Addersfield, or as casual with either Gren, Grey or even me. I guess this was what he sounded like when he had to act like a noble. It sounded odd to my ears, like an act or something.

I heard multiple metal-clad feet shift around at Azarus's words. "Well." The supposed Sergeant Hulisse said carefully. "I suppose that can be arranged. The captain is just over at the checkpoint. I can have a runner go fetch him if you'd like."

"I would appreciate that," Azarus said shortly.

A short, sharp creaking noise followed his word before the soldier spoke again. "Private Umnir." I heard Sergeant Hulisse say sharply. "Go tell the captain that Lord Azarus is requesting his presence outside the gate."

Another short creaking noise from what must have been one of the other soldiers that followed Sergeant Hulisse. "At once, sir!" A younger voice said excitedly. Loud clanking followed his words, as the soldier sounded like he took off at a dead sprint back up the road.

Everyone either sat or stood around in awkward silence for a few moments until Sergeant Hulisse broke it by clearing his throat. "Ah, is the cargo perhaps…dangerous, Lord Azarus? Should I gather a few more men?" he asked politely.

Azarus sighed. "That won't be necessary, Sergeant. It's not that kind of sensitive."

Everyone either in or around the wagon waited in awkward silence while the private fetched the captain. After a few minutes of waiting around, I heard the sound of more people approaching the wagon.

"What've you done now, Azarus?" A new voice asked tiredly. "Let me guess, it has something to do with the third person I sense in the back?"

I heard some muttering from the other soldiers outside along with the shuffling of feet.

Gren cleared his throat. "Ah, captain…"

Azarus cut him off. "I've got this, Gren." With a grunt, I heard and felt Azarus jump down from the wagon. "C'mon, Enzo." I heard Azarus walk away from the wagon, off to the side.

Captain Gastone sighed. "You, you." I heard him say. "Back in formation. Sergeant, stay with Mr. Freelith."

I heard multiple sharp, creaking noises followed by exclamations of, "Captain!" Afterward, two sets of feet walked in the direction of the city, while another walked off in the direction that Azarus had.

Azarus and Captain Gastone must have walked out of hearing range of the wagon because I didn't hear anything of their conversation. I waited around, mildly anxious, while they presumably discussed whether I'd be allowed into the city. After a while, I heard them walk back over to the wagon. Azarus sounded like was walking around the back towards me, while the captain sounded like he was walking to the front of the wagon.

"Sergeant." The captain sounded even more tired than he had been earlier. "Take this," I heard the clinking of coins. "And head into the city. Go to Madam Bella's, and buy a cloak with a high neck and a mantle. A nice one, mind. Bring it back as discretely as you can."

"Captain?" I heard the sergeant ask questioningly.

"Go." The captain's voice hardened. "You have your orders."

Another short creaking noise. By this point, I'm guessing it was that arm-bar salute that I'd seen the guards of Addersfield do. "Yes, captain!" I heard the sergeant jog away.

"Sorry about this, captain." I heard Gren say, with a slight pitying note in his voice.

The captain just sighed and began walking around to the back of the wagon. By that point, Azarus had reached the back of the wagon as well, where I could see him. I didn't say anything to him, I just splayed my hands out in a wordless questioning gesture. He just shrugged at me and waggled a hand. The captain reached the back of the wagon while Azarus and I were pantomiming at each other, allowing me my first look at him.

My first thought was that he looked like a tired office worker. Short-cut black hair, plain brown eyes, and the kind of face that seemed the definition of average, even on a dwarf. He was leaner than I was used to seeing on most dwarfs, with heavy bags under his eyes. But looking closer, I could see that he was more alert than he seemed. There was a sharpness to his gaze and his bearing that reminded me of a razor. He was outfitted in a similar set of plate mail that the soldiers had been wearing, except everything was slightly more elaborate, including the embroidery on his tabard. In addition, he had a bright crimson cloak thrown over his shoulders, with a sword in a scabbard tied to his hip instead of carrying a spear like the others.

I met his eyes from the back of the wagon and tried to smile at him. From the look on his face, it must have been more like a grimace. He hauled himself into the wagon and made his way back towards me. Taking a seat on one of the crates inside, he leaned forward to inspect me silently for a moment. Under his gaze, I felt like he knew everything about me. Logically, I knew he didn't. Ever since I'd gotten the hang of my Status hiding skill, I'd made sure that my Precursor status was always hidden. Even if he was Observing me, I didn't have much to worry about. Still didn't stop me from squirming slightly under his intense gaze.

Captain Gastone sighed. He seemed to do that a lot. "Mr. Hart, was it?" At my silent nod, he continued. "Azarus has informed me of your plight. I'm not unsympathetic, but you must understand that the city of Rhoscara has always strongly decried the practice of slavery. We can do nothing about it legally, but that would not stop others from acting on their own if they caught sight of you."

I piped in. "So…if I go into the city, I would be in danger?"

The captain looked surprised for a moment. "Ah, no. You would be perfectly fine, if not buried under a landslide of attempts to help you. No, it would be Azarus and Mr. Freelith who would bear the brunt of the citizenry's displeasure. Azarus would likely suffer a hit to his reputation that he would never recover from, as while he's generally well-liked, he still bears some suspicion due to his paternal ancestry. He could bear it, but Mr. Freelith on the other hand could potentially be in a great deal of trouble. He would likely lose a great many contracts and revenue streams from his patrons in the city, and could face potential ruin if his involvement in this issue came to light."

I took a deep breath and let it out slowly to tamp down my anxiety. "All right. Then what's your plan? I'm guessing you have one if you're not just turning us away at the door. Metaphorically."

"I do." Captain Gastone nodded. "Azarus is an extremely straight-forward thinker, more than willing to take a hit and bear it. On the other hand, Mr. Freelith is a strangely straightforward merchant, dis-inclined to more…clandestine maneuvers. I'm sure it didn't occur to them to present you as anything more than you are. Much less simply arrive separately on foot." He sighed. "I, on the other hand, am more than willing to help in this manner. No, rather than let them take a blow like this, we'll simply…pretend you're not a," He grimaced. "Slave."

I tilted my head in thought before remembering what I'd heard earlier. "You told that Sergeant to go buy a cloak," I muttered before looking back up at the captain incredulously. "It can't be that easy."

Captain Gaston grinned at me. "It is, indeed, that easy. The only people that can truly sense the presence of a slave collar are the Prin-cipality's highly-trained slave catchers. And *they* are barred from en-tering the city. I would suggest, however, that you attempt to change your demeanor and bearing as well."

"In what way?" I asked him curiously.

He shrugged. "Perhaps attempt to emulate a noble? All the better, if the people think Azarus is aiding a mysteriously cloaked foreign no-ble, fleeing his homeland for even more mysterious reasons. I would rather that than people gossip about how he's trafficking in slaves." He paused for a moment, tilting his head. "Ah, here comes the cloak." He turned around and raised his voice. "Azarus! Go get the cloak!"

I saw Azarus shove off the side of the wagon from where he'd been listening in. "Yeah, yeah." He walked around the wagon, out of sight. A moment later, I finally heard the sound of metal-clad feet nearing the wagon that the captain heard before me. Azarus must have inter-cepted him before he reached the wagon because all I heard was muf-fled conversation out of earshot. After a moment, Azarus came walk-ing back around into view, this time carrying a folded pile of brown cloth. Without a word, he chucked it at speed towards the captain. He caught it without blinking an eye.

Handing me the presumed cloak, the captain said. "Here you go, try it on."

Unfolding it, I could see that cloak was honestly pretty nice. Made from a rich, chocolate brown color with gold accents, it didn't appear to be the type that clasped together. Rather, it had a visible mantle that you were supposed to poke your head through, with a stiff, high collar that would presumably hide my own slave collar.

I bet this thing will make me look like a vampire.

Mentally shrugging, I put the cloak on. Once I'd done so, the Captain adjusted it slightly, I guess to better hide my collar. He stood up afterward and took a step back to look at me with a critical eye.

"That'll do." He nodded, after a moment of staring. "Hulisse picked a good one for you."

"Uh, thanks," I said, somewhat self-conscious.

The captain took a breath. "All right. Well, let's hope this works. Once the wagon is in the city, I'm guessing you and Azarus are going to head to the palace while Mr. Freelith gets his goods inspected. Hop out once you're at the checkpoint, and hopefully," he said the last word under his breath. "Azarus can handle it from there. Good luck."

With one last nod at me, which I returned, he turned around and strode out of the wagon. After a last whispered conversation with Azarus, he disappeared out of my field of view. A few moments later, I heard Gren speak.

"Ah." The captain's footsteps stopped momentarily. "Thank you for your consideration, Captain Gastone."

"Hmm." Was all the captain said, before moving on.

I guess Gren had heard most of my conversation with the captain, then.

Azarus had moved around back towards the driver's seat and hopped back up.

"All good, then?" Gren asked him.

"All good," Azarus answered.

With a shouted command from Gren, the wagon was back underway.

# Chapter 28
# Afternoon Stroll

I wasn't watching this time as the wagon entered the city, but I could feel it when we made the transition. The wagon went from rolling smoothly along the hard-packed dirt outside the gates, to trundling along atop cobblestones with a jolt. Shortly thereafter, we came to a stop again. The wagon must have reached the checkpoint that Azarus and I were going to get off at.

"Hey." I heard Azarus say to me from above. "Time to go. Get our bags, will ye?"

Taking a deep breath to settle my nerves, I answered in the affirmative. Standing up, I picked up mine and Azarus's bags from the hook they were hanging on, and shuffled my way to the back of the wagon. After jumping down onto the pavement, I took a moment to stretch and pop my back. The interior space of the wagon had been cramped enough that I couldn't really move around too much.

Opening my eyes after my stretch, I saw that I had attracted a bit of attention. While there didn't appear to be many regular people hanging around the entrance of the city, there were still some along with the soldiers. I could see them eyeing me from where they were standing and whispering to themselves. The soldiers at least kept their eyes to themselves, doing their best to ignore me. I shifted self-consciously in my fancy new cloak, nearly bringing a hand up to finger my collar before stopping myself. Don't think about it, I told myself. They're just curious about the weird human who was totally not a slave.

I jumped when a hand clapped me on my shoulder. Following the hand to its source, I found that it was Azarus looking at me with a raised eyebrow. "Alright?" he asked curiously.

I let out a breath. "Ah, yeah. I'm fine." I took another deep breath. "So, what next?" I asked him.

"Gotta finish up with Gren. C'mon." Azarus said, jerking his head towards the front of the wagon. I followed after him to find that Gren had jumped off of the driver's seat and was talking to another dwarf that looked like a clerk of some kind. They seemed to be exchanging papers. When the clerk saw Azarus and I coming, he said something to Gren and then walked away after bowing in Azarus's direction. Gren turned around to face us. When Azarus reached him, the two of them clasped arms.

"Thanks for the ride, Gren," Azarus told him. "I appreciate it, considering everything."

Gren nodded at him. "Well, it didn't end up being much of a problem, so it's fine. Just don't make it much of one after I'm gone, eh?"

"Yeah, yeah. Anyway, here's the rest of your pay." Azarus said dismissively, handing a clinking pouch to him.

Gren tossed the pouch in the air once, presumably to test the weight. With a satisfied look on his face, he nodded to Azarus. He then turned to face me. "Well, I hope you find what you're looking for, Mr. Hart."

"Yeah, me too," I said to him with a wry smile.

With a final nod to us, Gren walked off in the direction of the clerk that had been talking to him earlier. That left Azarus and I to ourselves, as it seemed that other dwarves were hesitant to approach Azarus.

"Well, let's get going," Azarus said to me before walking off down the road that led into the city.

I hurried to catch up with him. "So, where are we heading?"

Azarus snorted. "Where else? To the great bloody palace."

***

Azarus led me through the city of Rhoscara on foot. It wasn't a short walk by any means. The city was huge, and dense by any measure. We must have been walking for at least an hour and a half in order to reach the back half where the palace lay. During the walk, Azarus did his best to introduce me to the city. He pointed out historical monuments built by his maternal ancestors, he pointed out shops that he particularly liked, and he even pointed out building styles that he was knowledgeable about.

Sometimes I forgot that his second profession was Engineering.

He told me about how you could trace how old the city was like you could a tree. The oldest buildings were nearer to the center of the city, from before the palace had even been built. Newer buildings, and thus newer architectural styles radiated out from the center of the city. Apparently, the palace, or rather the palatial district, was a relatively new construction at only three hundred years old. The old Florens manor at the exact center of the city had been converted into an administration building from where the city could be governed by its apparently elected mayor.

I noticed during our hike that people recognized Azarus often. It wasn't uncommon for us to walk through a new area and for some dwarf to notice him and bow in his direction. Most of the time, this would lead to a bunch of other dwarves in the area copying them, even if they didn't know why. Azarus pretended not to notice as he took me on what was essentially a tour.

What I enjoyed the most, however, must have been the markets. Plural.

We must have passed through at least six of them on our journey to the palace. Each of them was different in some manner, each of them apparently catering to a different need. They were large and sprawling, filled with both people hawking goods or browsing for them. I was curious, so I asked Azarus about why Rhoscara didn't just have one huge market instead of multiple smaller ones.

Azarus scratched his chin. "S'pride thing, I think," he said musingly as we passed through one of the more sedate markets. This one seemed to be focused upon arts of one kind or another. There were paintings, drawings, and sculptures in this one. Hell, I even saw plenty of instruments on sale in shop windows. Many of them I didn't recognize at all.

"How do you mean?" I asked him distractedly, rubbernecking at everything we saw. I'd found that I was enjoying myself, truly having fun, for the first time I'd been stranded on this planet. Everything that I had seen in Rhoscara was just so interesting to me, so new to my modern sensibilities. It was like being a part of a massive Renaissance fair, except it was real, with real magic visible everywhere.

"Hmm, well." Azarus glanced at me. "I heard Gren talkin' to you about the Houses, yeah? Rhoscara belongs to the Florens, and they're the ones that the highest quality goods come from. At least, in the Principality. That's 'cause all the good crafters flock here. Common knowledge that you can get a writ from a Florens that'll subsidize your research if you impress 'em. Draws right from the royal coffers, as long as ya don't abuse it."

I turned to face Azarus at that, raising an eyebrow. "So, what, the Florens are patrons of the arts or something?"

Azarus shrugged. "'Something' like that? It's worked out well enough for 'em, I'd say. They're by far the wealthiest of the Houses. Anyway, the reason the markets are split up like this is 'cause the crafters can peacock at each other if they've got a writ and their rival don't. It's a way to breed competition or something like that. Always thought it was a mite inconvenient, meself. They like it though, so..." He shrugged again.

"Hmm." I agreed distractedly. I'd caught sight of a dwarven woman painting in the middle of the market to a crowd. From what I could see, she was painting a bleak picture. It seemed to be a landscape, but of an almost apocalyptically desolate view. I couldn't make out the details, but I thought I could make out some islands from on top of a cliff.

Azarus followed my gaze. He grunted disapprovingly after a moment. Surprised, I turned to face him. "What's wrong?"

"Drawing the Deadlands like that," he answered with a frown. "It's a bit disrespectful, ya know. Plus, you're just inviting trouble."

When he didn't hear a response, Azarus turned to face me. He found me wearing a deadpan look on my face. "No, Azarus, I don't. I don't know what a 'Deadlands' is, remember?" I stressed.

Azarus flushed slightly. "Ah, right. Well, don't worry about it for now. We're almost there, anyway. The palace is just beyond this district."

We traveled through the art markets for a few more minutes before we clearly exited them. On the other side of the markets was a very wide, cobbled road filled with people and carts coming and going. On the far side of the large road was a tall wrought iron fence that clearly divided the palatial district from everything else. I couldn't see much beyond the fence, only some trees that seemed to have been deliberately planted on the other side to block the view. The road, and the fence beyond, extended far off into the district, farther than I could see right now. Maybe it circled the entire district?

I followed Azarus as we turned left from where we had exited the art markets. After a few more minutes of walking, I could see a large gate on the opposite side of the road in the distance. The gate itself was huge, honestly. It was somehow shaped like a giant pair of bird wings that met in the middle. On either side were two huge, armored dwarfs. Their armor visibly differed from the other soldiers I'd seen. Bulkier, I couldn't even tell if the metal it was made out of was steel. It was a fiery red color with elaborate carvings, and even some parts visibly molded into avian shapes. They cut a fairly intimidating sight. Clenched tightly in their hands with the blade pointed downwards were large, single-edged curved great swords as well. I couldn't see anything about them through their strangely beaked helmets.

The avian-themed guards-dwarves didn't react as we approached the gates that all the other dwarves around us were avoiding. Finally, Azarus and I reached the gates and stopped in front of it. Slowly, the pointed helmet of the guard on the right turned to face Azarus.

"Be welcome in the Cardinal Halls, Lord Azarus." A deep voice rang out of the helmet. "The Lady has been made aware of your visit, and rooms for you and your," The voice paused momentarily. "Companion have been prepared."

Azarus frowned. "I guess Enzo sent word, then?" he grunted, visibly annoyed.

The guard didn't answer him. In a nearly synchronized move, both guards reached out with one hand, with the other still clutching their swords, to push open the monstrously sized gate. With a slight creak, the gates opened before us easily before their combined might. Azarus stepped through without a word, with me scurrying after him. The gates closed behind us with a clang, making me jump.

Before us wound a long and wide breadth of stairs that stretched up the gentle slope that led to the district proper. On either side of the staircase, beyond the trees, were huge flower beds that stretched off into the distance. They seemed to be organized in alternating sections of either red or yellow flowers of a kind that I didn't recognize off the top of my head.

I was snapped out of my admiration of the flower beds by Azarus letting out a huge sigh. Turning to face him, I could see that he had a put-upon look on his face.

"She's gonna do it, ain't she," Azarus muttered to himself.

I turned my head to face him. "Hmm? What was that?" I asked Azarus, curiously.

Azarus turned to me with a put-upon look on his face. "So, uh. Ya should know something about the person we're going to go see," he started awkwardly. "She—"

"Let me guess," I interrupted him, rolling my eyes. "She's the leader of House Florens or something, right?"

Azarus was visibly taken aback. "Uh…"

"Don't worry about it, man. I'm not that surprised, with the way you've been cagey about even mentioning whoever we're meeting." I said, unphased. "With the way that people here have been falling all over themselves around you, I can't say I'm surprised about it. You know, you essentially being royalty or something."

"It's not really like that." Azarus winced. "Prince is more of an elected position, ya know? It ain't like the human kingdom. And uh, yeah. You're right. My cousin is the Prince of House Florens."

"Whatever, man." I sighed. "As long as she's willing to help us out." I honestly had no more fucks to give for dramatic revelations, at this point.

"She'll help, yeah," Azarus told me. "I might catch some shit from her, 'cause of the whole. You know," he said, gesturing towards my neck. "But she'll help." When he was finished, he muttered something else under his voice.

"What was that?" I asked, raising an eyebrow at Azarus.

He shook his head. "Nothing. Don't worry about it. Let's get going, yeah? Sooner we get this over with, the sooner we can get to work."

Azarus took off in the direction of the stairs.

I followed him.

# Chapter 29
# Complications

Before long, Azarus and I had reached the top of the long winding stone stairway that led to the palace district proper. We made the trip in silence, as Azarus seemed anxious about something. Personally, I spent the time admiring the grounds that we were passing by. It really did seem like something I would see out of a magazine describing the lifestyle of the obscenely wealthy from back home. Huge plots of flowers, tastefully arranged on either side of us, with the occasional dwarven groundskeeper tending to them. Meticulously tidy individual gardens that seemed to double as pseudo-parks were also visible, with paths snaking every which way from the main path that we were walking on.

Every once in a while, I would see someone that very obviously wasn't part of the 'help' from where I was walking. To a one, they all looked faintly ridiculous to me. They almost seemed like a stereotype of an old-fashioned snooty medieval noble. Dressed in extravagant, impractical clothes, they were slathered in enough beauty products to look like a doll. Most of them were attended by an almost excessive number of servants and guard dwarves. However, I only saw a few of these peacock nobles.

I tried not to look at them too closely, or else I would burst into laughter and get shanked by their guards or something.

Reaching the top of the stairway, Azarus and I emerged onto an enormous courtyard that stretched all the way towards the palace proper. The courtyard itself was huge as well, with what seemed to be an arranged placement of five interconnected fountains within it. They seemed to be arranged with four of them in box formation surrounding the fifth and largest in the middle. The fountains themselves seemed large to my sensibilities, but it was clear that the middle one that they were all connected to be the largest of the four. It was as beautiful as anything else I'd seen on the grounds.

While I had been admiring the courtyard, Azarus seemed to have been scanning it for something. Whatever he had been searching for, he clearly found, as he let out a sigh. "And here he comes," he muttered in resignation.

I followed his gaze to see a dwarf hurrying in our direction from across the courtyard. As the dwarf got closer to us, I saw he was dressed fancily. He was wearing what almost seemed like a gilded, red and gold version of a butler's uniform. On the other hand, his uniform seemed to be much fancier than I would expect a mere servant to be wearing. The dwarf himself was about average height for his people, with greased-back blond hair and muddy hazel eyes. However, what caught my attention the most was the prominent curled mustache on his upper lip. Based on what Gren had told me, I guess that made this guy another noble of some sort?

"Lord…Azarus…" The dwarf gasped out in between breaths once he had reached us, hunched over with his hands on his knees. Azarus rolled his eyes visibly and stepped forward to help the other dwarf back upright with a slap to his back. The other dwarf winced and gave Azarus a shaky smile. Glancing back and forth furtively, the dwarf turned to me and waved me closer. Startled, I did as he bid. Once I was close enough, he whispered to Azarus and me. "Stay close, and follow me. I must explain how you will be presented to the Prince today." Having said that, the dwarf made an about-face and waited for the two of us to fall into place before slowly starting to make his way back to the palace. Azarus and I followed.

"What's this about, Piccio?" Azarus said softly, with a frown in his voice. "I didn't expect to cause this much trouble, this fast."

The other dwarf, apparently named Piccio, didn't turn to face him when he answered under his breath. "Normally, you would not. However, things have been…" He paused for a moment before continuing. "Delicate, lately. Lord Olgar has begun his campaign for the throne in earnest, I'm afraid." He paused again before turning his head slightly in my direction. "Ah, but where are my manners? I am Jadrath Piccio, Steward to her Ladyship the Prince of Cardinal. I'm afraid I wasn't briefed on your name, Mr…?"

I straightened up. "Ah," I said to him, careful to keep my voice low. "Nathan Hart. It's, uh, nice to meet you."

Piccio nodded slightly without turning to face me. "Indeed."

Azarus let out another sigh to my left. "Fuckin' of course that asshole would make a bid now, of all times," he muttered.

"Unfortunately so, Lord Azarus," Piccio answered softly. "Additionally, I'm afraid that Lord Olgar caught wind of the missive that Captain Gastone sent to the Prince detailing the situation."

Azarus visibly tensed for a moment before forcibly calming himself. "He didn't see it, did he?"

Piccio shook his head slightly. "Fortunately not. However, Lord Olgar is no fool. Once he was tipped off about an urgent missive to the palace in regards to yourself, he undoubtedly smelled an opportunity. For the past half hour, he's been gathering his supporters in the throne room. To counter him, her Ladyship has been doing the same. I'm afraid that the throne room is rather packed, as of now."

Azarus grimaced. "Goddamnit," he whispered harshly. "Why the damn throne room?"

"As blood of the Prince, you are entitled to a royal welcome. Technically." Piccio answered softly.

Azarus took a breath to calm himself. "Never had to do that shit before."

"Indeed," Piccio told him quietly. "However, Lord Olgar no doubt knows that you are entitled to this reception, and took it upon himself to force the issue. He is unmistakably attempting to force a scene in which he can tarnish your image, and thus the Prince's image. He does not know the reason for the captain's missive, but he seems to have smelled an opportunity."

By this time, we were passing the large fountain in the middle of the courtyard. We were walking *really* slowly.

"Fuck, okay," Azarus replied, his right-hand twitching. "What's the plan then?"

Piccio let out a sigh. "We don't have much of one, I'm afraid. With so little time between the gathering, your arrival, and your reception, there isn't much we can do. All I can ask, all the Prince can ask is that you follow her lead…and improvise."

"That's it?" Azarus asked incredulously.

The steward winced. "Unfortunately so. The Prince can handle Lord Olgar. Merely follow her lead. Perhaps she's thought of something in the last few minutes?" Piccio said hopefully, before turning his head to face me slightly. "You wouldn't perhaps have Acting, would you Mr. Hart?"

"What, the Talent? Um, no. No, I don't." At the look on his face, I couldn't help myself. "Sorry."

Piccio turned head back forward with a sigh. "Well, we can only hope, I suppose."

\*\*\*

We made the rest of the short walk across the courtyard in silence. Piccio was trying to project confidence, while Azarus was visibly girding himself for the coming confrontation.

Personally, I was strangely calm. I had the least to lose here, honestly. I wanted to do my best so that Azarus didn't catch any flak, obviously. But I wasn't scared of some uppity noble trying to verbally browbeat me or anything. I wasn't as scared of a social situation like this as much as I was of combat. Which was weird for me, honestly. Before I'd been dumped here, I'd been socially anxious. I guess everything that had happened to me so far was helping to cure that.

Yay.

Once we reached the front of the palace, we came to stand in front of the massive double doors that marked the entrance. The gates themselves were huge, at least three stories high alone, with a prominent engraving of a raven in flight upon them. Standing in front of the gates was a squad of four of the avian-themed knights that had been guarding the gates to the district. Without a word to us, they stepped out of the way of the gate, just in time for them to start rumbling open on their own.

Azarus sighed. "The main doors, really? Hells…"

Piccio shot him a sympathetic glance before motioning us forward. Inside, I found that the palace was as opulent as I had expected it to be. Gold seemed to be the preeminent theme, with red accents. We seemed to be in some kind of atrium or something, as there were multiple other doors that led elsewhere. On the far side of the room was another large set of doors, thankfully not quite as big as the palace gates themselves.

"Come along." I heard Piccio say to me, snapping me out of my rubbernecking. Flushing slightly, I glanced at him to see that he and Azarus were waiting for me. Piccio gestured towards the back. "The throne room is just beyond."

I nodded slightly at him and fell into step. As we drew closer to the large double doors, I began to hear a low murmuring through them. It sounded like a great many people were conversing in low tones just inside. Reaching the doors, Piccio glanced back at the two of us. "Brace yourselves," he said softly.

With a hard shove, belaying his short stature, Piccio opened the doors to the throne room with a grinding noise. With the sound of the doors opening, the conversation within audibly dropped from where we were standing.

"Announcing!" Piccio shouted from in front of us, blocking our view of the throne room. "Lord Azarus, of House Savoy! And his companion, Sir Nathan Hart!" When he finished, he smoothly stepped off to the side and bowed in Azarus's direction.

Sir? What the hell was that about?

With a hard look on his face, Azarus stepped through the doors to the throne room. After a moment, I followed him. Once I got a good look at the inside of the throne room, however, my steps faltered for a moment before I forced myself to continue walking. The throne room itself was massive, almost excessively so. Made of the same gilded red stone that the rest of the palace seemed to be, it must have at least been the length of a football field from back home. The room didn't have a normal ceiling, instead, it was lit by a glass ceiling that was letting in plenty of fading afternoon light. The orange hues of the setting sun lent an almost ethereal feel to the surroundings There was a main walkway that was laid out with a literal long, red carpet that ran the length of the room. On either side of the large, wide carpet were huge carved pillars that stretched to the monstrously high roof of the room, framing the glass.

However, what nearly stopped me in my tracks were all the damn people that lined the walls of the room. There were tons of them, with a large crowd visible in the distance blocking my view of what could only be the throne.

All of them had turned to face us in silence as we entered the room.

All right, I was wrong earlier. I was still damn socially anxious.

Taking a breath to steady my nerves, I continued following Azarus down the carpet further into the room. With a boom that nearly made me flinch, I could hear the throne room doors close behind us and Piccio follow us. I tried to copy Azarus as best I could as we made our way through the huge hall, trying to face forward and keep my anxiety from my face. I don't know how well I managed it.

Soon, we reached the mob of people that were blocking the view of the throne. Azarus stopped in front of them, stone-faced. I tried to remain slightly behind him. From out of the crowd stepped a bizarrely intimidating dwarf, with hair a darker red than even Azarus's. I was reminded somewhat of the painted fops that I had seen earlier in the gardens, but only slightly. On this dwarf, it seemed more like war paint. His face was painted a stark, pale white with large, artful black splotches covering the outsides of his shining golden eyes. Large, sharp red lines, almost blade-like in appearance ran down from under his face, to curl around his mouth and painted lips. This dwarf was very obviously a noble as well, not just from the superior quality of his clothes, but from his beard. He might have had both the largest and smallest beard I'd seen on a noble. He had nothing on his cheeks and lips, but he had a long, braided beard that extended from his chin that reached to his belt line, capped off somehow with a large chunk of metal.

He was smiling faintly at Azarus.

Off to his side, I was able to see Azarus start to scowl. "Olgar," he grunted.

"Azarus." The painted dwarf replied in a deep, rough voice with a mocking tone. "Welcome home."

# Chapter 30
# The Prince of Ravens

So, this was Olgar.

Not gonna lie, he was intimidating.

Azarus hummed noncommittedly in response to his greeting. He turned his gaze away from Olgar for a moment in order to drag it along the crowd of perhaps fifteen other dwarves at Olgar's back. Turning it back Olgar, Azarus spoke again. "Quite the welcoming party for little old me."

Olgar spread his arms, palms out. "A coincidence, I assure you. I wouldn't dream of impeding your business with the Prince," he said, somewhat insincerely. Someone in the crowd behind him snickered before they were audibly shushed. Olgar didn't blink. "I have business with her as well, you see."

Azarus crossed his arms. "Is that a fact?"

"Oh, indeed," Olgar said with a smile. "However, I will be gracious and allow you right of first meeting. After all," His eyes narrowed, and his smile took a more sinister edge. "It's always a pleasure to welcome the blood of the Raven back to the halls."

"Thank you kindly, then," Azarus said stonily. He took a step forward, putting himself within arm's reach of Olgar. Azarus met his eyes. "Now, if you don't mind, I have business with the Prince."

Olgar didn't move or say anything for a moment. He just stared straight back into Azarus's eyes without blinking. Slowly, I became aware that the hall had quieted to watch the confrontation between the two dwarves. There was a sense of tension rising in the air as the two of them just continued to stare into each other's eyes.

It was broken when Olgar's smile widened slightly and he stepped aside. "Of course, cousin." With an exaggerated gesture, Olgar swept his right arm out to the side in the direction of the throne. The crowd that had been standing with Olgar shuffled to the sides to allow a path through at his unspoken command. Without another word to Olgar, Azarus started walking again.

Letting out a breath I didn't know I had been holding, I hurried to catch up to Azarus as he made his way through the crowd. But as I was passing Olgar, I couldn't help but turn my eyes to look at him for a moment. I found Olgar looking right back at me.

A chill went down my spine when our eyes met.

If it was possible, Olgar's smile grew larger. This time with teeth visible.

Hurriedly looking away from him, I picked up the pace.

God, there was something wrong with that dwarf. I could see it in his eyes.

Catching up with Azarus, I let out a shuddering breath behind him. I wiped the back of my right hand across my brow, finding it soaked with sweat. "Fuck." I whispered quietly to myself, under my breath. Breathing in, I tried to calm myself down before we met with the Prince. After a moment, I stepped from behind Azarus to his right, but still behind him. Somehow, I knew I shouldn't walk beside him.

Looking up, I could see the throne now that we were past the crowd. It was, like most dwarven extravagances, mostly made of gold. Large and exquisitely molded, I didn't know if it was just gilded or entirely made out of gold. It didn't look like it had been sized for a dwarf, it was so large. The solid base of the throne was seated upon a raised dais that you had to look up at in order to view the throne. The stone on the far wall was much darker, and framed in gold prominently in the center of it was a large circular window. On either side of the throne were large banners of what must be the symbol of House Florens, the flying raven on a field of red clasping a flower, edged in gold. But what drew the eye the most was the statue that towered over the back of the throne.

It was a huge, golden raven. Massive, it was hunched over the throne as if it were protecting it. Two huge wings rested on either side of the throne, flat on the ground, each feather immaculately detailed. The head of the raven, with eyes made of two enormous rubies, stared out at the hall from just over the top of the throne. The fading afternoon sunlight danced in those eyes, making them seem almost alive.

But the throne itself was empty.

I didn't have much time to be surprised by this, as without a word Piccio hurried past Azarus and I. By the time we had reached the foot of the stairs that led up the dais to the throne, Piccio had ascended halfway up it before turning to look out at the crowd. I saw him make a small gesture with his hands off to the side. Without a word, two dwarves carrying long trumpets stepped out from behind a pair of pillars to stand at the base of the dais. Piccio visibly took a large breath before he began bellowing.

"Announcing!" His voice echoed through the hall, ending all other noise within it. "Her Highness, the Lady of Rhoscara! The Prince of Cardinal! Pentarch of the Principality of Velancia! Prince Elysael, of House Florens! Long may she reign!"

"Long may she reign." The hall echoed back in a myriad of voices, some more enthusiastic than others.

With a grinding noise, I could hear the throne room doors that had been closed behind Azarus and I begin to open again. I began to turn around only to be stopped by a firm hand falling on my shoulder. Following it, I found that Azarus had stopped me. He shook his head at me.

"Follow my lead," Azarus whispered to me. With his hand still on my shoulder, he led me off to the side of the carpet that spanned the length of the room. When we reached it, he knelt on one knee and gestured for me to do the same. I did as he bid, looking around curiously as I did so. Every other person in the room was doing something similar. They were all coming up to kneel at the edge of the carpet and bow their head, even Olgar and his companions. "Hey." I heard Azarus whisper to me. "Lower your head, yeah?" he said quietly, once I'd turned to face him. Okay, I guess. I lowered my head.

Once the doors finished grinding open, I heard metal-clad feet begin to march into the hall. At the same time, two clear trumpets rang out across the hall in a short tune that I wasn't familiar with. There were so many of them that I couldn't accurately make out just how many people were marching into the hall. Was the Prince armored or something?

The sound of marching armored feet grew closer and closer to Azarus and I, even though I couldn't see them with my head lowered. Before long, the procession had passed right by Azarus and I. I was incredibly curious about them, but I could see that Azarus hadn't raised his head from where it was lowered, so I didn't raise mine either. From what I could tell, the procession began to spread out along the dais as they reached it. Suddenly, all of the armored feet stopped moving to my ears. Straining them, I could hear something else moving. Where before all I could hear was metal-covered feet on stone, now I could hear what sounded like the swishing of fabric and much softer footsteps begin to ascend towards the throne.

After a few more moments of silence, I heard a firm, feminine voice ring out across the hall. "I, Elysael of House Florens, Prince of the

Cardinal Halls, do hereby call this session of the Scarlet Court to order."

The shuffling of feet and the creaking of boots whispered through the throne room as upwards of a hundred people rose to their feet at once. Out of the corner of my eye, I could see that Azarus was one of them, so I followed his lead. Rising to my feet I directed my gaze towards the throne, curious about the person that commanded so much power and respect in these parts.

I wasn't disappointed.

By far the most striking female dwarf I had seen so far, the Prince was almost ethereally beautiful. She possessed a slimmer build than I had typically seen on most other dwarves, who almost to one were stockier than humanity. I couldn't be sure, considering how she was sitting ramrod straight on her throne, but I would place her about average height for her species, so maybe about chest height on myself. She had the red hair that I was starting to expect was a telltale sign of House Florens members worn long and unbound, almost impractically so. As well, she had the same golden eyes that I had noticed in dwarven aristocracy. With her, the hair was a lighter shade than either Azarus's or Olgar's, while her eyes were shining far more noticeably than either of theirs. Possessed of fair skin, she was wearing a flowing silken dress of white with golden embroidery, with an almost militaristic cut to it. Instead of a crown, she wore a large golden torque around her neck, as well as a single large teardrop-shaped ruby seemingly set into her brow.

Standing at attention along the dais was a squad of those same avian-themed knights I've seen multiple times so far. Additionally, on the left and right of the throne were two more of the knights, this time holding House Florens banners. These guys must have been the procession I'd heard.

The Prince neither blinked nor took her eyes off of the hall when she spoke again. "Steward Piccio."

Piccio bowed his head in her direction from his position halfway up the dais. "Yes, your highness?"

"State the scheduled itinerary of the court, this day." The Prince said evenly.

"Of course, your highness," Piccio replied subserviently. Raising his head and drawing a scroll from his waist, Piccio turned back to face the hall. Unrolling the scroll and clearing his throat, Piccio read from the scroll in a clear voice. "Firstly, petitioners to the court this day include the honorable Lord Lozaki, the honorable Lady Hollawo, and the honorable Lord Olgar. Secondly, there is a dispute to be resolved in regard to pasture rights involving Houses Marino and Donnato. Finally, there is the welcoming of Lord Azarus during his scheduled visit to the Cardinal Halls."

Okay, I was a little confused, and judging by the murmuring in the hall, I wasn't the only one. Risking a glance over to Olgar, I found that he surprisingly had a wry smile on his painted lips. He didn't seem super upset about the news of a schedule, which I was a little confused by. Wasn't this supposed to be some big dramatic showdown between the Prince, Azarus, and Olgar?

"Hmm." I heard Azarus give an approving noise. I turned my head slightly to look at him with a questioning look on my face. He must have noticed because he turned to face me too. "It's a good move," he whispered to me. "Ely must have thrown together an itinerary real quick in order to make it seem like she planned this. 'Scheduled', yeah?"

Oh, I get it now. By making this seem like a normal day at court instead of a rushed confrontation, it makes it seem like Azarus wasn't here for anything important. I gave Azarus a slight nod to show I understood. Before I turned back to watch the Prince though, I gave

Azarus the side-eye as well. "Ely, huh?" I whispered to him. He gave me the stink eye back. The Prince drew our attention back shortly, however.

"Very well." The Prince continued smoothly. "Court is now in session. Proceed."

"The throne calls upon Lord Lozaki, of House Romano!" Piccio immediately called out into the hall.

For the next maybe half an hour, two separate dwarves approached the throne and aired their petitions to the Prince. The first wanted something to do with an inheritance. Sounded like he was pissed about an uncle. The Prince dismissed him and said to come back with the uncle in order to present a fair hearing. That guy veritably slunk out of the hall with his tail between his legs. The second one had some kind of routine business about zoning laws for her tannery business. I didn't understand most of the back and forth with this one, as it seemed to involve specific local ordinances. After a while, the Prince ruled in her favor and gave her some kind of concession? I didn't fully follow it, and judging by the attitude of the audience in the hall, they didn't either. A not insignificant number of dwarves had left the hall during both petitions, as it seemed like they might not get the show they were looking for. I didn't blame them, this was boring.

But enough stuck around, because it was Olgar's turn to petition the throne next. Now *this* I was interested in. What reason did he manufacture to be here?

I saw Piccio take a deep breath. "The throne calls upon Lord Olgar, of House Florens!" He announced.

The hall took up a low murmur. This apparently didn't sit right with the Prince, as she very obviously narrowed her eyes. "Silence." Her voice rang out in the hall, clear as a bell. The hall fell silent at her command. Shifting her eyes to look at Olgar, she spoke again. "Approach, cousin."

Olgar did as commanded and smoothly approached the throne from where he had been standing off to the side. Once he reached the foot of the dais, he bowed at the waist towards the Prince. "Hail the Raven Throne," he intoned in a strong voice. He stayed bent over, though.

The Prince let him stay bowed for several seconds before speaking. "Rise, cousin. State your petition." For the first time, her composure broke slightly. She sighed. "Even though I suspect I know what it is."

Olgar rose from his bow and smiled up at the Prince. "Your Highness is as wise as she is beautiful. Indeed, I have come before you today in order to reiterate a previous petition." In a grand gesture, he spread his arms wide. "I speak, of course, of my petition to intervene in the conflict further south. With your permission, I would rally my company and present myself to the human King in order to lend my aid against the Sculpted menace!" He finished, in a gallant tone of voice.

Polite clapping arose from the dwarves that he'd brought with himself, very obviously his supporters.

The Prince let the clapping stop before speaking again. "Denied." She said flatly.

Olgar didn't seem surprised by this. He stretched his right arm in her direction in an entreating direction, his left hand over his heart. "Will you not tell us your reasoning, my Prince?"

The Prince furrowed her brow slightly. "As I have told you before, the rebellion occurring within the Kingdom of Herztal is a purely internal matter. The decision arrived at by the Principal Convocation is that the Principality is not to intervene in a foreign affair of murky morality. No dwarven mercenary companies are to involve themselves in the conflict, under threat of exile. As you well know."

Olgar bowed his head in her direction. "It is as you say, my Prince. However!" He exclaimed, snapping his head back up. "Could you not entreat your fellow Princes to rescind their decision?! Even now, the poor citizens of Herztal suffer under constant threat of Sculpted terroristic acts! As a right-thinking noble, nay, as a moral *person*! Is it not our duty to liberate the frightened masses of humanity from the threat of the vile Sculpted?!" He cried dramatically.

"No." The Prince said flatly. "It is not. I will not gainsay the other Princes, nor will I challenge our collective decision. Furthermore, as you well know, it was my personal, on the record, stated belief that the situation within Herztal is too nebulous to support either side in the conflict. I will not allow members of my House to intervene in it."

Despite how enthralled I was in the drama playing out before me, I was still able to catch Azarus's face twisting out of the corner of my eye. Twisting my head in his direction, I could see that he had an almost uncomfortable scowl on his face. Noticing me, he just shook his head in my direction. I was curious, but I directed my gaze back to the scene before us.

Olgar sighed theatrically. "Very well, my Prince. I will abide by your decision," he finished mournfully. He bowed towards the throne again, but he was interrupted by the Prince before he could leave.

"Olgar." The Prince said coldly. Olgar stopped mid-motion from where he'd been turning to leave to look back up at the Prince. "You will not petition for this again. Am I understood?"

Olgar bowed again. "Yes, my Prince. As you command." At the Prince's slight nod, he turned and left the foot of the dais to return to his supporters. As he was turning to leave though, I caught a look at his face. He didn't look like he'd just been rebuked. In fact, from the look on his face, you'd think he'd just won something, instead of being denied.

The hall was quiet for a moment before the Prince broke it. She cut her eyes in the direction of Piccio and spoke. "Continue, Steward."

Piccio stepped forward from where he had stepped back. He brought his scroll back up. "The throne calls upon Lady Marien, of House Marino, and Lord Ronaldo, of House Donnato!"

# Chapter 31
# Performance of a Lifetime

I didn't pay much attention to the next couple of people that came to petition the Prince. I was more focused on the implications of Olgar's petition, instead.

It sounded to me like the human kingdom was involved in some kind of war.

Moreover, it sounded like they were at war with themselves, in some fashion. Olgar had called it a 'rebellion' involving some group called the 'Sculpted'. What the hell did that mean, anyway? What kind of name was 'Sculpted'? What did they want? People didn't typically rebel against their own government for no reason, after all.

What the Prince had said was interesting, too. When talking about it, she'd used words like 'murky', and 'nebulous'. That implied to me that she might have sympathies for these 'Sculpted', whoever they were.

Very interesting.

After all, one man's 'rebellion', could be another's 'revolution'.

I snapped out of my contemplation once I noticed that the last few petitioners had finished up with the Prince. I knew what that meant. It was our turn to be presented. The few people that had stuck around to see Azarus must have known this too, as I saw multiple other dwarves looking almost eager. Not Olgar, though. I could see that his followers looked more interested in us than he did, for some reason. He just looked…politely interested, I guess.

Hearing someone clearing their throat, I looked back up at the throne to see Piccio holding out his scroll again. "The throne calls upon Lord Azarus, of House Savoy, and his companion, Sir Nathan Hart!"

There was that 'Sir' again.

Azarus caught my eye from off to my left. When he saw that he'd gotten my attention, he nodded at me. I nodded back at him, trying to settle my nerves and mentally prepare myself. Azarus stepped forward and began making his way to the foot of the dais. I followed him, aware that all eyes in the hall were on the two of us.

When the two of us reached the dais, Azarus bowed at the waist in the direction of the Prince, right arm bent over his stomach and left behind his back. I emulated him as best I could.

"Rise, cousin. Rise, guest." I heard the Prince say, in a noticeably warmer tone of voice than she'd spoken to Olgar in. I did as she bid, aware that Azarus was doing the same to my right. Looking up, I could see that the Prince was looking at him with a small smile. "Be welcome in these halls, blood of my blood."

Azarus returned the smile. "I thank you for your kind words, my Prince," he said, ducking his head briefly.

The Prince then shifted her gaze to me. It was far more neutral than the look she'd given Azarus. "And you, Sir Hart. Welcome to the Cardinal Halls."

I took a deep breath before bowing my head to her. "Thank you, your Highness."

The Prince nodded ever so slightly in my direction before addressing Azarus again. "I assume it's your regularly scheduled business that brings you to my city?"

"Aye." Azarus nodded. "That and…some other business that I'll need to see done."

"I see." The Prince said slowly. "We can discuss any private business later. I invite you, and your companion, to dine with me after the conclusion of—"

"I apologize, my Prince." I heard a loud voice say. "But I must object!"

My stomach fell. I recognized that voice.

Olgar.

Turning my head to the side, I could see him walk back up to stand at the foot of the dais. This time, he stood at the foot of the dais in order to keep both the Prince, Azarus and I in his view.

The Prince stared disapprovingly down at Olgar. "You forget your place, Olgar. Your time to speak has passed."

Olgar placed his right hand over his heart. "I deeply apologize once more, my Prince. However, this man!" He said, suddenly pointing a finger in my direction. "Is highly suspicious! Who is he? Why has Azarus deigned to present him before the court? We know nothing about him! What if he was an assassin, with designs upon our beautiful sovereign?"

I could tell that Olgar's speech was starting to sway the crowd somewhat, judging by the murmurs throughout the court. The Prince could tell too, I could see, from the frown on her face. In my case, I could feel my heartrate skyrocket. Along with my anxiety.

"I assure you, Olgar." The Prince said carefully. "I've been briefed about the basics of the situation with Sir Hart."

"I beg you, your highness," Olgar replied passionately. "Illuminate us. I speak out of a deep sense of concern for not only your august self but for all residents of Rhoscara. We live in uncertain times, with barbarism rampaging beyond our southern border. Who knows what agents of disorder the vile Sculpted could slip into our midst!?"

271

Azarus stepped beyond me to stand in front of Olgar. "Leave it be, Olgar," he said warningly. "It's private."

Olgar stepped forward too. "I will *not*! You, sir!" He said in my direction, still pointing an accusing finger. "I demand that you explain yourself!"

Azarus clenched his hands into fists. "Olgar—"

"It's fine, Azarus," I interjected.

Azarus turned to face me with an almost panicked look on his face.

I took a deep breath and continued. "If Lord Olgar is so concerned about my presence, then I believe I *should* explain myself."

I took a step to position similarly to Olgar, half facing the Prince, half facing the rest of the hall. "Rest assured, my lord, that I have no designs upon the good people of Rhoscara. In truth, I've followed Lord Azarus to this fine city for the exact opposite reason! Please, will you not listen to my tale?" I cried passionately to the hall, in an attempt to match Olgar's theatricality.

Judging by the interested gazes I could see throughout the hall, as well as the raised eyebrow from the Prince, I was succeeding.

"As many of you know," I began. "My Kingdom—" fuck fuck fuck what did he call it "Herztal, is currently suffering a period of strife and unrest. Like many of my people, I too attempted to flee the anarchy across the northern border, as it is well known that the chaos has not touched our most illustrious neighbors!"

I DIDN'T KNOW THAT AT ALL.

Must have been on the mark though, from the 'sagely' nods I could see from so many of these painted fops.

"However!" I shouted bombastically. "Before I could travel even a league upon dwarven clay, I was attacked! By Elven raiders!"

Gasps rang out from many of the gathered nobles, while others just looked like they were enjoying the show. The Prince's other eyebrow went up.

I affected a sorrowful visage, bowing my head and laying a hand across my heart. "Sadly, the caravan of refugees that I, and my companions-" Me, myself, and I "were traveling with, could not fight them off. Nay, I'm afraid to say that those that were not slain, were enslaved by the barbaric raiders. Including my dear comrades…" I trailed off, forcing my eyes to well up. God, I hadn't done that in years. I was surprised I was still capable of it.

I could hear one of the sheltered popinjays in the audience start to weep softly.

Surging violently upright, I made a sweeping motion with my right arm. "But all was not lost! For before the elven leader could sentence me to a fate most foul, I was saved! By none other than Lord Azarus!" I spun in a circle, pointing a finger straight at him and causing more gasps to ring out across the hall.

I could see that the Prince was visibly fascinated by my show, leaning forward on her throne to watch more closely.

Azarus had been gaping at me with an open mouth during my speech, but when I turned to point at him, he visibly started. Closing his mouth, Azarus flicked his eyes to the audience to gauge their reaction. Looking back at me, he slowly nodded his head.

I nodded back at him, relieved that he was following my lead, but not letting it show on my face. "If it were not for him, I might not be alive this instant to address this august court! I shudder to imagine what would have befallen me had he not driven the foul elves away that day." I actually did shudder dramatically, before shaking my head sadly. "Lamentably, others were not so lucky as I. The raiders were successful in taking a number of poor, unfortunate souls as slaves that day, during their retreat."

A number of cries of outrage rang out, even from one of the dwarves in Olgar's retinue. The dwarf next to him elbowed him in the ribs.

God, I had these fops eating out of the palm of my hand.

Still facing Azarus, I mouthed something to him while I let the outrage in the hall die down. I'd had a fucking crazy idea, but based on the reaction of the room, I thought I could pull it off.

'Trust me.'

He just gazed back at me with wide eyes, as if he'd never met me.

"I am truly blessed." I near whispered once the hubbub had died down. Nonetheless, my voice still echoed in the dead silent hall, so enthralled was my audience. "Alas, I did not escape that day without my own scars. You see, the vile raiders did succeed in one manner. For while they did not manage to bind me, they did leave me with a parting gift. Behold!" I cried, grasping my cloak at the collar.

Azarus's eyes bulged in their sockets, guessing what I was about to do.

Ripping the cloak from my body in a violent motion over my head, I bared my body to the court.

Including my collar.

Shocked gasps rang out from every corner of the hall. The Prince lurched on her throne. Olgar gaped at me. Hell, I even heard some of the avian knight's shuffle in their armor.

I drank in their reactions, smiling near manically. I spread my arms wide, fully facing the hall this time. "Peace, my dear gentle dwarves. Peace. Did I not say that I was not bound?"

That quieted the hall.

Some.

"I," I started, before pausing dramatically. "Am not a slave! For while the raiders may have collared me, I retain my freedom!" I bellowed. "I may bear this collar, but I am not bound! Before this throne, and all gods, I proclaim! I will undergo any trial to prove this truth to you!"

Here I stopped speaking for a moment, praying to anyone that would listen that my hint would be picked up while my heart thundered in my ears.

Thankfully, my prayers were answered.

I heard a throat clear from behind me. I watched the stunned eyes of the hall shift to over my right shoulder. "Steward Piccio." I heard the Prince say smoothly behind me. "Were you not trained to detect the presence of the slave bond?"

"Ah, ah." I heard Piccio stutter behind me. "Um. Yes, your Highness. Right away, your Highness." I heard him shuffle hurriedly down the steps in my direction. I didn't turn to face him, still facing the hall with confidence written across my face. I didn't even turn to face him when he laid a hand on the back of my left shoulder. I heard Piccio mutter something behind me, but I wasn't able to make out the words. I felt a slight heat on my back, but nothing more.

"This man," I heard Piccio say behind me, after a pause. "Speaks the truth, your Highness. He does not possess a slave bond."

Cries of amazement arose from the hall before they were silenced by the Prince clearing her throat again.

"I see." I heard the Prince say calmly. Just as calmly, I turned to face her. I saw that she was nearly smiling down at me. Nearly. "Why, then, Sir Hart, do you still bear a collar?"

I bowed sweepingly in her direction, trying my best to emulate Olgar from earlier. "Your Highness, I bear this collar for two reasons. The first is as a reminder of my failure. For it was my weakness that day that allowed the elven raiders to massacre that caravan so. Before that day, and before the war, I did not take my training seriously. I am pathetically weak, your highness." I said, shaking my head sorrowfully. "I will bear this collar until the stain of my weakness has been erased, and my companions avenged. And so, my second reason ties to my first." I spun in place to face Azarus once more.

He was still frozen in place.

I stretched out my left arm in his direction, my right over my heart. "For his actions that day in heroically saving my life, I have pledged it to Lord Azarus!" I cried, dropping to one knee. "I am not his slave, but I have pledged myself to him! I will follow where he leads! I will fight his enemies in his place! I will be the shield that protects him from all harm! This collar may not be true, but I will bear it nonetheless, as a collar upon my heart!"

Oh, cringe, cringe, cringe. That last line was totally overblown.

I stayed kneeling in that position, my arm still stretched to Azarus, hoping I hadn't screwed everything up. But I didn't think so.

Cheers arose from the audience, echoing through the halls.

"Hail, Sir Hart!" I heard one dwarven voice call. "Hail, the Collared Knight!"

The other nobles took up the chant.

"The Collared Knight!"

"The Collared Knight!"

I rose to my feet to face the crowd and bowed in their direction, before turning back around to face the Prince. The crowd quieted again, seeing that I wasn't finished.

"And so, I come to my petition, your Highness," I said solemnly. "By now, from my tale, you should be aware that there are roving gangs of Elven raiders upon your southern border, waylaying innocent refugees. I have heard your arguments against interfering in the Herztalian war, and will not gainsay you. However, will you not find it in your heart to deploy soldiers to protect the downtrodden castaways that even now flee the violence of my homeland, to the safety of yours?" I finished, bowing my head.

Silence fell upon the hall, the audience holding their breath.

"Hmm." I heard the Prince say, my head still bowed. "I have heard your tale, Sir Hart, and you have my sympathies for your plight.

Intelligence so close to the border with Herztal of late has been lacking, due to the difficulties of gathering it within the Barren Forest. Neither I, nor my forces, were aware that the elves had grown so bold as to attack Herztalian refugees upon my lands. I will speak with my captains and *tentatively*," she stressed. "Agree to the deployment of forces, in order to increase patrols in the area. Hopefully, this will discourage any further raids."

I let out a shuddering sigh, relieved for many reasons. Raising my head, I smiled up at the Prince. "Thank you, your Highness. I am truly grateful for your magnanimity."

The Prince merely nodded back at me, a wry cast to her lips.

Thunderous applause overtook the hall.

The Prince raised her voice for the first time to be heard over the din. "Court!" She shouted. "Is adjourned!"

# Chapter 32
# Judged

"Well," The Prince began delicately. "That wasn't quite how I was expecting things to go."

Once the Prince had ended court for the day, Azarus and I had followed her out of the throne room through a small, recessed doorway off to the side after I had collected my cloak. She had led us through a small corridor in silence before we'd emerged into another hallway. From there, she'd led us through the mostly empty halls to a stately room that must function as an office, based on the décor. Gesturing to a pair of chairs for Azarus and me to sit in, she sat behind a large wooden desk that dominated the back half of the room.

"Yeah," Azarus said faintly, collapsing into a plush red chair. "Me neither." He turned his head to the left to watch as I sat down as well and worked his jaw for a moment. "I...I don't even..."

I held up my hands defensively. "Hey, I saw a chance and I took it. It seemed to work out, right?" I said, looking from Azarus to the Prince.

They exchanged their own look before the Prince delicately cleared her throat. "In the moment, yes. I would say that your...performance did work to put Olgar off balance. In some ways, I would also say that you achieved the exact opposite of Olgar's intentions. Rumors of today's court session are no doubt already spreading across the city, and working to bolster Azarus's reputation." She paused. "However…" She shook her head, before opening a drawer on her desk. Out of it, she pulled out a crystal bottle of some kind of dark, nearly pitch-black liquid and three glasses. Setting the glasses out, she uncorked the bottle and poured a generous portion of the suspected liquor into them, before sliding two of the glasses across the desk.

Azarus grabbed one of them before immediately shooting the contents of the glass back. I picked up mine as well and tried it. Tasted like rum, to me.

"However, the consequences of such a…grandiose show are difficult to calculate." She said, drumming her fingers on the desktop. After a moment, she stopped and fixed me with her gaze. "Ah, but my apologies. We haven't been properly introduced, have we?" She mused, before extending a hand in my direction. "I am Elysael, of House Florens."

Somewhat hesitant, I reached across the desk to grab her hand in mine. Despite my expectations, it wasn't quite as soft as I would expect the hand of a royal to be. Rather, it was a strong grip, with prominent calluses on it. "Uh, nice to meet you, your highness. I'm, well, I'm Nathan Hart. You…can call me Nate, if you want." I said, shaking her hand.

She nodded at me, dropping the handshake. "Then I insist you call me Elysael. In private, you may do away with formalities." I nodded back at her and sat back in my chair. Elysael took a deep breath before raising a perfectly sculpted scarlet eyebrow at me. "Out of curiosity, how much of your tale was truthful?"

"Um." I floundered, before looking over at Azarus. Leaning over to him, I got his attention. "So, how much are we telling her?" I said, trying to whisper as quietly as I could in his ear.

Azarus didn't bother to keep his voice down when he answered me. "Everything," he said tiredly.

I was taken aback. "What, even the…?" I said, pointing to myself. "Yeah."

"And…?" I mimed as if I was stroking a beard on my bare chin.

Azarus rolled his eyes at me. "She already knows about Grey," he said, emphasizing the name.

"Uh, alright," I said, turning back to Elysael. She was watching us with a mildly amused expression, as if we were a pair of mischievous children. "I'd say maybe sixty percent was accurate-ish, and forty percent was bullshit I made up on the spot."

She didn't look surprised. "And what was false, exactly? I'm assuming you are not actually a wandering Herztalian Knight?"

I choked on a laugh, slightly hysterical. "God, no. I'm really," I said with emphasis. "Really not from around here. Your Highness, what do you know about Precursors?"

For the next half hour, I explained everything that had happened to me since I had arrived on this planet to Elysael. I spoke about my abrupt appearance outside of the doomed caravan. I spoke of the elven raid that had killed most of the refugees, and our transport to Addersfield. I spoke of my purchase by Magnus, and how I'd narrowly escaped being inflicted with a slave bond thanks to Azarus. I told her about being Awakened, and learning what and where I was.

I didn't, however, tell her about our plans. Little as they may be.

When I finished, my throat hurt from talking so much that I couldn't help but grimace. Seeing my discomfort, Elysael poured me some more of the rum. The burn of the alcohol helped to numb my throat. The Prince had mostly let me speak in silence, only asking a few clarifying questions throughout my tale.

"I see," Elysael said quietly. "To think, a Precursor would appear during my reign." She grimaced slightly, furrowing her brow. "And that he would fall victim to the darkest part of dwarven culture when he did." Standing up from her desk, the Prince shocked me by actually bowing in my direction. "On behalf of the Principality, I apologize for the actions taken against you by Lord Magnus." Slumping back down into her chair, she sighed. "Unfortunately, there is little I can do to aid you. As Azarus has no doubt explained, while you are indescribably lucky to have dodged a bond, you are still legally a slave in the eyes of the Principality. Not even the highest authority of the land can forcibly dissolve slave contracts. And that maggot Magnus would deny me, or any of my agents, if I expressed interest in purchasing your contract, purely out of spite." She finished bitterly.

This time, it was Azarus and I that exchanged looks. Looking back at her, I cleared my throat. "Yeah…" I started. "I know. While it would be great if you could just wave your hand and fix all our problems, I didn't expect it. I tagged along with Azarus for a different reason, something that you *can* help me with."

That caused Elysael to sit back up in her chair. "Oh?" She said, surprised. "And what is that?"

I leaned forward, excited despite myself. "So, it turns out that as a Precursor, I get unique racial talents, yeah? One of mine is the ability to learn all seven of the Professions." At that, Elysael gave me a strange look. "Yeah, seriously! So far, I've picked up six of them. The only one that I'm missing at this point is Artistry. We looked around Addersfield, and there was nobody around but Magnus that I could get to teach me, so obviously that was out. Azarus mentioned that you had it though, and could teach me. So, uh, yeah. Here I am." I finished, somewhat lamely.

Elysael stared at me disbelievingly for a moment without blinking. "Are you telling me…" She started slowly. "That you traveled for nearly a week, braving the monster-infested wilderness, to show up in my city and cause such a scene in my throne room, that my courtiers

281

will be speaking about it for years. All so that you could have the Prince of Rhoscara teach you...Artistry?"

I coughed into my right fist. "Well, I didn't actually see any monsters on the trip," I said weakly.

When Elysael transferred her gaze to Azarus, he just shrugged at her. She shook her head at the both of us slowly. "Well." She said weakly. "I have no objections?"

"Hey, thanks!" I said, smiling at her. "So, do you want to do it now, or later or something?"

Elysael took a deep breath for a moment before nodding. "Now is fine, I suppose." She said, extending her right hand in my direction. I reached out across the desk and took it in my own right hand. The Prince adopted a somewhat stern look on her face and spoke authoritatively. "Do you wish to learn Artistry?"

I smiled widely at her. Finally, after all this time, I was going to find out what was going on with my Professions! "I do," I said excitedly.

That familiar little tingle happened again, between our two palms. But...

That wasn't all that happened, though.

Pressure.

Enormous pressure suddenly exploded into the room. It was charged, as if energy was suffusing the very air that we were breathing. It bore down on us, driving Azarus, Elysael and I out of our chairs. In fact, the chair that Azarus was sitting on exploded underneath him, sending him flat on his back. Because Elysael and I were leaning over, we merely slipped out of our chairs. I think she might have hit her head on her desk though, on her way down to meet me on the floor. Vaguely, I was aware of glass shattering and the furniture Elysael's office groaning and splintering.

It was as if a colossal weight was bearing down upon me, pitiless and unrelenting. I couldn't move, I couldn't breathe, I couldn't even scream. Even the act of moving my eyes was somehow a gargantuan undertaking. Slowly, terrified out of my mind, I dragged my eyes to meet Elysael's own terror-stricken gaze through the gap under her desk. I could tell from the wild panic growing her in eyes that she didn't know what was going on either.

What was worse, however, was that the pressure continued to grow.

With every passing second, I could feel the pressure increase upon me, as if I was sinking ever further into the abyssal depths of a callous ocean. I could feel my bones begin to creak within my body. I could feel my lungs compress, driving the little air I had in my body out.

I could feel it when my heart began to slow.

As blackness began to creep across my vision, I was certain that I was about to die. Somehow, I'd managed to survive this far upon this damn planet, but something I'd done had ended up killing me, nonetheless. If I'd been capable of it, I might have laughed.

Suddenly, the pressure suffusing the room disappeared in an instant.

In that same instant, not only did three simultaneous gasps of air explode from the three people in the room, myself included, but the door exploded as well. I was still too dazed to lift my head to look in that direction, but I heard the clang of multiple pairs of armored feet rushing into the room.

I may not have seen them enter the room, but I sure felt it when a rough, gauntleted fist seized me by my shoulder and flipped me on my back. Above me was one of the avian knights I'd seen so often, staring coldly down at me.

Oh, and pointing his enormous curved great sword down at my throat, close enough I swore I could feel the tip on my Adam's apple.

"Don't move." I heard a low, menacing voice echo out of the knight's pointed helm.

I was still too out of it to really pay any attention to him, however. I could still remember the feeling of my heart slowing in my chest. It seemed to be fine now, though. I wanted to bring a hand up to my chest to clench at it fruitlessly, but at the last second, I remembered the orders of the knight.

Above me, I could see the eyes of the dwarven knight narrow slightly down at me through his helmet, as if he could somehow tell.

Out of the corner of my eye, I could see another knight, similarly poised with his great sword over Azarus. I guess not even being the Prince's cousin saved him from suspicion with these guys.

Behind me, I could hear another one of the knights speaking in a low voice to the Prince, as they presumably helped her to her feet. Whatever they were saying was too quiet for me to hear.

"Enough." I heard the Prince say in a rough voice. "Enough, my Corvid Knights. I do not believe this was an attack."

I heard the knight above Azarus do as she said and step away, but the knight above me didn't move for a moment. He just continued to hold my gaze, sword poised above my throat.

"Sir Ofrean…" I heard the Prince say in a warning tone, voice still coarse.

After a moment, the knight above me complied. He took his sword away from my throat, and slung it across his back in the same instant that he stepped away from my prone body. "By your command," he murmured.

Once he was away from me, Azarus appeared in his place. "Ya all right?" he said in a concerned tone.

I just gazed at him for a moment before blinking. I opened my mouth to try and answer, only to find that I couldn't. Only a croaking noise emerged from my throat.

Azarus grimaced. "Dumb question," he said under his voice. Reaching down and grasping my arm, Azarus hauled me to my feet. When I was finally upright, I was able to see the damage done to the office.

It was wrecked.

Where before the office had been stately, with a sense of under-stated elegance to it, now it looked like someone had rampaged through it with a sledgehammer. Everything glass in the office had shattered, including the windows. The chairs and the bookcases were either shattered or half collapsed, with the books themselves somehow looking as if they'd exploded as well. Scraps of paper lay everywhere, some of it still floating in the air.

I looked around a little, lost.

What the hell had happened?

# Chapter 33
# Uncertainty

After the incident in the Prince's office, nobody seemed to be in the mood to talk anymore. Elysael told Azarus and me that we would finish the conversation later, before calling a servant to lead us to the rooms that had been prepared for us. Shortly thereafter, I found myself in a small, relatively opulent room that I suppose I was going to be spending most of my time in while I was in Rhoscara. Azarus had been led to the room to my right and bid me goodnight, but not before shooting me one last puzzled look. Before they left, the servant had apologized to me and said that dinner would shortly be brought to my room, instead of taking it with the Prince.

Meanwhile, before my food arrived, I sat on the edge of my bed and stared blankly into space, lost in thought. Once again, I felt like I'd just barely dodged death. What had that pressure been, anyway? If it had lasted any longer, I wasn't sure I would have been able to survive it. Thinking about it, it wasn't hard to realize that it had happened because I had accepted the final Profession I needed. Something else must have happened because of that.

Did it have anything to do with Grey's theoretical eighth Profession?

Guess it was time to find out.

I used my skill and pulled up my status.

**Hidden Amidst the Spheres.**

**You have learned the General Talent Acting!**
**Acting has reached level 3!**
**You have learned Artistry!**
**You have created Aetherial Melding!**
**Would you like to review your Professions?**
**Y/N**

Uh, okay.

I'll take it from the top, then.

I wasn't surprised to see that I had gotten Acting as a talent. After my performance earlier in the throne room, I would have been shocked if I didn't get *something* out of it. I'd gotten quite a few levels in it too, I noted. Next was Artistry, and something was bothering me about that. After a moment of thinking about it, I realized that I had apparently only learned Artistry and not some kind of derived Profession. Every time I'd learned a Profession, I'd also immediately learned something else, like Medicinal Alchemy, or Material Enchantment. It was a weird difference, and I guess I was going to have to ask Elysael or Azarus about it later.

And then there was the truly weird thing, the third notification that I had gotten. 'Aetherial Melding', huh. I had apparently 'created' it, rather than 'learned' it. It was an interesting choice of words that the System had chosen, there. It implied that whatever I had 'created' was something entirely new, rather than something I had merely 'learned'. Was this the mysterious eighth Profession that Grey had nearly peed himself over?

Guess there was only one way to find out.

I mentally selected the Yes button on my notifications, mentally opening my Professions pane.

Which had changed.

Massively.

With a mounting sense of anxiety, I reviewed it. Where before my Profession pane had had seven circles surrounding an indistinct picture of a fist, six of them with symbols in them and glowing blue, now it had changed. The empty circle had been filled with a picture of a paintbrush, but it hadn't started to glow blue. No, instead none of the circles were glowing blue anymore. Each of the seven symbols representing my Professions had lost their light and were now a dull gray. Similarly, both the circles they were in, and the connecting lines of the heptagram between them had lost their glow. Instead, it looked like all of the light had transferred to the middle of the Profession star, leaving only a glowing blue heptagon in the center. The light inside of the heptagon was pulsing rhythmically, like it was a heart.

I couldn't see the fist symbol anymore, through all the light.

Slowly, I breathed in and out.

In.

And.

Out.

Trying to control my anxiety over whatever this could mean, I changed my status back to the main page away from the Profession pane. I had a suspicion.

| Name | Nathaniel Eugene Hart |
|---|---|
| Titles | N/A |
| Level | 5 |
| Age | 24 Sol |
| Race | Human (Precursor) |
| Affinity: | Terrestrial |
| Classes | N/A |
| Profession | |
| Health | 240/240 |
| Stamina | 100/100 |
| Vitality | 14 |
| Strength | 10 |
| Spirit 10 | |
| Dexterity | 18 |
| Perception | 14 |
| Intelligence | 22 |
| Wisdom | 22 |
| Free Points: | 0 |
| Options | Talent Page, Skill Page, Profession Page |

There it was, clear as day.

I didn't have *any* Professions anymore. Not even whatever this 'Aetherial Melding' was. Where before I'd had six different ones listed on my status sheet, now the Professions section listed as just blank. It didn't even have an 'N/A' like my class section because I hadn't gotten one yet. It was just *blank*.

I started hyperventilating, no longer able to control my breathing.

Oh fuck, what did that mean? Did I screw myself trying to get all of the Professions, just because I could? What if Grey had been wrong? He'd told me early on that Awakenings could go wrong for people that underwent it later in life, resulting in corrupted Statuses. What if that was what had happened to me?! What if we had been wrong about what 'Dream of the Infinite' did?! We'd guessed that it was what was allowing me to learn all of the Professions, but what if we had been wrong?! That could have just been an indication of a corrupted status or something!

Grey had been telling me all about how Professions were important for advancing with the System, because of Impact. If I had accidentally erased all of my Professions, was I screwed now?! If I didn't have Professions, I couldn't generate Impact. If I couldn't generate Impact, I couldn't get good classes! And if I couldn't get good classes I couldn't escape from being a slave! I was going to die a fucking slave because I'd fucked up my Professions!

I was going to die.

In a mad panic, I jumped to my feet and began moving towards the door. I didn't know if Azarus was still awake or not, but I was going to wake his ass up if he was asleep. I needed to know If I hadn't just fucked all of our plans.

Suddenly, before I could reach the door, a knock rang out on it.

I froze, before trying to clear my throat. "Ah…who is it?" I called out weakly, unable to stop my voice from cracking.

"Excuse me, Sir Hart." I heard a soft, female voice say on the other side of the door. "I have your dinner, compliments of the Prince."

Oh, yeah. That butler guy earlier had said something about dinner.

Snapping back to reality, I realized I'd just been in the middle of a panic attack. I was soaked in sweat, to the degree that I could smell myself. I was trembling too, shakes still running all up and down my body. Additionally, I ran a hand through my hair, finding it dripping as well. Realizing that the maid on the other side of the door was still waiting on an answer, I tried to get ahold of myself. It was surprisingly easy, actually. As soon as I focused on it, I could feel my shaking stop, and my stance firm up.

"Ah, excellent!" I called to the other side of the door. Striding up to it and concentrating on my breathing, I opened it with false confidence. On the other side of it was a dwarven woman in an almost stereotypical French maid outfit. She had her hands on a push cart, upon which was resting what must have been my dinner.

When she saw me, her eyes widened in surprise. "Oh! Excuse me, my lord!" She said, curtseying behind her cart. "If…if you're indisposed, I can return later!"

I crossed my arms and beamed at her, as a proper overly-theatrical knight would. "Not at all, not at all!" I said boastfully. "I, ah. I was merely engaging in some late-night calisthenics! Yes! I need to keep up with my training, even now!"

The maid cut her eyes away from me for a moment, before looking back and fixing a polite smile on her face. "Of course, Sir Hart." She said gently, as if speaking to a small child. "As you say."

My own smile grew wooden. "I'll. I'll just be taking that, then."

The maid curtseyed to me again. "If you can, my lord." She murmured. "Once you're finished, leave the cart outside and the staff shall collect it."

"Very well," I said, my smile becoming more awkward by the second. I hurriedly grabbed the cart and wheeled it into my room, jostling it somewhat and closing the door behind me. Through the door, I heard the maid sigh slightly before moving on.

Once the door was closed behind me, I let my act fall. Slumping, I hunched over the cart containing my dinner.

Breathe in.

Breathe out.

After a moment, I managed to catch my breath. All right, now that I wasn't drowning in anxiety, I was thinking more clearly. Furrowing my brow, I considered my Profession situation. I kind of doubted that I was as fucked as I thought I was earlier. Clearly, something was going on with my Professions that I doubted anyone, even Grey, knew. I might have lost all of my other Professions, but something was telling me that I was going to get something else. The pulsing blue hexagon

291

on my Profession pane was too suspicious in of itself to just dismiss it as losing everything. Call it gut instinct.

Speaking of guts, the smell of food now wafting through my room was making me aware of just how hungry I was. Wheeling the food trolley to a small desk in the corner of the room, I transferred my dinner tray to it. The cart had also come with a bottle of red wine and a glass as well, so I uncorked the wine and filled the glass before setting it next to the tray. Sitting down, I opened the tray to see what I had gotten for dinner. Looked like a pork chop with some kind of raspberry sauce, as well as assorted greens. But, you know. Fancy.

I settled down for dinner.

***

When I was finished with dinner, I put the cart out into the hallway like I was asked, and then took a quick bath in the attached en suite. Immediately after, I flopped down in the sinfully comfy bed and conked out. It had been such a long and…interesting day that I had been exhausted.

A polite knocking on my door awoke me the next morning. Groggily lifting my head, I squinted at the door with bleary eyes. When the knocking came again, I groaned and dragged myself out of bed. Shuffling my way toward the door, I opened the door and squinted at who I found. "Yes?" I said slowly.

The dwarven maid, different from the one last night, curtseyed and bowed her head to me. "Your pardon, Sir Hart." She said, politely. "The Prince requests your presence in the Coral Room, in order to break fasts."

I took a deep breath. "Yeah, uh, okay," I said, starting to wake up. "Give me a minute." I started to close the door, in order to get ready, before pausing. "And...where is the Coral Room?"

"Do not worry, my lord." She answered, head still bowed. "I was sent to guide you, as well."

"Ah. All right. Just, give me a minute." I said, still somewhat sleepy.

I shut the door in front of her and turned around. Stepping away, I considered what to do next. I ended up taking a few minutes getting myself presentable in the en suite, before getting dressed in some nice clothes I found in a drawer. I made sure not to forget my cloak as well, in order to conceal my collar. I might have revealed it to the whole court yesterday, but that didn't mean I was comfortable parading it about.

When I was ready, I left my room and let the maid lead me through the palace. It seemed much quieter than it had been yesterday. I guess now that the nobles had gotten their show, they weren't inclined to stick around in the palace proper.

After a while, we reached a set of double doors that were being guarded by a pair of the Corvid Knights. They didn't pay me any mind. The maid turned around and curtseyed at me again. "The Prince awaits you within, Sir Hart."

"Ah, thank you," I said to her. She merely bowed her head at me before hurrying off down the hall. I took a deep breath before opening the door and stepping through and closing it behind me.

Pink, was my first impression. The room was very...pink. This room was much more casually decorated than the rest of the palace that I had seen. Very frilly. Very...girly. Rather than stately portraits and solemn busts, it had paintings of cute animals and delicate little statuettes decorating the walls and shelves.

Coral Room, huh. I get it. Not the sea creature, then.

Inside, I found the Prince sitting at a (relatively) small table with a number of plates and dishes upon it.

Just her, though.

"Ah…" I said, hesitantly. I wasn't sure if she was pissed about her office from yesterday. "Good morning."

Elysael looked up at my greeting, taking her eyes off the papers she was considering. She nodded at me. "Nathan. Good morning to you, as well. Please, take a seat." She said, gesturing to a chair across from her.

I made my way across the room to do so. "Is it just us?" I asked questioningly, as I took my cloak off and sat it on the back of the chair. "Azarus not up yet?"

She shook her head. "Azarus has already left the palace. He still has business that he must begin within the city. It's just us, this morning. Please, feel free to help yourself."

Just us, huh.

Taking a deep breath, I nodded at her. "Okay, thank you."

Don't be nervous, man. You're only alone with a startlingly beautiful and powerful woman. Er, dwarf.

No reason to be nervous at all.

I sat down and then carefully began to load my plate from what was on offer.

# Chapter 34
# The Coral Room

For the next maybe quarter-hour, we ate our breakfasts in awkward silence. Well, awkward for me at least. In a casual setting like this, I didn't know how to speak to Elysael. What kind of chit-chat did you have with literal royalty? I didn't know. I was aware of how awkward I was, and I'm sure I was making a fool of myself somehow. Elysael didn't indicate in any way that she noticed, though. She just ate her meal with a quiet poise, seemingly unbothered by the silence.

God, Azarus, did you have to leave me alone here?

Once the two of us were finished, Elysael folded her napkin over her cleared plate. I stiffly tried to emulate her as best I as I could. Once I was done, a more tangible awkward silence descended over the two of us.

Uncomfortable, I cleared my throat. I at least did have one thing I wanted to speak about. "Ah, er, your High-Elysael," I corrected myself. "I'd like to apologize for what happened to your office last night. I, uh, I had no idea something like that was going to happen."

Raising an eyebrow, Elysael shook her head. "Think nothing of it. Last night's…" She paused, visibly searching for the word. "Phenomenon, was completely out of my experience as well. Truthfully, I would have been surprised if you *had* expected it, considering your unfamiliarity with the System. Such a thing is unheard of, in circumstances such as those."

My eyebrows shot up. Leaning forward, I forgot some of my awkwardness in my curiosity. "That almost sounds like you know what happened."

Elysael smiled slightly. "That would be because I do. I was curious, so I spent some time researching the matter before bed. It is an exceedingly rare event, but not an unheard-of one. What occurred last night is colloquially known as System Judgment. As the words imply, whatever happened when you accepted Artistry from me directly called the attention of the System itself. In rare occasions, such as whatever happened to you, it is known that the System must step in, in order to…facilitate whatever Status changes are taking place at the time."

I furrowed my brow. "Really? But I thought that the System was almost entirely automated for use?" I asked confusedly.

Elysael hummed. "Not entirely." She said after a moment's thought. Directing her gaze to meet mine, she asked a question. "When you were Awakened, I assume that whoever did so explained some aspects of the System to you?"

Tilting my head, I nodded at her question. "Yeah, Grey explained some things."

"Did Headmaster Greycton perhaps mention how the System is…flawed?" she asked leadingly.

"Yeah, he—" I paused and then narrowed my eyes at her suspiciously. "'Headmaster Greycton', huh?"

Elysael was visibly taken aback. "Yes?"

"I've only known him as 'Grey'," I said, frowning. "Exactly what is he Headmaster *of?*"

"Ah…" Elysael grimaced. "I appear to have overstepped. If…Grey has chosen not to speak of himself to you so far, it is not my place to gainsay him."

I nodded slowly. "All right, I guess."

Whatever, I'll just badger Azarus about it.

"In any case, we were speaking about the System and its flaws, were we not?" Elysael said pointedly. I held up my hands in surrender. "What has he mentioned?"

"Uh." I took a moment to think. "He told me about how some Awakenings can get corrupted? And…something about the System being inefficient?"

"Truly, that's all?" Elysael said in surprise.

I shrugged at her. "We've been kinda busy."

She shook her head. "Very well, then. System Judgements are one of those inefficiencies that he told you about. The System is imperfect. Very rarely does it impart power in and of itself. Rather, it is an…automated guide stone on how to refine Aether safely, resulting in 'levels'. It may interest you in knowing that soul refinement before the advent of the System did, in fact, exist."

"Huh," I said, leaning back in my chair. "I swear Grey said something about not much being known about from before 'System Initialization'."

"Not much, is not nothing," Elysael said knowingly. "In the before times, it was known as the 'Thousand Steps of Divinity'. *Very* ancient records indicate that it was uncommon, to a startling degree, especially compared to how ubiquitous the System is today. The 'steps' of the old method, could be roughly equated to our modern 'levels'. Of course, the old method did not possess the advantages that the System does. There were no Skills nor Talents, Racial or otherwise. No Professions, in order to impart Impact."

"What did it have then?" I asked, curiously.

"Virtues. Records tell us that the Soul masters only truly had the refinement of their Virtues. And it was an intensive process indeed. They could not spare the time to learn anything else, such as Magic or Cultivation, where the majority of a modern classer's strength lies." Elysael told me passionately, leaning forward, eyes bright. It was interesting. This was by far the most animated that I had seen her. "They were apparently formidable warriors in their own right, however. Where ancient Magi could call upon the elements to smite you, and ancient Cultivators could cut you down, swift as the wind, they were different. The ancient Soul Masters could instead touch upon the otherworldly, and battle that which was eldritch. Primalists, they were called. Curiously, one particular country still practices this art, if only in a diminished manner." Elysael must have caught sight of the amused expression that I was wearing, because she leaned back in her chair visibly fighting a blush.

"So, is that what you're into then? History?" I asked her, genuinely curious.

"Ah," Elysael answered, visibly embarrassed. "Apologies, that wasn't relevant. Getting back to the topic at hand, it's a widely held belief that the System is, somehow, unfinished. Modern scholars believe that the System is an attempt at formalizing and combining all three methods of self-improvement into one, coherent whole. However, it has very obviously failed at this task, as it only ever managed to assimilate one of them. Primalism. The refinement of the Soul."

"Yeah, Grey told me about that some. The System is apparently using raw Aether to do it, and that results in levels, right?" I said, nodding along.

"Yes, but it's meant to do more than that. The System very obviously is supposed to support Magic and Cultivation as well, but it almost…flails about helplessly whenever it attempts to do so. It can only cursorily assist in those matters, and often only in indirect ways. This is where a System Judgement comes in. Can you perhaps guess why?" Elysael asked me encouragingly as if she were a teacher.

I took it in stride, tilting my head back in thought. Could it be…

Looking back at Elysael, I began hesitantly. "Maybe…because my Status tried to do something that verges on Magic or Cultivation?"

Elysael smiled at me. "Close. A System Judgement occurs when an individual attempts to forge a skill that veers off the beaten path and touches upon those disciplines in order to do so. When they attempt something unique. It's a good sign, truly. It's rare these days because it's been millennia since the advent of the System, and most paths are already beaten with our limited access. Which is why I'm terribly curious as to how one was triggered by the acceptance of a *Profession* of all things."

Ah.

Shit.

I hadn't thought of what I would say to her in regard to what I had seen last night. Azarus and I might have told her a ton last night, but he'd been very obvious in not sharing everything.

He hadn't said a word about escaping anywhere with Grey.

Elysael must have seen the hesitance on my face because her expression visibly cooled. "My apologies if I've overreached—".

I waved my hands frantically. "No, no! It's fine, really! I just…don't really understand what it did myself."

Ah, screw it. Based on the history lesson, she might be as big of a nerd as Grey, and I was still a little anxious over my Professions. She might be my best source of information until I returned to Addersfield. Something told me Azarus would have no idea what was going on with me when I told him about it. Besides, my gut was telling me I could trust her.

Huh, I was really relying on my gut a lot these days.

Probably not a good sign.

I proceeded to tell Elysael about what I had seen on my status last night. About my missing Professions, and the state of my Profession pane. Her expression opened back up as I talked, with open fascination crawling across her face.

"How interesting," Elysael whispered to herself. Looking back up at me, she shook her head slightly in regret. "Unfortunately, I have not the faintest idea of what could be occurring with your Professions, Nathan."

I slumped. Well, damn. Never mind then.

"However…" I heard her voice continue. I looked back up at her to see her looking off into space, ponderingly. "However, I do not believe you have anything to worry about. In fact, I believe you should look at your Status again. Sometimes, it can take time for truly momentous changes to bind to it," she said, looking back at me and nodding.

"Uh, okay," I said to her, confused. A moment later, Elysael handed me a small, decorative mirror she must have been hiding in a pocket in her dress. Taking it and trying to ignore how warm it was, I focused on bringing up my Status. I knew I could open it without a mirror now, but I didn't need to show off all of my secrets to her. She hadn't asked about my other talents at all, other than the one that allowed me to get the other Professions.

Right away, I could see a difference on my Status screen. Barely holding in a gasp, I focused on it. I was a little startled when my Status screen changed to focus on the difference I'd seen.

### Profession    *Locked*

"Is aught amiss, Nathan?" I heard Elysael ask in a concerned tone.

"One sec," I muttered distractedly, holding up one finger.

I maneuvered around Status some more, bringing up my Profession pane. I couldn't help but let a confused frown creep onto my face at what I found. Mentally closing my Status, I set the mirror down. "Huh," I said, absent-mindedly staring at a small figure of a horse behind Elysael. After a moment, I focused back on her. "Yeah, I'm...glad? I did that?" I said still, confused. "There was a change to my Status sheet, but not my Profession pane, since last night. What does it mean to have a locked Profession?"

Both of Elysael's eyebrows shot up. "Locked? That was the exact wording you saw?"

I nodded back at her. "Yeah."

"Hmm, well, I believe I know what has happened in that case, as baffling as it is." Elysael shook her head. "You most assuredly possess some kind of Profession. When something is termed as locked on a Status, it means that you have acquired a Skill that is too powerful for you to attempt to use. It's one of the few safety measures that the System provides. However, I have never once heard of a Profession, of all things, being too powerful. This 'Aetherial Melding' must be truly exceptional."

I perked up. "So, how do I unlock it then?"

"Simply grow more powerful, is my guess," Elysael answered wryly. "You are currently without a class, yes?" At my nod, she continued. "Colloquially, that means you rank as Tier Zero. Once you choose a class at level ten, you are termed as Tier One. It's possible, even probable, that once you have acquired a class, whatever Profession you have stumbled upon will be unlocked. I highly, highly doubt that the System would deliberately hobble someone by locking a Profession of all things until Tier Two."

At Elysael's words, I could feel a knot of tension I wasn't even aware of begin to unravel inside of me. Despite managing to calm down last night, I'd still been experiencing a low level of anxiety about my Professions. It was good to know that I was probably not completely screwed.

"Okay." I breathed. "Thanks for your help, then."

"It was my pleasure," Elysael told me, smiling. Standing up from her chair, she picked up a small bell that had been sitting on the table and gave it a ring. Immediately, one of the maids shuffled her way into the room and began to collect the plates and cups from our meal, expertly balancing them on a tray. Once the maid was finished, she bowed in the direction of the Prince, still balancing the tray, and scurried out of the room. Elysael paid her little mind, looking at me instead. "Shall we take a walk? I'm interested in continuing our conversation, and I have little to do for the next hour before I must begin my duties."

"Ah, sure," I said, startled. I stood up to match her and grabbed my cloak. Settling it around my shoulders, I hurried to catch up with Elysael, who was waiting for me near the door. She opened it as I grew closer and stepped through, without a backward glance.

I followed her.

# Interlude 3
# Kragsdwarf [Vol. 1 End]

The fading twilight stretched across the city of Rhoscara, glittering among its crimson and gold spires. Beneath them, the work of the city began to die down, after another frenetic day of creation and trade. Carpenters and masons, bakers and chefs, most daytime workers began to close up shop and head for home. Gradually, they streamed from their workshops and their patisseries, leaving only the fading dust of a hard day's work in their wake.

While the working public of Rhoscara closed their doors, another kind of resident began to open theirs.

The nightlife.

Unique among the Five Points of the dwarven Principality, Rhoscara possessed a thriving night culture that catered to those that sought entertainment under the moonlight. Streetlamps were gradually lit by lamplighters, made much easier in the modern age since the invention of enchantment discs. Where before they needed to painstakingly light each individual gas lamp, these days they only needed to activate individual discs that required a specific key.

Taverns and dens of iniquity opened their doors en-masse, eager to welcome in the hardworking dwarves of the city. They were equally eager to take their coin. Carousers and drunks of all sorts came and went from establishment to establishment, either seeking more amusement or having worn out their welcome. It was a common sight among Rhoscaran pubs for disagreeable patrons to be literally thrown out the door by one of the employed guards.

Bront Stonebin was one of those guards. A former military dwarf, he'd served in the Rhoscaran guard for three years before being court marshaled over a simple misunderstanding, if you asked him. All he'd done was a bit of flirting, after all. How was he supposed to know that dame he'd goosed had been a Count's daughter? All those hoity-toity types looked the same to him, after all.

After he'd done his time, Bront had drifted as a tough for hire among the underbelly of the city. But after a while, Bront'd had a thought. 'Bront,' He had thought to himself. 'Bront, yer getting' on in yer years, and ye ain't going to be gettin' many more levels. This is it fer you, bucko. Time to settle down.'

And so he had.

Bront had looked for honest employment among the scenes he had been most familiar with and had eventually ended up as a guards-dwarf for The Gilded Mare. He'd known that most bars in the city were always looking for ex-military to help handle people that'd had a little too much to drink. The Mare was a decent bar that paid decent wages. It wasn't as high-end as some of the places that the nobs went to, but it wasn't a slum bar either. Today, he was working the outside door.

Bront was happy with his life these days. He'd settled down and found gainful employment, astonishing his poor old ma. He'd even started making inquiries about a nice girl he fancied. Marva Kegborn worked over at a bakery on fifth street, and hadn't spat in his face when he'd given her flowers!

He was sure they were going to get married any day now.

Bront snapped out of his daydreaming when he heard the sound of a loudly singing group coming up the road. Shoving off the wall next to the door of the Mare he'd been resting on, he directed his gaze that way.

He was puzzled by what he found.

It looked like a group of nobs. Like, the *really* fancy ones, even.

All dressed up in crimson silk and more gold than Bront was sure he'd ever see in his life, their faces were even painted in the new style that was all the rage with the higher class. It must have been a group of at least ten dwarves, in all. He couldn't tell though, because they were surrounding one dwarf in the center of them closely.

The group was singing at the top of their lungs in the old tongue, so Bront didn't understand a word of what they were saying. Uppity lot this, then. Only people that deliberately didn't want to be understood turned off Language Adaptation. They weren't very good, anyway. Bront had heard better from some of the regulars, once they'd gotten a few ales in them.

Once the group reached the street in front of the Mare, they started to make their way to the door, without a care in the world. Bront stopped them, for the simple reason that he had stepped in front of the entryway. The group of nobs halted, with some of the group visibly shocked. Hell, some of them looked as if they had only just now noticed them.

"Oi, oi," Bront grunted, crossing his beefy arms across his leather-padded chest. "What are you lot thinkin', then? We're full up, yeah? Shove off, and find someplace else to get yer piss on."

A few of the group looked more astonished than ever. A couple of them even began to look around, as if they were looking for someone. One of the nobles spoke up, though. "Now, look here—"

"No," Bront said, unfolding his arms and looming over the foppish noble. "*You* look here. Fook off, all of ye. I won't tell ye again."

"Calm yourself, my good dwarf." A smooth voice echoed out of the circle of dwarven nobles. At some unseen signal, they peeled away in front of Bront to let the speaker step forward. It was another nob, but this one was different somehow. He was taller and was dressed in a way that was both fancier than the rest of them, and yet somehow less ostentatious to Bront's untrained eye. But it wasn't his clothes, or even his bearing that gave Bront pause about this new nob. It was his face. Unlike the other nobs, who were all done up in foppish cosmetics, he was different.

He looked like he was wearing war paint, instead.

The new nob smiled evenly at Bront before he spoke. "I assure you, doorman, we are expected by the owner. We have a reserved room."

Bront shifted uncomfortably. Something about this new dwarf was throwing him off. "I dunno," he muttered doubtfully. "I ain't heard no—"

Bront was cut off by the door slamming open behind him, causing him to jump. Before he could turn around to see who had slammed the door open, he was astonished to see his boss, and the owner of the Mare scurry past him to bow repeatedly in front of the painted nob.

"I'm so, *so* sorry milord." His boss, Fanziel Brightbrew, stammered cringingly between bows to the nob. "I-I was busy in the back, and I lost track of time, and I deeply, deeply apologize for the actions of my doorman. He's new, and—"

The painted nob laid a hand on Mr. Brightbrew's shoulder and drew him upright. "None of that now." The strange dwarf said with a small smile. "We have a business, don't we? It wouldn't do to delay it even more." Turning his eyes back to Bront, the painted dwarf didn't have to say another word. Mr. Brightbrew looked up at him as well, with a wide-eyed, murderous gaze.

Bront stepped out of the way of the door.

Not giving Bront another look, the painted nob directed Mr. Brightbrew back into the bar, followed closely by the rest of his entourage. A few of the other dwarves glared at Bront on the way inside, but he didn't pay them any mind. He was still puzzled by what had creeped him out about the guy that Mr. Brightbrew had been bowing and scraping to.

After a moment, he managed to pin it down and shivered. It had been his eyes. The painted nob may have smiled at him, but his eyes had been dead. It was like they hadn't even actually seen Bront when they were looking at him. Bront resolved to stay out of the way of that nob in the future and tried to put him out of his mind.

Thoughts of Marva Kegborn were much more pleasant, after all.

\*\*\*

Lord Olag of House Savoy calmly folded his hands on the table in front of him as the last of his subordinates shuffled into the room. The proprietor of this…hovel, shut the door behind the last dwarf to enter the room. Once he was finished, the commoner made his way to the corner of the room, where a chair was waiting for him.

It was good that he knew his place.

Olag waited patiently as his followers seated themselves along the sides of the long table that lay in the meeting room he had rented. Of course, he sat at the head of it. Once the last of his peons had seated themselves in proper silence, Olag let it stretch on for a moment longer.

Shifting his eyes to the dwarf closest to his right, Olag broke the quiet. "Report," he said simply.

The ostentatious dwarf, the second son of some no-name coin counter, rose to his feet and cleared his throat. "Of course, my lord," he simpered. "This week…"

What followed was almost entirely drivel. For the next half hour, Olag did his best to pay attention as the worthless peons that had flocked to his banner prattled on about court gossip. Olag truthfully didn't care a whit about who had diddled who, or who had been spreading rumors this week. However, it was important for him to at least pretend that he did. If he wished to retain the support of the merchant faction, then he needed to retain at least the image of cordiality with their scions.

Olag repressed a sigh.

These fops were so tiresome. They crowded around him for attention and praise, when he despised them in his heart. They aped the trappings of nobility after their families had purchased their titles, instead of inheriting them like true nobles. They spent money as if it was water that fell from the heavens in a vain attempt to appear important. Gods, they had even begun to paint their faces in cosmetics in a fruitless attempt to mimic his tattoos. That had irked him when they had first started that. He had made the commitment to permanently mark his face in the traditional manner of the old Kragsdwarves, and these fools thought to mimic him with powders? They likely knew nothing of their history, choosing to dishonor their ancestors so. He'd had to stop himself from challenging the fools.

No doubt Ely knew how much the practice irked him, from the way she had to hide a smile whenever one of the dunces presented themselves to her.

Still, they had their uses.

Olag raised a hand to stop the current fool from rambling on, something about this week's menu. "Stop. Repeat the last thing you said," he said commandingly.

The fop stopped speaking to stare at him in surprise. "Ah, about the lobsters, my lord?"

Olag's eyebrow twitched slightly in annoyance. "No. What were you saying before you began to speak of...the menu?" he finished, unable to stop a hint of distaste from creeping into his tone.

The painted fool cringed slightly before trying to rally himself, unconvincingly. His 'peers' watched hungrily, eager for any form of drama. "Ah, I-I was speaking about how that dreadful human knight has been spotted in the library recently?" he asked plaintively.

Olag hummed, leaning back into his chair thoughtfully. Ah, yes. 'Sir' Nathan Hart.

Hah.

That had been a very, very interesting series of events. Since the court session nearly a week ago, he'd done his best to keep eyes on the 'knight'. From what his incompetent spies had told him, he'd spent most of that time either in the royal library or in the presence of Ely. His supposed liege lord, that lumbering oaf Azarus, had been busy with his usual contracts in the city and thus absent from the palace. You would think that a sworn knight would attend to the needs of his master, but no. The human had spent his time in the palace instead.

Olag wondered who he really was. A Herztalian agent of some kind, perhaps? Not everyone possessed either a skill or artifact powerful enough to veil his status, as he had so obviously done. Certainly not a 'low-level' hedge knight of no renown.

Still, let it never be said that Olag of House Savoy couldn't appreciate a good spot of subterfuge among the court. He'd intercepted a missive sent from a spy in the court about the recent going ons. He believed the rat in this case belonged to that Savoy deviant, Magnus. He'd had one of his agents do some careful editing of the message before sending it along its way. After all, if the human 'knight' was pretending to be Azarus's slave, no doubt he was also spying on that feculent toad. He wished him all the luck in *that* endeavor.

Really, he was almost disappointed in Ely. If she had wanted to insert this 'Sir' Hart into her court, she should have thought of a better cover for him. What was more interesting, however, was the role that Azarus was playing in this performance. Whatever could he have done to attract the attention of such a skilled operative?

Olag focused back on the fop in front of him. "Are there any other reported movements concerning Sir Hart?" he asked sharply. At the startled look on some of the faces surrounding him, he reigned his temper in and attempted a smile. "That is, if you've heard anything?"

The fool smiled back at him nervously. "A-ah, the only other thing is that I've, well, I mean, one of the servants overheard him telling the Prince he was leaving soon?" At Olag's raised eyebrow, he continued. "Ah, er, apparently Lord Azarus is finished with his business and they're leaving? Soon?"

"I see," Olag said quietly. If that buffoon was done collecting the rocks he needed to beat with his hammer, then that must mean that the 'knight' was finished with his business as well. Olag felt another surge of irritation with the incompetencies of his so-called spies. If only he had been allowed to bring any of his scouts into the palace, he wouldn't have needed to rely on these fools for information. Alas, old Morok had ruled long ago that soldiers not under the command of the Prince of Rhoscara were barred from the palace. Ely hadn't re-scinded that order once the old man had carked it and she had risen to power. Honestly, probably a good idea, if not somewhat inconven-ient for his purposes.

Olag made a show of nodding thoughtfully at the idiot's words. "Very well then," he said, rising to his feet. Everyone else in the room, even the proprietor in the corner, scrambled to copy him. "I believe that we've covered everything we need to tonight, my friends. I bid you goodnight," he finished with a pointed stare at the door.

One by one, the painted fops began to bow in his direction before exiting the room. Before long, the only people left in the room were Olag and the proprietor. He bowed to Olag as well. "If you'll excuse me, my lord, I'll have your dinner brought along shortly," he said nervously. Before he could leave, however, he was stopped by Olag clearing his throat.

"Brightbrew." Fanziel Brightbrew turned back to face the noble, anxiously. "You should begin looking for a new doorman. I'll be having a word with Don Thraggec about your...current one." Olag smiled slightly.

The smile didn't reach his eyes.

# LitRPG Resources

For more Level Up titles, visit https://www.levelup.pub/books

There you can sign up to be an ARC reader for our books, find out about new releases, apply to join the WhatsApp group, or get news on offers.

The Reddit community r/litrpg is really lively and a great mix of discussion, memes, news and recommendations.

LitRPG Forum is a terrific Facebook group, as is the related page LitRPG Reads (the former is better for discussion, the latter for announcements). Another really lively Facebook group is LitRPG Books. LitRPG Releases is good for keeping up to date. Although smaller, LitRPG Reviews Group (Viewers Choice) is fun, as is LitRPG Adventures: Reviews & Discussions.

Discord has a large LitRPG server under that name and the less obvious Silver Pen server has a lot of LitRPG news.